THE DARKEST VALLEY

GROUP X CASES · BOOK 2

J. A. BOUMA

PROLOGUE

You know what I wish for, friend—above all else in the universe?

Smell, that's what.

Sometimes I wish I could smell. Taste, too, but those sort of go hand in hand. Or, so I'm told. Yessiree, of all the five senses, smelling would be at the top of my list.

Sight I've got. Same for touch and hearing. Talking, too—though I know that's not really a sense, in the traditional sort of things. It is in my neck of the universe, the back and forth between us and our kind, you and your kind.

Though that's another story, for another time.

Smell. That's what I want, in the traditional sense of it. Where hundreds of molecular chemicals skate across thousands of olfactory sensory neurons until they land in the brain just right.

Take that bakery across the street, selling fresh-baked bread and sticky buns, along with cups of Joe. From what I hear, those dueling scents of baked goods and coffee are the bomb. Nothing like it in all the world. At least, according to one of my confidants.

Others would rank grilled steak or chicken right up there

with bread and coffee, slathered in BBQ sauce and charbroiled with the smell of woodsmoke or charcoal still lingering. Not my cuppa, but to each their own. Got enough of that charbroiled stench in my neck of the universe, if you get my drift.

So, yes, smell.

And yet, I've adapted, growing to appreciate the lesser obvious scents from humanity that waft my way. Not what is conscious or obvious. No, no, no. The stuff of life, my friend. That which simmers just below the surface but manifests itself upon my own olfactory, the only one I've got.

Fear.

Anxiety.

Dread.

Now *that* is worth sniffing—like the finest bouquet of roses, they are! It's also far more lucrative in my neck of the universe than a loaf of bread.

And much more fun.

I have heard it said around my parts, quoted from my compadres from time to time, there once was a god who claimed to have become death itself.

I am become Death, this god quipped, destroyer of worlds.

Death. How pedestrian. How finalizing.

What a yawn.

In fact, I'm doing it now. Yawning in the face of such a ridiculous ambition! Why kill when you can devastate sheeple to the point they're curled up in a corner bawling their eyes out without an ounce of hope left? Why end life when you can make sheeple wallow in its miseries?

I am become Death, destroyer of worlds. *Bo*-ring!

Not me. I am something better than death itself.

Despair…

I am Despair, destroyer of worlds!

Not *the* world, but individual ones. The mousy sheeple that trot across this ill-begotten land, full of insecurities and unfulfilled desires. Those so wrapped up in their neuroses and marinating in panic-porn fueled fear that they're one neuron firing on the wrong cylinder away from losing their marbles.

Or worse…

Tossing the whole kit and caboodle overboard.

And the quickest way I have found to leapfrog from the sunny side of the fence headlong into the clawing, cloying oblivion of mawing darkness is to leverage the worst of human emotion and the inner workings of their very souls.

Comparisonitis, envy, jealousy.

Hopelessness, gloom, misery.

Impulsiveness, passion, rashness.

The world is awash in it all.

Not the least of which is my own specialty—

Despair…

These are the tools of the trade—the tools of *my* trade. The ones I've been using for generations, hammering and honing their application to take down the mousy, mewy, miscreants that tread upon the world crafted by the Name-Who-Shall-Remain-Nameless. What he sees in them, I'll never understand it.

What *we* see in them…now that's another story.

When I look upon the expanse of all that exists—all that has existed over the generations—what I see are poor, helpless souls in need of an extra push. Something to send them barreling into that which they deserve, yet don't have the guts to go after.

Yet our Adversary puts up roadblocks at every turn. Stymying our progress to eliminate his Image from the face of Earth. Or at least bring it to the belly of life's darkest valley.

Chief roadblock: his Church, inspired by his own heroics.

Some think we are unfamiliar with the Good Book. Nay, that is incorrect. The farthest from the truth, actually. For it was the Master who first perfected the art of memorizing the Nameless One's words, then spitting them back into his face! As well as those who bear his Image, the bipedal creatures that deserve far less than his love.

And yet, as I consider this town of mine, and all the others like it scattered across this Third Rock from the Sun, those words spring to mind. I cannot avoid them. The one's from the book penned by the chap known as Matthew:

> *Then [the Nameless One] went about all the cities and villages, teaching in their synagogues, and proclaiming the good news of the kingdom, and curing every disease and every sickness. When he saw the crowds, he had compassion for them, because they were harassed and helpless, like sheep without a shepherd.*

Then again, from that wretched Mark's tract on the Nameless One: '*As he went ashore, he saw a great crowd; and he had compassion for them, because they were like sheep without a shepherd; and he began to teach them many things.*'

I snort a laugh, my breath billowing from these heights.

Like sheep without a shepherd is right.

Sheep are the dumbest animals on the Nameless One's green earth—especially humans. So easily led astray, sheeple are! So easily manipulated and managed, conned and coaxed into giving up the only thing that truly sets them apart from the rest of the created world.

Freedom.

If there is one thing I've learned that greases the skids for part of their identity being wrenched from their cold, dead fingers, it's dragging them through the valley of death's shadow.

And now is the moment to make our move.

My move. To ruin all that the Nameless One holds dear.

His Image Bearers.

Time to stay the sheep's bleating; time to provoke the sheep's bleeding.

One by one.

For I am not Death, but Despair.

I am Despair, destroyer of worlds.

Your world.

And I've got you in my crosshairs, bucko.

CHAPTER 1

Elijah Fox was in a real pickle.

He was supposed to meet his boss, Silas Grey, Master of the Order of Thaddeus, at 10:00 a.m. sharp for coffee—which also happened to coincide with his daily morning bagel-coffee ritual, something he never missed. Win-win for him.

But he was lost.

Took a wrong turn somewhere several blocks back and was now heading north when he should be heading south, then west toward destiny. But these blasted DC streets were all wrong.

All wrong, they are!

No thanks to some Frenchy who prided himself on symmetrical city planning but managed to absolutely screw up what any sane person would view as logical urban navigation.

That's the French for you.

Pierre L'Enfant, he was. How's that for a perfectly ridiculous French name? Although, it means Peter in English, so Elijah figured he shouldn't be too snooty about it, since he was named after one of Jesus' three amigos.

Anyhoo, Pierre L'Enfant came to fight in the Revolutionary War and later became George Washington's trusted city planner. Had grand plans for the city, envisioning it to be laid out like a grid, where east-west streets were lettered and north-south streets were numbered. But that wasn't all. No siree! Had he left it there, it would have been fine. But on top of those streets, he introduced other "grand avenues" (yeah, right!) intersecting those letter-number streets at 45-degree angles, forming circular and rectangular plazas. Sort of like those crazy British roundabouts that gave him a headache at grad school in Cambridge University years ago.

One of the most idiotic parts of the whole cockamamie plan was the fact the numbers and letters started over! With the U.S. Capitol Building anchoring the center of the grid, numbers radiated east and west, then the letters radiated north and south, with Independence and Constitution Avenues serving as those starting points—repeating them in both directions!

Madness, I tell ya. Madness!

But that wasn't all of it. No siree! After all, it's the French we're talking about.

To interpret it all, you need the cypher. The key, the code, the abracadabra incantation to navigate the cockamamie scheme! Without it, you're screwed.

Which probably explained Elijah's current pickle. That, and he disavowed smartphones a few months ago, content with his dumb phone now. A Jitterbug Flip2 that was advertised as an easy-to-use flip phone for seniors.

Now though…lost in some sector of the District, hot and sweaty and becoming more anxious—wished he'd disavowed his disavowal and joined the rest of humanity staying plugged into the WeShare matrix. At least he'd have a map, directions, the cypher to his destination. Because his granny phone wasn't going to cut it. Neither was the Frenchy's grand plans.

The quadrants were the key to it all, see. Northwest, Northeast, Southwest, Southeast. 8th and M Southeast versus 8th and M Northwest was the difference between getting a glass of Côtes du Rhône with beef bourguignon for a hot date or getting mugged and shot in the kisser for your sneakers.

Probably the dumbest part of it all was there was no J Street. Nope. Skips from I to K. Something about some grudge against someone whose name started with the letter (rumor has it, Chief Justice John Jay). Same for X, Y, and Z Streets (except there's no discernible reason why, because: French!). After W, the roads were named after trees, flowers, presidents and other local figures.

And right now, Elijah was about to cross one of those other roads!

Quebec. Figures. There's a Frenchy for you.

So there Elijah sat, idling at a red light behind an over-the-top, bright yellow Hummer, which for DC was saying something. Thought those things went out of style back when the Backstreet boys tried to kiss and make up with their comeback album that only landed them in a revolving Vegas Strip gig at the Bellagio.

At least its shadow offered some relief. Because on top of lost, Elijah was stifling and sweaty to beat the band in the middle of a DC summer straight from hot Hades. Oh, yeah, another brilliant move by the Frenchy: He built his grand plan on a swamp! Again: the French for you!

He revved his BMW R 18. Definitely not one of those hippy Harley hogs that smacked of biker cliché. Not a Honda, either, or other Japanese variety. No Yamaha or Kawasaki for him as well.

Nope. What Elijah rode was the only motorcycle worth its salt.

Pure German-engineered mechanics, sporting the dexterity and temerity of a modern cruiser combined with the nostalgic sense of classic beemer design.

And yes: beemer. With two Es and one R. Not a bimmer, with one I and two Ms, which is the American bastardization for cars of the original moniker for BMW motorbikes.

Beemer, not bimmer.

Boy, did Elijah love his motorcycle, mostly thanks to Dad. He'd been a hog guy himself, riding a hippy Harley to his pastor gig. But he didn't hold it over Pops since it was a mid-life crisis buy. Would ride that thing day in and day out to their country church down the road from their country house in Paducah, Kentucky. Or Kenturkey, as he liked to call it. Then to get groceries or get nails for the endless honey-do list Mama kept tacked up on the refrigerator.

Took Elijah along, of course, the pair of them racing through the country roads, wind whipping their hair, the smell of pine and pigs heavy.

He smiled at the memory, Dad gone nearly two decades now, revving his engine while he waited. With all of the potential power in those handlebars, and the 91 horsepower at 4,750 revolutions per minute propelling him forward, giving him all the control he needed to go wherever and whenever—and as fast as ever—he wanted.

Power and control.

The two things in his life he'd never had. Not over his life, certainly not over where it went. Not even his own body, his emotions and brain and body triggered by stimulus and circumstances outside of his control, and leading to less-than-ideal reactions he had little power over.

But now, without knowing where he was and where he was going—and this blasted red light still red, on top of the hideous view of the backside of a Hummer from before he still had braces—he felt himself starting to fray at the edges. Not good.

The mounting anxiety triggered his stimming trick, or tried to anyway. Except his gloved hand gripping the throttle wouldn't allow for it. No way for his thumb to press against his index finger, then his middle, and to his ring finger and pinkie. So he'd have to settle for the next best thing.

Whistling "Amazing Grace."

Was especially effective inside his helmet, the high pitch music to his ears along with the vibration of his lips a balm to his rising anxiety. Stimming or stimulating for autistic people like him was like drinking water. Couldn't not do it when the thirst came. Was a matter of mental and emotional survival.

Elijah pushed his sleeve back to check his watch—a Christmas gift from Dad.

And yelped.

"Oh my cheeps!" he exclaimed, his grumbling, rumbling stomach putting the exclamation point where his helmet muffled his surprise.

It was quarter past 10:00!

Not only was he late for his meeting with the boss man. He was missing his mid-morning coffee and bagel break!

Raisin bagel with cream cheese. Plain, non-fat. And a cup of dark coffee.

Every morning.

With. Out. Fail!

He couldn't deviate from his rhythm, his routine. It would throw off his entire day, his equilibrium!

Had to take action. Set the world back in order.

So he did.

Spinning out from his spot, he punched it in the middle of the road named after some Midwest state, nearly clipping the front end of a black Audi and getting pancaked by a rusting delivery truck and sending up angry horns and even angrier words.

Elijah blamed the Frenchy for his ridiculous roads. You could blame the French for a lot of things, if you thought about it.

He raced down the road—Wisconsin Avenue, apparently— spotting the spires of the Washington National Cathedral as he zoomed between cars giving him the middle-finger salute (how rude). Its Indiana limestone shone bright in the clear morning, the HQ for the Order of Thaddeus. Didn't know how he got so turned around, and an embarrassing heat raced up his neck at the realization. Should know the city like the back of his heel after working in it for so long before getting canned by J. Edgar

Hoover's boys and sent packing. But he didn't get out much, so he'd never really explored the city.

Now he wished he had, because he was late. Not only for his meeting with Silas but also with his belly.

As if putting an exclamation point on it all, his belly turned sideways, forcing him to put away his pride and ask for directions. See, men could be taught.

Blowing through a yellow-turning-red light, he pulled into a Sunoco gas station, asked the attendant for directions to Saxbys, and was righted back on the straight and narrow.

Took a bit more negotiating with L'Enfant's nonsense, but soon he was parking his beemer (two Es, one M) between a silver Civic and blue Camry. Then he raced to a two-story, brick corner building painted the color of vanilla ice cream, windows accented by a tasteful navy trim. Not bad. Perhaps there was hope for the morning yet.

Elijah threw open the grayish-blue door and was overcome with the force of brewing coffee, baking blueberry muffins, and the rumble of conversations. The red-brick space anchoring the corner of 35th and O Street since the eighteenth century was packed with students grabbing a caffeine and sugar fix before class at Georgetown University up the road.

Offering a dose of cheer was a display of orange flowers sitting on top of cases filled with cookies and breads and bagels and scones, greeting and tempting patrons waiting in line. Gray plastic tables and chairs lined the walls and filled small alcoves in the back and across from the register, all brimming with folks putting last-minute touches on papers or cramming for tests, or both.

Elijah wrenched off his helmet and scanned the space searching for Silas.

There he was, settled in a high-back chair in the bay window with a large coffee and chocolate croissant. Too much sugar for his liking, but at least the man was a coffee guy, so he figured they could be friends, though he hadn't spent much time with the man.

Silas Grey was the Master of the Order of Thaddeus, ancient defender and protector of the Christian faith. He spent most of his time directing the Church's special ops agency SEPIO, the Order's more muscular arm that kicked bad guys' butts and took names. A Latin acronym for *Sepio, Erudio, Pugno, Inviglio, Observo.*

Protect, instruct, fight for, watch over, heed. Based on Jude 3, Saint Jude Thaddeus's exhortation to *'contend for the once-for-all faith entrusted to God's holy people.'*

First time Elijah met them during an operation to expose a massive political conspiracy involving UFOs and aliens (don't ask), the agency felt vaguely like if the Navy SEALs and Knights Templar had a baby. As Silas explained, around a decade ago, near the start of the Church's existence, the good Apostle had already seen forces inside and outside the faith working against it. So he launched a religious order about five centuries before that was a Christian thing, historians pegging the first Christian order with Saint Benedict in the 6th century.

For centuries, the Order had worked tirelessly to instantiate Thaddeus's vision for faith-contending—all the while battling nemeses from the shadows of history. Especially one particular bad actor who happened to be headed up by the Order Master's little bro, Nous.

Although formerly a Roman Catholic outfit, the Order of Thaddeus itself was an ecumenical mission, with members from every Christian denomination. Protestant, Catholic, Orthodox, even some Southern Baptists on the force.

And now a Messianic Jew who formerly taught at an evangelical Protestant seminary, who was the director of operations for Group X—the Church's investigative agency solving *inexplicitus* cases, his specialty.

Elijah was just glad he'd landed with that new agency rather than SEPIO. Was much more his style, the whole detective PI gig than the Navy SEALs for Jesus one. Although, the last case sure gave him a run for his money. Had seen more action than in all his half decade with the Federal Bureau of Investigation. Was just glad he wasn't doing it alone.

His former partner, Georgina Anderson, from the FBI had joined him after a bad run-in with the Bureau. The pair had cut their teeth on solving cases of the more paranormal variety that stumped Uncle Sam's men in black. And there they were, back in the saddle of an investigative arm solving cases of the more supernatural variety—only this time for Jude Thaddeus, or at least his long-lost religious order.

Gina was seated in another navy high-back chair, scrolling through her phone and sipping tea in an attractive pink sweater with a tan leather coat draped around her back. She tossed him a wave, and he pointed at the counter where he stepped up to order.

A chic in a black Grateful Dead T-shirt and matching black skirt asked him for his order. He had a hard time concentrating with the silver gauges the size of cantaloupes in each ear staring back at him. Said he'd have a large coffee to match his friend, but traded the chocolate croissant for a raisin bagel.

"Sorry, we're out," she said, lips glistening hot pink he guessed was meant to make the vinegar news go down like honey.

Didn't work.

"Out?" he snapped, the heat rising up his neck only outmatched by irritation.

"Out."

"Like, out out, or are you only saying you're out because you just don't want to take the time to check to see if you're really out. Because any cafe worth its coffee beans can't be out of raisin bagels at 10:43 in the morning!"

She shrugged, her silver gauges dancing a waltz. "Sorry, toots." Tapping the glass cover with a single long fingernail painted black (how cliché), she added, "I've got blueberry left. It's yours if you want it."

Elijah scoffed. "Sweet mother of Melchizedek, are you mad?"

She planted a hand on her hips that meant business. "Look, I've got other customers, so if you—"

"Fine," he interrupted, waving a dismissive hand and trying not to lose it.

This was not the way it was supposed to go.

Raisin bagel with cream cheese. Plain, non-fat. And a cup of dark coffee.

Every morning at 10:00 a.m.

With. Out. Fail!

Could things get any worse?

A minute later he snatched his bagel and coffee, left a fiver for a tip (because, hey, it wasn't her fault upper management were doofuses who couldn't order right), then hustled to his awaiting seat next to Gina across from Silas.

"Everything alright?" he asked.

"Peachy." Elijah looked down at his bagel, revising his senti-ment: "Blueberry, actually. Hey, Gina."

"Howdy, partner," she replied, sipping her tea.

Settling into his chair, he took a sip of coffee before tearing into his bagel. Cream cheese was thick and smooth, sticking to the roof of his mouth, with the mild, sweet taste and pleasant slight tang he'd come to love about his ritual. At least he had that going for him.

Heaven…

Elijah swallowed and regarded the joint. "Different digs from the bowels of the Basilica of the National Shrine of the Immacu-late Conception, that's for sure."

Silas chuckled. "I'd say. How are your offices? I know they're not the Hoover building, but hopefully your HQ does the job."

"It does the job." Throwing back a swig of brew, he asked, "Why the change of venue?"

Silas glanced around the joint, taking a swig himself.

"Needed a break from the stuffy confines of limestone and paperwork."

"Ain't that the truth!"

"Besides, this was an old haunt from back when I was a student at Georgetown. Figured a little sunshine, some coffee and a pastry, would do us all some good."

Except for the blueberry bagel, Elijah agreed.

Silas asked, "So, how's Abraham Patel working out?"

"Nice enough fella," Gina answered.

"A bit overeager," Elijah added, chewing a bagel bite, "and a little wet behind the ears, but seems competent enough."

"So things are working out alright?" Silas asked.

"So far, so good."

He smiled. "Good, because I've got another case for you."

"Where?" Elijah asked, taking a sip of coffee.

"Back home."

Nearly burned his lips with surprise. "Kenturkey?"

Silas furrowed his brow. Gina clarified, "He means Kentucky. Little pet name he has for his childhood state."

"Ahh, no. The other hometown."

"Grand Rapids?" Elijah said, twisting up his face.

Had been a professor of biblical theology at a graduate school for pastors there—until a rogue government agency destroyed his office, and he was called to lead Group X. Wouldn't call it a hometown, however. Never had one of those, actually. Not really, having been an orphan before being tossed between eleven foster families until ending up in his forever family home. Probably spent as much time in Grand Rapids as he did anywhere else, maybe more.

"Mill Creek Junction," Silas clarified. "Remember Pastor Peter Young from last year?"

Elijah nodded, taking another swig and waiting for more.

"Well, something's happened, and he called me for help."

"What's happened?"

Silas hesitated, then reached into a brown leather satchel at his feet and pulled out a manilla envelope. He handed it over.

Elijah snatched it, butterflies doing the conga line in his stomach. Always got that way at the front end of a case. When all the possibilities were wide open, and a myriad of open boxes just waited to be investigated and closed, one by one, until the one that held the golden goose popped out the golden egg that hatched the big resolution prize.

Not necessarily solution prize. He'd been around the block enough to know not every case gets solved. But every case must get resolved. Any mystery writer worth their salt knew that.

And Elijah Xavier Fox was the author of his detective story.

Envelope was labeled with an X-000002 case identifier. He smirked. How original. Was heavier this time around, so at least they had that going for them. Their first case was a single sheet of paper. Can you believe it? Was a miracle of Yeshua Almighty, of Jesus Christ himself that they solved the dang thing. But they did. Barely.

Elijah unwound the red twin and peered inside.

Then he frowned.

Not what he was expecting.

Not in the slightest.

CHAPTER 2

Gina Anderson had a headache.

Used to get them all the time as a teenager, then as a young adult. Searing buggers in the middle of her head, accompanied by brain fog and fatigue. Not so much anymore, not after she found out she had a non-celiac gluten intolerance. Who knew?

Certainly not Mama, who raised her on Wonder Bread and mac & cheese. Sometimes both together. Mac & cheese sandwiches were a specialty of Gina and her sister Grace, the pair heaping spoonfuls of Kraft's best between two slices of buttered white bread. And that wasn't even counting the cereals (Count Chocula was her fave!), chips (ditto for Doritos), gravies, tacos, and all other manner of gluttony foods.

Now, not so much. No more processed grains for her, a medical necessity rather than the latest celebrity-fueled fad, like the low-fat, no-fat craze of the '80s and '90s. Not that she minded. Her gluten headaches reminded her of Toledo, which reminded her of the family double-wide, which reminded her of family. Memories she'd rather leave buried in the dustbin of history, along with those boxes of Kraft and bags of Wonder Bread.

But this headache wasn't that gluten one.

Right between the eyes, it was. Needling and blooming. Happened like this every morning for a few weeks after their first Group X case. Right after she woke up and geared up for another day on the job. It was often accompanied by a tightness in her chest and a sour stomach. Any first-year psych student knew exactly what was going on. And any psychologist worth their University of Michigan degree—like her—knew she was suffering from acute anxiety.

She'd always been an analyst, a desk jockey pushing papers around and solving the FBI's unexplainable cases from the cozy comforts of a basement room in the bowels of an office building. Not getting hosed down by lead in a Cracker Barrel, and certainly not firing her weapon at another human, even killing one. Of course, it was for a good cause—justice and public safety always were—but still…Didn't think it would affect her so much, coming under fire, opening fire, and coming face to face with something not of this world.

Literally…

And there they were: saddling up on another pony that would take them only the good Lord above knew where!

At least she had Elijah, and prayer. The latter had been particularly key to her surviving the past few months waiting for the next case to land in their lap. There was one in particular she'd relied on to carry her through, from her Catholic upbringing. She prayed part of it now:

> *Saint Michael, prince of the heavenly hosts, who stands*
> *always ready to give assistance to the people of God;*
> *who fought with the dragon, the old serpent, and*
> *cast him out of heaven, and now valiantly defends*
> *the Church of God that the gates of hell may never*
> *prevail against her, I earnestly entreat you to assist*
> *me also, in the painful and dangerous conflict which*
> *I have to sustain against the same formidable foe. Be*

> *with me, O mighty Prince! That I may courageously*
> *fight and wholly vanquish that proud spirit, whom*
> *you have by the divine power, so gloriously over-*
> *thrown, and whom our powerful King, Jesus Christ,*
> *has, in our nature, so completely overcome.*

"Amen..." she muttered to herself, the prayerful promise of protection from the crazy already lessening the pain.

Elijah asked, "What's this?" jolting Gina back to the moment.

Gina took her tea mug in both hands, its warmth against her fingers a balm, then took a sip. She hummed with surprising pleasure, the peach notes to her herbal tea re-centering her. Was more a black tea gal, only sometimes dabbling in herbal flights of tea-drinking fancy. Today seemed like one of those days to dabble.

"Your case," Silas answered.

Eli pulled out a single piece of paper, holding it like it was a live scorpion or a rotten banana peel. His face said it all: not a happy camper.

"Is there a problem?" asked the chief.

"Uh, yeah." He eyed it, turning up a brow before turning up a corner of his lip in disgust. Then: "It's another one-pager!"

Silas gulped down a swig of coffee and shrugged. "Welcome to the big leagues."

Elijah muttered something under his breath as he scanned the briefing.

Gina took another sip of her own, suppressing a smile. Their last gig with the FBI afforded them certain investigative comforts this new gig did not. Primarily, full case files ready for their consumption. Not the new agency they'd joined.

It was becoming clear that Group X was more a bootstrapped endeavor, the Church's answer to a rising darkness posing confounding, unexplainable mysteries. Or *inexplicitus*, rather, the Latin word inspiring the X in the agency's name—along with inexplicable, incomprehensible, inconceivable. Also had the advantage of mirroring the Greek letter *Chi*, which was the first letter for Christ, an X.

The pair had worked their own set of *inexplicitus* cases for the FBI, the kind of the more paranormal variety. She had been recruited out of the University of Michigan—go Blue! Her thesis on cultic ritual abuse had gotten her noticed by the muckety-mucks up the Bureau food chain, and she was assigned with Eli, a fresh graduate of the Academy. They were handpicked to work the same magic for Group X.

After everything went down in their operation last year with the Order, Silas Grey had realized there was missing a crucial element to the Order's mission to preserve and contend for the once-for-all faith entrusted to God's holy people. An investigative arm to the Order that was separate from the operations part that SEPIO took care of, the Order's more kinetic, special-ops agency.

Irregardless, or perhaps *regardless*—always messed that one up—anyhoo, their outfit took seriously the Apostle Paul's exhortation in the Book of Ephesians to stand against the darkness: *'For our struggle is not against enemies of blood and flesh, but against the rulers, against the authorities, against the cosmic powers of this present darkness, against the spiritual forces of evil in the heavenly places.'*

Last time that meant going toe to toe with Chaos, a supernatural Being straight from the Unseen Realm that had concocted a plan to ravage humanity and murder any who stood in its way. What it would mean now…only the good Lord above knew!

Silas gestured to the envelope. "There's something else inside."

Supposed now *she* would know…

Gina snatched it from Elijah's lap. Furrowing her brow, she reached a hand inside the manilla case file and felt something hard, something blocky.

She pulled it out. A brown, leather-bound book the size of a paperback. Wound around it was a leather strap keeping the book closed, its creamy-page contents secured, secret.

"Looks like a diary."

Silas swallowed a swig of coffee. "That's right."

"From who?"

"Whom," Elijah corrected. "It's from whom."

Gina frowned and threw him not-now eyes; sometimes he needed them kind. He looked at the ceiling, taking a sip of coffee and shutting his yapper, as well as taking the hint.

"As I was saying…" she went on, "Whose diary is this?"

Silas answered, "One of Peter's parishioners, actually. He overnighted it after he called yesterday, beside himself with grief at his loss."

Eli smirked. "A pastor with his parishioner's diary? Sounds like they had a deep connection. It also sounds like the punchline to a racy TMZ gossip article."

Silas frowned. "She's like sixty."

"Hey, I'm not judging. Cougars can be fun."

Gina threw an elbow in his ribs; Elijah yelped.

"She's also dead," Silas said.

"Sucks for her," said Eli as he looked over the one-pager.

Gina rolled her eyes. Loved the man to pieces—in a platonic, co-agent sort of way. But sometimes he could be a bit much. Blunt and honest, to a fault.

She unwound the leather strap holding the book together and opened it, lavender and vanilla rising from its pages. Flipping through the pages, she could see it was clearly the diary of a woman, with cursive script in pencil, an odd choice. As if the musings and memories of this woman were impermanent, erasable.

Elijah asked, "What happened?"

"Suicide."

She snapped her head up with wide eyes. "Suicide?"

"Oh my cheeps," Elijah said. "That's deep."

Silas nodded. "Sure is."

"And I take back my snark."

"Good man."

A chill skated across Gina's skin, raising a coat of goose pimples where her milky smooth Irish skin had been; that was her dad's doing. And not only because some blockhead decided to crank the AC, and she was sitting directly under a vent belching a polar vortex on her head.

No, it was that word. The one that was apparently at the center of this case.

Suicide.

There it was again, at the mention of that word inside that noggin of hers. Raised flesh skittering across her arms and back and neck, her hairs standing at attention, joined by an insufferable itch!

She brought her tan leather coat up around her shoulders to stay the chill. An Ann Taylor red-line special she swiped at the end of last season. A $300 bad boy she got for sixty buckeroos! She might be Irish in hair and skin tone, but she was a little Dutch girl at heart, spotting a steal-of-a-deal from a mile away; that was her mom's doing. As they say, if you ain't Dutch, you ain't much.

Felt bad for the baby goat that gave his life for her fashionista find. It was sure cozy, and Gina needed the extra touch of baby-goat love, given the memory attached to that word.

Suicide.

The very personal one…

Hated when that happened, when cases she worked on connected with her past. Unfortunately, given her upbringing in Toledo, one of America's armpits, there were endless connections to the memories of FBI cases she'd soon enough forget about.

And apparently, Group X cases too…

Gina reached for a ginger lock swaying in the frigid AC, wanting to twist it and pluck a single strand of hair, but caught herself. One of her many flaws, a tick from childhood when anxiety rose. Instead, she reached for her tea, sipping the peach nectar gone ice cold and swallowing, flushing away the memory. For now.

She continued flipping, the cursive becoming less precise, messier as the dates went flashing by. Until—

"Egads!"

She dropped the diary as if it were a searing hot plate, the book tumbling and flopping to the floor.

"Where's the fire, Gina colada?" asked Eli.

Taking a breath, then taking a beat, she pointed at the book lying face down.

Silas asked, "Did you find something?"

Gina collected herself, another ripple of goose flesh racing across her arms and up her back.

"Just…take a look."

Elijah glanced at the Order Master before snatching the book from the floor. Opening it on his lap—he yelped with a start, slamming back against his chair.

"Sweet mother of Melchizedek!"

She swallowed and chanced another glance. There it was. The stuff of nightmares.

The two-page spread had been completely covered by dark gray shading, scrawling impressions from the pencil evident in furious tracks grated across the pages.

But that wasn't all.

For an eraser had peeled back layers of the dark graphite, revealing a ghoulish figure etched in triangular, right-angle white lines, with a wide mouth and razor teeth, eyes blazing white triangles. Joining it at the bottom was a curious line, not in the cursive found elsewhere in the journal but in jagged capital block script:

I AM BECOME DEATH, DESTROYER OF WORLDS

"Creepo…" Elijah said, back still pressed against his chair.

Gina shivered. "That's one way of putting it."

"It's from the Bhagavad Gita," Silas said, "that quotation."

"And J. Robert Oppenheimer," Elijah said. "He was among those who observed the Trinity test in New Mexico, where the first atomic bomb was successfully detonated on July 16, 1945. Afterwards, he uttered those words because the explosion brought to mind a phrase from the Bhagavad Gita: *'Now I am become Death, the destroyer of worlds.'*"

"But what does it mean?" asked Gina.

"In the context of Oppenheimer, he seemed to have come to the horrifying realization that his work on the atomic bomb would facilitate the killing of so awesomely many people. So he invoked Eastern mysticism to sound awesome and profound."

Silas chuckled. "Sounds about right."

"It's also a phrase that was apparently posted on someone's WeShare account the day before they shot up a school in Michigan."

"Did you say Michigan?" the chief startled.

"Michigan?" echoed Gina with the same surprise.

Elijah frowned. "Is there an echo in here? Yes, the Great Lakes State."

An interesting connection given the case from Mill Creek.

She grabbed the diary back from Elijah's lap, flipping backward through its pages. The creepo drawing was the last entry, undated but coming after the previous one from three days ago.

Eli asked, "Drawn by this dead woman, we presume?"

Silas nodded. "Presumably…"

Gina glanced through the other pages, disturbing entries about voices in her head and despairing thoughts, feelings of being trapped inside of herself and worthless to the world. An unrelenting desire to run away, to escape, to end it all. Classic suicidal ideation. Painful to read, and very familiar.

Snapping the diary closed, she asked, "How is Peter taking it?"

Silas shifted in his chair. "Not good. They weren't close, the man only having assumed the pulpit a few years ago. But…well, he was her parishioner."

"Sure."

"And there's more."

"More?" Elijah said, snapping his head to attention. "More what?"

"More suicides," said Silas. "And in Peter's church."

"Oh my cheeps…"

"For the love…" Gina added, giving her head a shake in disbelief. "I assume the authorities are worried that a suicide cluster has formed, brought on by a brewing suicide contagion."

"Suicide cluster…" Elijah turned to her. "And suicidal contagion? What are those?"

She smiled. "Don't tell me the venerable Elijah Xavier Fox isn't in the know about something, what with that eidetic memory of yours and all?"

He frowned. "Shocking, I know."

Now she giggled. "Just playing, Eli. Anyway, it's long been held that when a suicidal contagion occurs, a suicide cluster can develop. A cluster defined as several suicidal ideations or actions within a community that bloom within an accelerated time frame, even within a particular geographical area."

"Like Small Town, America?"

"That's right. The exposure to suicide or suicidal behaviors within one's family, one's peer group, or through media reports of suicide can result in an increase in suicide and suicidal behaviors. Just like a viral contagion takes hold of a community, so too can psycho-social dynamics infect a group. Like Small Town, America."

Silas said, "I'm not sure what the authorities are thinking about the case. Peter called me up after this latest…episode asking for help. There were some strange happenings in that town a few years ago that SEPIO dealt with, and he wondered if there might be a connection."

Gina leaned forward with interest, the psycho-social dimension of the case definitely intriguing her. "What sort of strange happenings?"

"Some upstart charismatic faith healers had rolled into town promising a strange blessing."

Elijah smirked. "What, like a mansion on the ocean in Orange County and Botox-like skin for life?"

"Something like that." Silas went on, "Turns out, all they were offering was deadly hope, a conspiracy to rake in the millions through infecting people around the globe with a contagion concocted in Mill Creek Junction."

Gina said, "And you think this…suicidal contagion is somehow linked?"

"Don't know," he said with a shrug. Then he grinned, adding, "That's why I pay you two the big bucks."

Elijah laughed, loud and from the gut, the guffaw echoing in the bay window and eliciting a stern look from the goth chic at the front counter.

Silas frowned. "At any rate, I'd like you two to see if something's going on. Can't be a coincidence six people have committed suicide in the span of one week in the same church."

"Six?" Gina exclaimed, her gut sinking to the floor even as disbelief bloomed in her head. "How big is this town of yours?"

"Something like five thousand."

"Egads!"

Elijah turned to her. "What's up, Gina colada?"

"The annual age-adjusted suicide rate in the United States is 13.42 per 100,000 individuals."

"Egads is right…" he whispered, sinking into his chair. Looked like he was picking up what she was putting down.

"Something seriously messed up is going down to spark a tenfold increase—and in one week! Something inexplicable…"

"Don't you mean…*inexplicitus*?" Elijah deadpanned.

Gina chuckled, smacking his leg; her partner yelped.

Silas stood. "Which is why you best get going."

Gina nodded. "Suppose so."

"Wait a minute," Elijah said, sitting stiff with wide eyes. "You said Mill Creek Junction."

Silas nodded. "Right."

"That's, what, like 645 miles from here."

"Sounds about right."

"That's like a day's drive!"

"Well…I sort of need you there by dinner."

He swallowed hard, eyes growing wider. Gina knew exactly what was coming.

"But that means flying!"

Silas shrugged. "That a problem?"

Gina knew it was, her partner having a fear of flying. Nearly as bad as her own fear of elevators, but not as paralyzing. But knowing him, he'd overcome it for the sake of the investigation.

He sighed, then nodded. "I knew I should have stayed in bed."

Gina understood completely.

CHAPTER 3

The quiet hum of the LearJet 85's engines lulled Elijah to sleep as he reclined in the soft, tan leather chair. Add to that the dark-mahogany minibar stocked with hundred-dollar bottles of booze at the rear and the same wooden accents around the windows and baseboard, and he might get used to this kind of flying.

Might.

Because Elijah Xavier Fox hated flying. Had a phobia about it, in fact. Mostly brought on by claustrophobia, the thought of zooming around through the heavens in a metal tube breathing other people's air on top of other people's germs (yeah, add germaphobia into the mix, too!), combined with speeding hundreds of miles an hour thousands of miles above the ground —he was dumbfounded there weren't more people averse to flying!

But this...

At just under $21 million, the luxe jet was the latest in top-of-the-line air travel for the uber-rich. Or a Christian religious order flush with Vatican cash footing the bill for two former-FBI investigators on their way to the Midwest.

Part of him wondered what he'd gotten himself into zooming

through the sky in such luxury. The Order of Thaddeus sounded suspiciously like the kind of fronts that populated religious conspiracy action-adventure thrillers perched on the shelves of airport bookstores than anything he'd normally be associated with. His was a life that was neither action-filled nor adventurous. Certainly not thrilling—he'd been a professor of biblical theology at a no-name graduate school for Pete's sake!

But now look at him. Headlining the Church's investigative agency sussing out unexplainable, supernatural mysteries.

Elijah gripped the soft feeling of privilege beneath his fingers while resting his hands on the leather-wrapped armrests. He took another deep breath of filtered, ionized, private-jet air unsullied by a hundred grimy passengers, then took another swig (from a Waterford crystal glass, no less) of Meritage red wine he found in the back.

Which really didn't mean much, since Meritage was sort of an American invention trying to circumvent trade import laws for red and white Bordeaux-style wines without infringing on the Bordeaux region's legally protected designation of origin. So the fact the Order stocked that kind of red wine instead of an actual Bordeaux—say, a Chateau Margaux, with 94% Cabernet Sauvignon, 3% Cabernet Franc, 2% Merlot, 1% Petit Verdot—told Elijah what kind of low-brow outfit he was working for.

Although, they were zooming through the stratosphere in a LearJet. Supposed that counted for something.

As he brought the freshly poured wineglass to his mouth, the plane dipped, sending some of the crimson liquid over the sides.

Elijah held the glass steady as they hit another shuddering wave of turbulence, then took a sip and set down the glass before the next one rolled them. He licked the spilled Bordeaux blend off his hand, then glanced over at Gina. Who was completely checked out, head lolling to the side as one final bump of air knocked them around.

He threw back another mouthful of the heavy red wine, his taste buds dancing with the mouthy blackcurrant flavors and candied violets, and nose now confused by a mixture of cigar box with subtle wafts of lavender and oolong tea. Wowie was that an interesting mix! If he wasn't careful, he might overwhelm his olfactory senses. But…man oh man was that wine the cat's purr!

Maybe the Order wasn't so bad after all. And maybe he just found a new wine blend to love!

Meritage…whoda thought?

Elijah settled back in his seat and closed his eyes, wondering what on earth he was doing traveling halfway across the country again to chase down the truth about some mysterious deaths.

Bad enough he'd chased down mysterious minister deaths earlier in the year, and now he and Gina were being sent to suss out parishioner suicides? Sort of beneath him. And sort of felt out of his league on this. Suicides had never been on the FBI's radar, unless some high-profile muckety-muck was the victim, and it looked like foul play could be involved. So, not much experience on this end of the investigative scale.

Which ratcheted up a rising sense of anxiety about next steps.

Heart started rapping a foreboding beat against his ribcage; lungs searched for more air; head bloomed with the voices of his childhood that told him he was never good enough, couldn't hack it, would never amount to anything. Before he knew it, he was strumming through his tick.

Thumb to index finger, thumb to middle, thumb to ring finger, thumb to pinkie. Then rinse and repeat.

Another two rounds of that, the droning hum of the jet engine reminding him he was sailing through the stratosphere 45,000 feet above Earth, sent him for that mouthy Meritage with backbone again.

The dueling tastes of blackcurrant and tobacco skated across his tongue, filling his head with delight and grounding him back to reality—his reality, the one Yeshua Almighty had mapped out for him. Accompanying the grounding alcohol was a calming verse, from the Book of Jeremiah: *'Before I formed you in the womb*

I knew you, and before you were born, I consecrated you...Do not be afraid of them, for I am with you to deliver you.'

Elijah smiled, thanking the Holy Spirit for giving him all the grounding in his investigative operation he needed, and courage: his very Word.

The case still weirded him, though. A cluster of suicides in a small-town church. Now that took the cheesecake.

Nothing like the glory days when he and Gina colada brought down a child sex ring fueled by satanic ritual abuse down in Albuquerque, New Mexico. Or the mysterious killings in Dubuque, Iowa, brought on by the psychedelic extracts from some ayahuasca shaman. Now that was a trip—literally, as he'd downed a glass of the stuff while undercover and had the loopiest dreams ever.

But then he took a deep breath, enjoying the tart scent of supple leather and sighed, enjoying, even more, the tart feeling of his mouthy Meritage. He knew why he was annoyed. It was the reason he did most things in his life, the ones that eventually got him into trouble, anyway. Those double-trouble deadly sins of pride and envy.

If he wasn't careful, that deadly pair would be his ruin.

Almost had been, a time or two...

Half a bottle of that Meritage that was growing on him (he'd have to swipe the label and hunt it down) did the trick, numbing his nerves and settling his anxious brain enough to complete the quick hour and a half flight time. The Order-issued jet banked toward Grand Rapids and started coming in for a landing.

He looked out across the familiar Interstate 196 running from Detroit to Lake Michigan, and down around toward Chicago, a blanket of foliage putting a bit of a skip in his heartbeat. Which was odd. Hadn't really bonded with his old hometown. Had never really bonded with anywhere he'd lived, having bounced around so much between foster homes as a child. Kenturkey was about the only place he'd gotten attached to. Even then, after Dad was murdered, it was hard to go back.

The Order jet landed half an hour outside Mill Creek Junction just after noon with a bounce before skidding to a shuddering stop at the end of the runway at Grand Rapids International Airport.

Elijah gripped the supple armrest as the jet recovered from its halting landing, the sweet scent of leather rising at his tightening grip.

"Breathe, Eli, breathe," Gina said with a chuckle across from him.

Exhaling through pursed lips, he smirked. "Easy for you to say. You're not the one with aerophobia."

"True, but the wicked combo of acrophobia and claustrophobia ain't nothing to write home about. Hence, my special candies."

She gave an orange prescription bottle a jiggle, pale rectangular pills jostling around inside.

"Xanax?" Elijah asked, bringing his seat upright.

"Sure thing—"

"—chicken wing," he said, finishing her rhyme. Was always rhyming all the timing, she was. One of the things he liked about her. He raised his Waterford crystal, saying, "I prefer my anti-anxiety meds in a glass."

"And the power of the Holy Spirit, right?"

"Of course."

As the jet continued onward, Elijah glanced outside at the familiar scenery—which wasn't much. It was flatter than a flapjack out there, the airport a plainspoken concrete monstrosity without any character that was surrounded by low-slung office buildings and warehouses.

Home sweet home.

Waiting for them when the LearJet parked in a darkened hangar was a Cadillac Escalade, white and with gold accents. Another SUV, and a pimped-out one at that. What was it with this religious order outfit? First a Mercedes G-Class, then some yuppy's American Dream ride? Not a fan of cars, and definitely not a fan of the oversized monstrosities that bespoke the rank consumerism that held the West in a death-grip.

He'd have to have a chat with Silas Grey about that, but supposed the oversized chrome wheels and supple tan leather and SiriusXM hook-up would make the journey bearable.

Elijah offered Gina the captain's chair, but she said she was too loopy from the Xanax and flying to drive. He threw up a complaint, but she was already in the passenger's seat flipping through the radio before he knew it.

"Fine," he said, slipping into another cabin of creamy leather. "But I'm picking the tunage."

"Whatevs," Gina protested, flipping through the stations and throwing up a whole heck of a lot of weird tunage complaining about ex-lovers.

Bringing the beast to life, he said, "I drive, I pick the tunage. My rules."

"For the love…"

Finding a good jazz station on the satellite radio—Kenny Burrell working an electric guitar like it was nobody's business —he pealed out of the garage on toward destiny.

The drive to Mill Creek Junction wasn't much better than the airport, the highway cutting east through farmland being tilled by bright green John Deeres working the fields and suburban sprawl composed of cookie-cutter plastic houses that made his skin crawl.

Not that he expected anything more. After all, it was the Midwest; it was Michigan. Flatter than a flapjack, though, without all the conifers and deciduous trees and rocky hills from his childhood and even his young adult. One of the things he'd missed the past few years was backpacking through mountainous forests. None of that in these parts.

It was mid-afternoon by the time Elijah pulled off the interstate and made for Mill Creek, the sun full and sky wide open with possibilities.

He asked, "Do we know anything about the town?"

"Thought you could clue me in," Gina said, "since you were from around here."

"Didn't get out much. And definitely didn't get over to Mill Creek. *Oof*," he said with a grimacing shudder.

"Now, now, Eli. No room for snoot on an investigation where lives are concerned."

"Touché," he mumbled.

Gina swiped through her phone. "Here's something on the town's website, a bit of their history."

"Oh my cheeps!" Elijah exclaimed. "Mill Creek Junction has a website? Can't be too backwoods, I suppose."

She cleared her throat and read:

A hundred and forty-four years ago, our ancestors saw fit to start a new town along the mighty Grand River that would also be a new way of life. A life built on working the land and feeding the world, the windmill at the north end of town still standing as a monument to that vision. A life built on gumption and ingenuity, where anyone could make something of themselves if they put their mind to it. A life of morals and ethics and religious conviction. A life of learning and working and building and marrying and raising a family. A life of giving and sharing and communing and supporting one another. We are Mill Creek Junction. Welcome!

"Sounds homey," she added. "Like a good place to raise a family."

"Looks like it, too." Elijah pointed forward, the Escalade firmly riding on Main Street now.

They were leaving the flat farmland for something a bit more interesting. Oaks and maples and sycamores towered above the road ahead on either side, full and flowering, followed by neat rows of turn-of-the-century homes telling a story that plucked at Elijah's heartstrings. Lawns were well-manicured and the bright, cheery day made it all look like something from a Norman Rockwell painting, it was so perfect.

There were inexpensive bungalows painted brown and beige and white, along with red and brown brick, tree swings hanging from those large, old trees. Then more modest craftsman-style homes—some last century, some this century; two-stories and split levels; some all bright and others painted with contrasting trim; all with generous porches that bespoke an era long gone in America. Down a wide side street overhanging with more of the same towering trees, generous two and three-story colonial revival houses bespoke of a wealthier side of town Elijah wouldn't have expected.

Got lost marveling at the small town, and the shops and cafes along Main Street. Turned around at a Kwikimart before barreling back through the Norman Rockwell dreamscape again.

"So, what are you thinking about the case?" Gina asked as they passed a Starbucks. Generally, wasn't a fan of Big Coffee, but at least he knew of a joint that he could get a decent cup of Joe, if it came to it.

"Sure takes the cake…" he said, apprehension rising again.

"Don't you mean *cheese*cake?"

He threw her a grin. "Oh, yeah. The bane of my corporate restaurant chain existence."

"*Psht*. Corporate restaurant chain my hiney. What about Cracker Barrel?"

"Doesn't count."

"Why?"

"Because they've got the best breakfast this side of the Mississippi."

"No, that's Bob Evans."

Elijah almost hit a granny crossing the street at that one. He slammed on the brakes and scoffed.

"You're seriously comparing Cracker Barrel to Bob Evans."

Gina shrugged. "Their sweet tea is to die for."

He frowned and got back to it. "You better watch yourself, Gina colada. I know where you live. Besides, that cheesecake factory joint has 85 different chicken dishes. No restaurant should have 85 different chicken dishes. That's insane."

"Whatever. How about we stop arguing about culinary capitalism and get back to the case."

"Right. Suicidal parishioners."

She sighed. "Sure does take the cake."

"Nope. Cheesecake. Besides, a one-pager isn't enough to have an opinion."

"But that diary…Freaky-deaky is what that thing was."

"I'll give you that. There was also something familiar about it."

"Like what?"

Elijah shook his head. "Not sure. Just a feeling."

"Hopefully, Pastor Pete can shed some light on it all. Because things could get interesting."

"Speaking of which…"

Elijah turned into the Mill Creek Baptist Church drive. Cracked blacktop led to a modest lot of the same, with faded yellow parking lines, empty but for two cars anchored next to the handicap spots in front of a rather sad looking structure. A one level building, sided with beige plastic siding, jutted off toward the left from a large hall with a sharply peaked roof.

Elijah figured that was the sanctuary, as a tall cross was anchored to the roof at the far end. Looked like a whale with a spout of holy water spraying from the top. Could never understand why his fellow evangelicals were more content to worship in spaces decked out in metal chairs and stage lighting than the glories of stained glass and crucifixes, with ceilings that soared high with buttresses and walls decorated with bright saintly icons—something he'd taken to while studying at Cambridge University, as well as Anglicanism.

But Gina was right: snoot had no place in an investigation where lives were concerned. Even if he was right.

Elijah parked the Escalade in a spot a few rows back, then the pair made for the entrance.

He led them into a dimly lit lobby smelling not much different than the church he grew up in. Mold and mildew, old wood and stale Folgers. Funny how churches smelled the same, no matter the denomination. Wide windows offered a glimpse into the sanctuary. Honey wood pews with crimson cushions arrayed in neat rows dutifully faced a large wood cross emptied of Christ's body anchored to the wall behind a large wood pulpit —a typical-looking Protestant sanctuary.

"Home sweet home…" he muttered.

Gina said, "That's right. I'd forgotten you were raised a Baptist. So the same family of Protestants, eh?"

"Nope." He gave his head a shake. "Same flavor, different family. Believe I saw this one's an Independent Regular Baptist church."

"As opposed to irregular Baptists," she quipped.

He laughed. "Good one! I'll have to use that someday."

"Hello?" a voice called out from behind.

Icky fluorescent lighting shuddered to life down a darkened hallway. Appearing through the sickly lit corridor was a man of modest height, wearing a white V-neck shirt and dark skinny jeans. Hair was cropped short on the side, the rest of it long and slicked back. Looked late thirties, around Elijah's age. Remembered the man from last year, when he graciously took him and Gina and the rest of the SEPIO agents in after the Feds blew up his former place of employ.

Peter's face brightened on approach. "Hey, I remember you two."

"Elijah Fox," he said, then gestured to his partner. "Gina Anderson. Investigators with Group X."

"Group X?" The pastor raised a brow.

"Think the Vatican's x-files. Silas Grey said you needed some help. Something about a string of suicides."

He heaved a breath and sighed, running a hand through his hair. "That's right. Good of you two to come. And x-files is about what we've been dealing with."

Elijah crossed his arms and asked, "And what exactly is it that you've been dealing with?"

"Let's go my office. I can lay it all out there."

CHAPTER 4

Peter led them through the fluorescent-lit hallway that looked like a set of offices, that stale coffee more pronounced now, along with the scent of copier ink and some sort of pine candle.

Gina smiled, the memory of her office from Quantico, Virginia, springing to the surface. Always kept a lit pine candle, she did. A Yankee Candle Co. candle. None of those cheapie Walmart knock-offs that smelled more like a truck stop bathroom air freshener than the Pennsylvanian forests her dad had taken her camping. Her real one, not the stingers that came through Mama's double-wide.

Samuel Anderson was his name. And while he walked out on the family when she was ten, on account of Mama's pain pill problems and nasty fights, he did find her after Grace passed. Made a real effort to reconnect and be the father he failed to be for all those years.

And one of those ways was camping trips in the Allegheny National Forest a few hours into Pennsylvania. The scents were positively heavenly! Pine and cedar, joined by moss and earth. That wasn't even touching on the woodsmoke from campfires and grilling hot dogs and coffee. Well, not the coffee part. Hated the scent of it with a passion that burned bright and strong.

Anyhoo, a blessed relief from all the Toledo factories and plants belching carcinogens into the air every second of the day, it was. As well as the time she'd spent with Dad, her only family left. A psychology professor, of all things.

"It's hot as Hades in here," complained Elijah, undoing his top button to his starch-white shirt and loosening his blue bow tie dotted yellow. Loved that about him, dressing all proper all the time. Especially donning those bow ties. Had been a trademark of his at the Bureau, and the fellas had ribbed him for it.

Peter turned to him. "Yeah, sorry about that. Air conditioner is on the fritz, so it might get a little toasty as the afternoon rolls on."

"Just our luck…"

The pastor headed left at a T-juncture and stopped at a reception area lit by more bright fluorescent lights that made Gina squint with discomfort. Hated those things, something she and Eli shared. Made life in the bowels of the J. Edgar Hoover Building bearable, the pair of them preferring a darkened workspace with some floor lamps to government-issued, OSHA-approved lighting.

A corner copy machine was spitting out a stack of what looked like bulletins, those half-folded, multi-colored sheets of paper with the Sunday morning schedule and weekly list of events. A phone rang on the desk, its incessant ring wailing for attention going unanswered by a woman in her 60s.

"Hey, Kat," Peter said, "I'd like you to meet some friends of mine."

The older woman, sporting gray curly hair with a silver hummingbird clip in a tasteful mint-colored dress, startled at some Herman Miller leftover, beige and dented and probably donated, looking wide-eyed at a laptop—which she promptly snapped shut on their arrival.

Elijah smirked. "Hope you weren't watching *Fifty Shades of Grey*. Because that would be *real* awkward."

Gina jammed an elbow in his ribs; he yelped. She had to do that sometime.

For obvious reasons.

Sometimes she'd wished the good Lord above had sought fit to sew a verbal filter on his creatures. Especially the male species. And definitely those named Eli Xavier! That boy had a mouth on him that didn't come with a filter. One day it would get him into mega trouble, mister—the both of them!

The poor woman named Kat, or something, seemed to choke on her tongue. Embarrassment bloomed crimson in her cheeks, and she looked down while bringing a hand to coke-bottle glasses to adjust them while shifting in her seat. She brought a white shawl closer around her shoulders for comfort.

"Kidding!" Elijah said with a half-hearted chuckle and waving jazz hands.

Peter just stood there with wide eyes, clearly not knowing what to do.

"Well, I for one," Gina said, trying to diffuse things, "thought *Fifty Shades of Grey* the movie was a pale comparison to the book. They always are, aren't they?"

Peter's eyes went wider, and Kat went fifty shades of even more crimson.

"Kidding..." Gina mumbled, bringing a hand to her hair and twisting it.

Elijah said, "Now that both of us put our feet in our mouth... I'm Elijah Fox. This is Gina Anderson."

Peter explained, "They're here to help with the Warner case."

"Ahh," the woman said, face drawn and pinched and going white now. A curious woman Gina couldn't get a read on. Seemed troubled, on top of embarrassed. Good going Eli...

"Katrina Hanson, here," the pastor continued, gesturing to the woman, "is my sweet-mannered administrative assistant.

Reminds me more of my grandma than anyone who should be assisting me."

Katrina smiled now, sitting a little straighter.

"Not that I don't need administrating. Certainly not one of my spiritual gifts! Just felt weird when I started pastoring at Mill Creek bossing someone around who looked like the woman who slapped me around and set me straight my whole life."

Now she laughed, making another adjustment to her glasses.

"Not much fond of giving orders, but Katrina's been more than willing to help out and put me on a good administrative footing. Even slapping me around a bit!"

"Oh, stop it, Pastor Young," Katrina said. "You're a peach to work for."

Smirking, Gina leaned over to Eli. "You need someone like that to slap you around a bit when you need it, methinks!"

He turned to her. "Isn't that what you're for?"

"Don't you know it!"

"Hey, Kat," Peter said, "hold my calls for me, would you? We're going to be meeting for a while."

Katrina nodded, her silver curls bouncing at her shoulders and her coke-bottle glasses sliding down the bridge of her nose. The pastor led the way, and Gina glanced behind.

Catching the woman heaving a heavy breath before hoisting an oversized tan cloth purse up on her desk. She eased her laptop open again, a blue glow casting wicked lines on the woman's widening face. Sat there for the longest few seconds, unblinking, unmoving.

Except for her lips. They were doing a sort of pantomiming dance before she bit at her bottom one and returned to her purse.

Interesting. Real interesting…

Gina hustled to catch up to Eli and Peter, who was pushing through a windowed door into a cramped space lit by more of that awful fluorescent lighting. A few bookshelves lined one wall behind a CEO-style desk with two brown herringbone wingback chairs in front and a complementary tan couch along one wall.

Elijah crossed his arms and regarded the space. "Say, pastor—"

"Peter's fine," the man said with interruption.

"Alright. Say, Peter, what's the difference between a high-church minister and a low-church pastor?"

"Like me, you mean?"

Eli shrugged and nodded. Gina jammed another elbow into his side as she passed. "No offense or anything…" he quickly added.

The pastor chuckled. "None taken. And, if I recall the joke, pastors have offices, priests have studies."

Eli dropped his arms. "Hey, you stole my thunder."

"Hear, hear!" Gina clapped and took a seat in one of the wingback chairs.

Her partner joined her in the other. "Like Gina said, no offense or anything. But your office passes muster."

"Gee, thanks." Taking a seat behind his desk, Peter asked, "So what are you guys, anyway? Silas was pretty coy about your identity."

"Group X," Elijah said.

"What's that?"

Gina explained, "We're the investigative arm for the Order of Thaddeus, joining the operational one SEPIO, the Order's more kinetic wing responsible for protecting the faith."

"Kinetic wing…" Peter chuckled. "That's one way of putting it. Nearly got blown to bits a year ago while in the thick of one of their *kinetic* operations."

Elijah smirked. "Sounds about right."

Gina added, "And sounds like you've been in the thick of it once again."

Peter frowned, and he heaved a sigh. Looked like he was carrying the weight of the world on those thirtysomething shoulders of his. He was going to need something stiffer than skinny jeans to get through this one.

He said, "You could say that."

"Why don't you take it from the top?"

First, he stood. "How about I get some refreshments. This could take a while."

"Herbal tea for me, please."

"*Herbal* tea?" Elijah said with surprise. "I thought it was black Red Rose all the way?"

Gina shrugged. "Can't a girl branch out?"

"Nope."

She smacked his knee; he yelped.

Now he grimaced. "*Blech.* Coffee for me. But none of that cardboard Folgers church special."

"Don't worry. From one coffee connoisseur to another, I think you'll be pleased."

He disappeared for several minutes before reappearing with a tray of mugs.

Setting the tray down on his desk, the pastor handed a mug of hot water with a tea bag draped across the edge to Gina. She took it and smiled, fresh mint hitting her nose and sailing straight to her head.

He promptly poured coffee into the other two mugs. Surprisingly didn't smell half bad.

Taking a swig of brew, Elijah hummed with pleasure. "Not half bad. Nutty with some caramel notes thrown in for good measure."

"Glad it sits right," Peter said.

"So, the top of the cheesecake."

He raised a brow. "The top of the what?"

Gina said, "He means, start from the top."

Throwing back a swig, Peter nodded. "It all started a few months ago. A teenager from my congregation jumped into Mill Creek. To her death…"

Peter went silent, casting his eyes down into his mug.

"By Mill Creek, you mean…"

He took a breath, then explained, "The river that runs on the north end of town."

"River? That doesn't compute," Elijah said. "Why isn't the place called Mill River Junction?"

Peter shrugged. "Was a creek back in the day, back when the town was settled some 150 years ago. Something about widening it to compete with the Grand River for waterway commerce and make way for the mill that made the Junction a thriving town back in the day."

Eli scoffed. "Thriving. I bet."

Gina threw him eyes that said enough's enough; she had to do that sometimes.

He nodded and looked off at the ceiling, as if he both understood but was annoyed; he did that sometimes, too.

"You said," she went on, drawing a spiral notepad from her back pocket, "that a teenager jumped. And it sounded like a girl."

Peter nodded. "That's right. Abby Johnson. Fourteen."

"Fourteen…"

Gina had to catch her breath at that revelation. Same age as Grace when she herself passed…

She found the pen knocking against the pad of paper, a tremor taking hold of her hand. She clenched it tight, crossing one leg over another and casually reaching for her ginger locks, twirling them to stay the rising sense of dread. The memory of her own sister's death still smarted; would for anyone. So young, so early.

And here was another sweet angel, taken from this world for God only knows why.

God only knows is right. Sometimes that idea made Gina hopping mad—the idea that God knew what was going on inside people tormented by fear, anxiety, despair, dread, misery, hopelessness. Yet what did he do about it? Bupkis! Took everything within Gina sometimes not to just give up entirely on their being a God, let alone a benevolent Father who loved the world with a crazy love—enough that he sent his one and only Son to die on that wretched cross for the world's rebellion against him.

Took a long time to talk with him again after her own sister's death. And now fourteen-year-old Abby. How could a good God allow someone so sweet and innocent to die—to take their own life?

Apparently, there were more…

Elijah said, "Silas said six people had…well, died by their own hand," drawing Gina back to the moment.

"Right. There were four more. Well, five, including the latest one."

"Abby was the first?" Gina asked, returning to her notepad.

"That's right. Then Carrie McLaughlin, Trisha Lyndon, Jessica Briggs, Maggie Atwood—she was the youngest."

Gina gasped. "Younger than fourteen?"

"Twelve…" Peter whispered, swallowing hard with a rise in emotion springing to his eyes.

"Oh my cheeps…" Elijah said.

Gina agreed.

"Who was the latest?"

Peter sniffed and batted at his eyes with his shirt sleeve. "Gloria Warner, a longtime member of Mill Creek Baptist whose husband is on our church council."

"And also a longtime Christian," Gina said. "Who would have presumably understood such a thing to be—" she paused, searching for words.

"Not Christian?" Elijah said, giving her what she was looking for.

"Presumably," Peter simply said.

"How did she die?"

He sighed and leaned back in his chair. "I'd prefer you deal with the authorities on that one. They've got all the details that I'd rather not get into."

Gina said, "Understandable, pastor. Same for the others?"

He nodded. "As you can imagine, Mill Creek PD has been all over this. Six suicides, in the span of a few months. Makes folks skittish, you know?"

"How old were the others? You said fourteen and—" She took a breath and swallowed. "Twelve..."

"Two were sixteen. Trish and Jessica. Carrie was twenty-one or twenty-two."

"Then Gloria, who was sixty-something?"

"Sixty-four."

"You said months," Elijah clarified.

Peter nodded again. "Since just after the new year."

Gina asked, "Were these girls, and these women, close friends?"

"The four girls were in the same youth group. Pretty active, too. Since we're a small church, I also double as the youth pastor."

"Makes sense," Eli said. "Especially with that hair and those skinny jeans."

Crimson raced to the hipster pastor's cheeks, and he shifted in his seat with a chuckle.

"What about the women?" Gina asked.

He shrugged. "Not sure. I mean, they knew one another. Small church and town and all."

"Sure. What about any history of mental instability or suicidal ideation in any of the victims?"

Peter opened his mouth to answer but snapped it shut instead, drawing his lips into a thin line and jaw clenching shut. His eyes went down, and they started blinking. Avoidance and hesitation, while mulling over how much to reveal.

Or not.

"Listen, pal," Elijah said, "you sought our help."

"And priestly confidentiality doesn't apply after death," added Gina. "Especially given the nature of the travesty."

That emotion rose to Peter's eyes again, along with his face going blotchy and that jaw working like it was nobody's business. The man was clearly bothered by something.

"It isn't—" His throat tripped over itself, and he coughed to recover. "It isn't that. The confidentiality and all."

"Then what?" asked Elijah.

Peter heaved a sigh, as if the weight of the world were on his shoulders. Supposed at least the weight of a small town was.

"I knew that the girls were having trouble."

Gina leaned forward. "What sort of trouble?"

"Abby and Maggie said they'd been bullied at school, and it had been extending online with social media."

Elijah smacked a closed fist against his hand. "Kids can be such bastards sometimes."

Peter startled at that, but didn't respond.

Gina knew Eli's past, with his own bout of bullying at the orphanage, then during his gauntlet of foster families. She herself had known the raw end of verbal sticks and stones during high school. Double-wide living wasn't the golden ticket into the "in" crowds, even in Toledo.

"What about the other two girls?" she asked.

"Both Trish and Jessica," Peter answered, "had been dealing with eating disorders. Tried my best to see them through, connecting them with a counselor teaching at the local college, but…"

He trailed off, emotion rising again. Have to imagine pastoring in this day and age was a real bugger.

"And the women?" asked Elijah.

Peter shrugged. "Not too sure about Carrie, but Gloria—well, she was different."

"What do you mean, different?"

"Our counseling sessions, that's what!"

Gina asked, "What was different about Gloria?"

Something shifted in the pastor. Sudden and overwhelming. His back went straight and rigid. His eyes widened and face drained of color. That jaw was set again, lips thin and almost trembling. He took a shuddering breath before easing it out through his nose.

"The diary," he whispered. "Did you bring it?"

Gina turned to Eli, who had it in his jacket.

When he bolted to his feet.

Brow furrowed and spinning around. As if he was searching for something, but unsure what. His sudden movement cut off the man's reply, and messed up Gina's mojo.

But that wasn't all.

His face had drained a shade, like Peter's, and he started up his finger tick.

Thumb to index finger, thumb to middle, thumb to ring finger, thumb to pinkie. Then rinse and repeat.

Which meant something had shifted.

"Eli, what's wrong?" she asked.

He snapped his gaze to her, his eyes saying it all.

Nothing good.

CHAPTER 5

The last thing Elijah heard before the other thing he heard was something about the diary. The one with the cursive writing and crazy goblin drawing with the weird Oppenheimer quote that was really a pagan Hindu one.

Then he bolted to his feet.

Brow furrowed and spinning around. Searching for the faintest of sounds that pinged his ears. Was sure his face had drained of color, too, because something inside his lizard brain told him exactly what it was. That part in the back that had helped his distant ancestors survive being run up the rear by a mastodon's tusk, or shredded by a saber-toothed tiger.

But what he'd heard wasn't the grunt or growl of some prehistoric beast.

It was a muffled pop. Almost like a balloon in the next room. Or one of those air pillows he loved to pop in packages from Amazon, the sweet, sanitized air giving him a peck on the nose after keeping his next vinyl record safe and secure.

Except what he'd heard wasn't either of those things.

One might have interpreted the pop as a firecracker, from maybe some kiddo playing hooky up the road. But target practice with Dad as a teenager had clued him in long ago the difference between one of those and something else far more deadly.

Which ratcheted his heart rate and started up his finger tick without him even knowing it.

Thumb to index finger, thumb to middle, thumb to ring finger, thumb to pinkie. Then rinse and repeat.

"Eli, what's wrong?"

Gina's voice jolted him from his contemplation sussing out the faint noise.

Elijah snapped his gaze to her, his eyes seeking her corroboration at what he swore he'd heard.

"Did you hear that?"

She furrowed her brow, neck craning and eyes roaming around the room. "Hear what?"

"Was that gunfire?"

Peter chuckled, then turned toward the window. "Probably fireworks. This state has some of the dumbest, permissive laws about that sort of thing, and Chief Roller doesn't enforce what little—"

"It wasn't fireworks," Elijah said with interruption, heart racing with recognition now and lungs searching for breath.

Where Peter was still craning outside, his attention was trained on only one part of the room.

The vent, perched at the ceiling behind Peter's desk.

Should have been pumping out cold air into the joint, except it was on the fritz. Which allowed something else to travel through those corridors of galvanized steel, the absence of any HVAC hum giving it all the room it needed to channel something other than air.

Sound.

Like the muffled pop of nothing good from somewhere inside the church. Amazing how far sound waves can travel when nothing else is getting in the way, bouncing from one angle to the next until it finds its escape.

Like through a vent perched at the ceiling behind a desk in a pastor's office.

"Eli…" Gina said lowly again. "What is it?"

Elijah frowned, turning back toward that vent and giving his head a shake. "Not sure. But we should check it out."

Hustling to the door, he motioned to his partner and reached for the Glock at his waist for such a time as this.

Gina stood and followed him, removing her own Glock at her waist.

"Umm, is that really necessary?" Peter said, shoving off from his desk and joining them with a concerned, furrowed brow.

Elijah glanced over his shoulder. "Not sure. But better safe than sorry."

Then he pushed out into the hallway—weapon ready, willing, and able, but not outstretched like some low-brow limited streaming series. Not yet, anyway.

It was quieter than before.

Too quiet.

No copy machine doing its office thing. No clattering keyboard keys at the front desk. No ringing telephones and chatter. Nothing that would signal someone was still waiting out in the reception area manning—or he supposed *womanning*, as was the case—the phones and pretending like she wasn't watching *Fifty Shades of Grey*.

He padded down the cinder block hallway of chipping white paint and drew up to the corner that led out to the front office.

Then he drew his weapon to his chest—yes, just like in some low-brow, limited streaming series—and sprang from around the corner. Glock outstretched and ready to put it to good use. Should it come to it.

Empty.

But for that hideous fluorescent lighting, no one and nothing else was around. Expected Katrina to slam her laptop closed again with concealed embarrassment at whatever it was she was peeping, but nope. Must be on a potty break.

Or something…

Gina hustled up behind, weapon outstretched as well before bringing it up for a rest, followed quickly by Peter.

"Where's your assistant?" Elijah asked, already making for the T-junction toward the rest of the church.

Peter was breathing hard, like he'd just run a marathon. He shrugged, then checked his watch. "Quitting time, I suppose."

Elijah glanced behind, wondering…

Then noticed something on the reception desk.

The laptop from earlier. Still opened, faint blue light skating across the clean desk. Chair was perched out from the desk, turned slightly, with an opened purse resting on it. As if its occupant had shoved off, stood, then left—abruptly even, with whatever had been nestled inside her lady bag. The white shawl he'd noticed her wearing was still there, so why would Katrina leave for the day without her shawl?

"Where's the woman's bathroom?" he asked.

Peter glanced down at the other end of the T-junction. "There's a uni-sex bathroom down that way."

"Gina—"

"On it." She left for a moment, Elijah's heart rate picking up pace as the minutes ticked by.

Half a minute later, she returned. "Empty."

His bowels now felt weak and watery, and he gripped his Glock tighter, wanting to strum through his finger tick, but knew it was neither the time nor the place.

"Any other bathrooms?" Elijah asked instead.

Peter answered, "Just a main set in the foyer."

"Let's check it out."

"But why, when Kat—"

"Let's check it out!" he insisted before shoving off toward the way they arrived.

Temperature had really ratcheted up with that HVAC on the fritz. Humidity too, the air cloying and clawing through the hallway. Heat was really amplifying those old church smells as well.

The dampness and musty smell of a basement, the old wood and Folgers. *Blech!*

Foyer was dark, but for the sunlight streaming in through the double glass doors. A card table was set up on one wall with some sign-up sheets for Bible studies and a Tuesday morning prayer meeting. Old-time tracts were dutifully arrayed, all recounting the horrors of hell and blessings of heaven.

A few missionary pictures were tacked on a bulletin board papered over with a Rand McNally map, strings spider-legging to their place of ministry overseas. Tonga, Thailand, Timbuktu. Quite the alliterative bunch—

And then he saw it.

Scratch that. First he *felt* it—a sort of tugging force, tingly and insistent, that drew his attention to the large picture window looking into the sanctuary he'd raised his nose up at upon arrival. It was the Holy Spirit, cluing him into something.

The vaulted space was dark, but for a muddy mess of stained-glass colors filtering the late-afternoon sun inside and brightening the boring off-white walls—casting their gaze on something propped up in one of those polished honey wood pews cushioned with crimson.

That's when he saw it.

Scratch that again. Not *something* propped up in one of those polished honey wood pews cushioned with crimson.

Someone…

And not propped, either. Not even sitting.

Reclining, a body slumped against the hard wooden back. A head of curly gray hair lolled to the side. Still, unmoving. And something glinting in the light.

Elijah's head bloomed with instant recognition. Bile rose to the back of his throat, tasting like sour milk. He swallowed hard, his mouth suddenly dry and sandpapery.

"Oh my cheeps…"

"What do you see?" Peter whispered, stepping to his side and following his gaze.

He put out a staying hand and lowered his Glock. "Stay here."

The double doors into the sanctuary gave easily. Typical cheap church doors of light-weight wood, their hinges throwing up a squeal. Heat slapped him in the face, as well as an odd smell.

Real odd.

Gunpowder. From a discharged weapon.

Made sense on one level, the faint pop thrown up through the ventilation having to come from somewhere. Large galvanized steel ventilation tubes ran down the center of the gabled ceiling, clearly a later addition to the sacred space built several generations ago. The perfect carrier for the sort of faint pop he'd heard.

And yet…on another level, the scent of gunpowder made not a lick of sense.

Because there was no lingering scent of gunpowder from a discharged weapon! At least in modern weapons.

Elijah smirked to himself at the absurdity of those low-brow limited streaming series and bargain-bin Kindle mystery yarns. Didn't know jack about firearms, they didn't. Gunpowder hasn't been used in firearms for a loooong time. And no, the air doesn't smell of cordite (black gunpowder's replacement), a ridiculously specific detail on the level of someone eating a handful of blueberries and it tasting like potassium! Just flat inaccurate and tedious.

Same for cordite, which has been rarely used in any weapon since the mid-20th century! A smokeless propellant is what's used in modern gunpowder. It isn't even powdery, more like the little sprinkles you might find on a donut than anything.

Back to the sanctuary's smell.

Because there was definitely gunpowder in the air. A bit sulfurous, a bit metallic.

And something else…

Couldn't place his finger on it. A bit musty, a bit mossy. Like wet newspaper or wood. Exactly what he remembered from his childhood parish church, actually. Like he'd said when they'd arrived: Amazing how similar churches smell, regardless of which denominational team they played on.

But that wasn't all of it. Because the tang of a zoo was also present. The reptile exhibit, by the stench.

Elijah swallowed hard at that thought, his Adam's apple a lump of clay, then gripped his Glock tighter.

Steady Eli…

Topaz carpet ran under his feet, flat and scuffed and definitely in need of replacement. Color reminded him of a broach the head guardian of his orphanage wore, sending a sour shiver ratcheting up his spine.

He shoved away the memory and centered his concentration on the figure up ahead, Glock a little higher now on approach, but only because his FBI training was kicking in.

One by one, the polished honey wood pews ticked by as he padded forward. Like the metronome during his piano lessons ticking off the beats. Really more like a countdown to the explosive revelation waiting up front, the twenty-three rows he'd counted on arrival halved now and winding down to zero.

Eleven.

Ten.

Nine.

Didn't much want Numero Uno, sensing in his gut what he'd find, but he kept at it, passing—

Six.

Five.

Four.

Before the glinting something resting in the nest of gray curls became clearer. Something silvery, a hair clip.

A hummingbird.

Elijah's breath seized in his chest. All the confirmation he needed.

And now he saw it more clearly.

Dark liquid, thick and sticky, was winding down the back of the polished honey wood, joined by pale matter that looked like his morning oatmeal—from a hole blown clear through the back of the head.

Padding forward, Elijah glimpsed an arm resting across a mint-green dress, fingers lodged inside an unusual weapon. A pistol, clearly from early last century. With a wooden barrel and scuffed silver handle. The sulfuric, metallic smell was heavier there, the olfactory echo marking the spot from which the sound he'd heard had ricocheted.

A gasp from behind startled him.

"Kat?" Peter said, barely above a whisper.

Then again: "Kat?"

Louder as he pushed past right before he yelled: *"Oh my God!"* and spun around toward the horrific scene. Neither with a hint of blasphemy nor with any intention of breaking the Second Commandment taking the Lord's name in vain.

Was more an emotional utterance at seeing his assistant sitting at the front of his sanctuary with half her face blown to bits.

Elijah understood the sentiment completely.

Oh, my God…what the hot Hades happened?

Even Gina was looking green, his partner's face whiter than those sanctuary walls, her hand trembling at her mouth and tears winding down from the corners of her eyes.

My God…*dear* God—this poor woman! What was going on inside herself to bring her to the brink. To bring her to *this* brink.

And now look at things.

Elijah's chest was tightening in a vice grip, his ticker galloping away from him now and lungs screaming for air. He yanked off his blue bow tie with yellow dots—a gift from Mama for Christmas last year—and threw it into a pew row. Then he fiddled with his top shirt button, his fingers jelly and fumbling for relief, eventually finding it.

He stretched his neck, searching heaving helpings full of

stale, staid sanctuary air that had gone warm and warped by old paint and even older wood pews.

But it was no use.

Throat was like a closed fist had jammed itself down inside. Or maybe wrapped itself around Elijah's neck. Didn't know the proper way to describe it; didn't care to. All that mattered was something began welling within that made him feel like he was sipping air through a coffee stir stick!

Something long buried since Dad's death that was now scrambling for the top, scraping along his throat and screaming for release.

Emotion!

There's an unrelenting stereotype that autistic people like him don't have a single empathetic bone in their body. That they cannot understand emotion or offer others emotion—or even feel it themselves when life dumps a pant's load of banana peels in your path. That they're just these unfeeling, unemotional robots that are liable to fry up your brain and eat it with a bottle of Chianti and fava beans (cue Hannibal Lector reference).

Nope. Not true. Not in the slightest.

Autistic people feel! No, really, they do!

Just because it might be expressed differently than the way the average allistic, neurotypical John or Jane express it doesn't mean it's not there.

Laugh, love, cry—the whole shebang taco is the way autistic peeps roll.

Even Elijah Xavier Fox.

Except...

Had been a long time, a real long time since he'd allowed himself to feel. Was a time when he blubbered like a baby whenever a roommate at the orphanage scraped a knee or when the older kids force-fed his bunkmate their underwear (yeah, that happened). And by blubber, he meant Blubber—capital B!

Snot running down into his mouth and dripping off his chin.

Barely able to catch his breath from hyperventilating over the suffering of another.

Nope. Elijah's problem wasn't that he didn't feel at all. Problem was, he felt too much. Even physically painful, experiencing other people's trauma with an emotional intensity—until it was beaten out of him, that is. By those older boys, by the guardians and then foster families after that.

By the time he'd reached his forever home, he'd learned how to stuff his emotions down into the basement of his very soul. Into a place that would never, no, never again come out.

Even when Dad was shot between the eyes in front of him by a lunatic one Sunday morning at the front of his church. Even when his Rabbi at Beth Yeshua, the Messianic Jewish community he'd attended in the District more than half a decade ago, was run through by a machete during one Shabbat service. Even when he worked countless cases plumbing the depths of human depravity—through all of it, Elijah Xavier Fox had played the perfect autistic cliché.

Emotionless. Robotic. Unempathetic.

To a fault.

But now…something about seeing that woman with that bullet between her eyes (just like Dad), dark crimson still pulsing down the ridge of her nose and collecting beneath the pair of coke-bottle lenses…something about seeing Pastor Peter doubled over and wailing at the violence, the injustice, the agonizing despair that must have brought her to the brink—*that* brink—all of it was too much.

To handle, to process, to keep down inside stuffed deep in that basement within his soul.

Something in Elijah broke. A dam of emotion that he'd perfected at keeping at bay for years (decades!) came cascading out in a terrifying, furious, stream–of–conscious rant against the universe—against Yahweh himself!

Throwing his head back, the sounds of three decades of bottled emotion came cascading out in a wail that felt he was joining Peter in his retching—expelling from his very being the sorrow and agony he felt in the face of death, in the face of Katrina's agony and anguish roaming through the darkest valley that had led to her death.

All of it was because he deeply felt the emotional agony of what had just gone on inside that room. What Peter was going through, losing his partner in ministry. What Katrina must have gone through believing that Smith & Wesson still lodged in her hand was the only solution. What all those victims from his Bureau days had gone through at the hand of satanic ritual abuse, serial killers, traffickers, and every other depraved scheme straight from the pit of hell.

What Mama had gone through losing Dad like that, in that way.

What he himself had gone through losing his forever-family dad…

Didn't know how long it all had lasted. Somehow he'd ended up on the floor, his shirt soaked through with sweat (maybe tears and snot), voice hoarse and chest aching from heaving his emotion.

When he was done, when he was spent, at least for now, Elijah took a breath then crossed himself. Was the only thing he thought to do in the moment.

Because he had not a clue—flat no clue what to make of what had just happened, not in the slightest.

So he did the only thing he could think of at that moment.

He prayed.

Channeling a prayer from the Book of Common Prayer, he intoned, "O God, whose mercies cannot be numbered: Accept our prayers on behalf of thy servant Katrina, and grant her an entrance into the land of light and joy, in the fellowship of thy saints; through Jesus Christ thy Son our Lord, who liveth and reigneth with thee and the Holy Spirit, one God, now and forever. Amen."

He was met by another retching sound, followed by a whimper. Peter, at the front, near his pulpit.

Understood completely.

Things had just gotten real, real quick.

And dark…

Unseen Realm dark, it just had to be.

Time to take a stand—again.

And he did, bringing a trembling hand to the pew bench armrest and taking a faltering step back to his feet but making it.

One way or another, this *inexplicitus* case from hot Hades would be resolved.

Nope. None of that bargain-bin Kindle mystery nonsense.

Solved is what.

For Katrina.

For the others.

CHAPTER 6

Gina padded carefully down the sanctuary aisle toward Peter sitting in a pew half way down. Not only because she was carrying a microwave-hot mug of coffee the good pastor had brewed for their sit-down, but also because she didn't want to disturb him in his grief.

And boy, had he grieved.

You would've thought his very own mama had passed, he was so beside himself. Collapsed and doubled over on the floor. Sobbing and snotty and slobbery, liquid running out his eyes and nose and mouth. Face beet red and slicked hair all askew, going this way and that. Mournful cries springing from him like a trapped cat.

Which she understood completely.

She'd been a wreck for months after going through something similar with her sister way back when. Only she didn't have the whole town's police and rescue infrastructure coming to the rescue.

After everything had gone down, Gina had been the one to call nine one one. For Elijah's part, he had been a real champ guiding Peter away from the gruesome scene and consoling the pastor. In fact, an empathy sprang from him that she hadn't seen before—defying one of the crude clichés a neuronormative world had broad-brush painted across the backs of the autistic world.

How many Hollywood yarns had portrayed autistic people as these stone-cold zombies—uncaring, unsympathetic? A persistent stereotype that really got Gina's goat sometime. Her and Elijah's kind weren't the social nincompoops they were portrayed as.

Case in point: Elijah's almost mothering of the good pastor. Got him a blanket and glass of water and a roll of toilet paper (said it would last longer than tissues); sat with him and prayed with him, even sang some old hymn ("The Old Rugged Cross," where Peter broke down at the words *I will cling to the old rugged cross, and exchange it some day for a crown*; Eli did not); and played the part of pastor to the good pastor while she dealt with the incoming police and rescue peeps. Reminded Gina why she liked him so much.

But before then…well, that was enough to freak her out from here to Sunday!

Elijah had thrown back his head and wailed something fierce. Sounds she'd never heard since the day Mama had learned of Grace's death sprang from the man. Hadn't heard or seen anything like it from him in all their years serving together. He'd been so stoic, so robotic even—playing the cliché autistic person while she had offered up enough empathetic emotion for the both of them. Probably the estrogen, but it was more than that.

Gina would get physically ill unless she let it all hang out. Almost like before she discovered she had a gluten intolerance (not the fad kind; the genuine kind), her gut clenching and souring until she made herself puke. This was like that, feeling like unless she let her emotions out with full-on, five-point-one operatic weeping, with physical motions that made her look like a Go-Go on steroids, with expelling more tears than a sprinkler —if she didn't join in with all the feels sitting with someone in their grief then she would explode!

Was a hyper-empath, it turned out (who knew?), that was triggered by that fateful autumn day when she came home from school. It was like some prehistoric amoeba or something came alive within her after what she endured.

Had wondered where her sister was all day, the two of them sharing trigonometry (blech) and chemistry (double-blech, except for Mr. Beel, who had a nice pair of loafers, a wicked tan, and the body of Michaelangelo's David—at least according to her dreams) with nary a sign of her twin.

Turned out, that's because she was hanging by her bedsheet from an exposed rafter in her double-wide bedroom. Had used one of Mama's gardening trowels to claw through the cheap-o ceiling tiles, exposing their double-wide's innards enough to loop her purple Groovy Chick bed sheet through after making her own slipknot (thanks to five years of Girl Scouts).

One might wonder where Mama was when all this went down. Working her cleaning gig, perhaps, or out grocery shopping. Negatory. She was passed out in the other room from a hit of smack. Never knew what was what until she heard Gina's panicked cries after finding her dangling by her tippy toes after school, face purple and tongue hanging out.

Police found a diary tucked under her bed explaining it all. Girls in gym class had taunted her for years. Same ones, too. *Fatty, fatty, two-by-four, can't fit through the kitchen door!* they'd sing with wicked taunts, the catcalls of bullies.

Had never been the same since that day, something breaking inside that connected everyone's pain to Gina's own, ratcheting her hyper-empathy up in ways that were greater than even the average neurotypical person expresses.

Got her into trouble a time or twelve at the Bureau, with Agent Pendergast, their special agent in charge. With Eli, even, the man exploding with irritation when she couldn't hold it together. Eventually found a way to manage it through therapy.

And gum.

Standing in the middle of the aisle dealing with her own feels from that dear woman recapitulating her sister's death, and now dealing with her partner's unraveling emotions, Gina had promptly withdrawn a packet of Wrigley's Doublemint when Eli exploded in his supernova of emotion, burning hot and uncontrolled. "Double your pleasure, double your fun," as the commercials from her '90s childhood had promised. Boy, were they right.

Two sticks wrapped in shimmering foil did the trick, Gina unwrapping them to reveal the white sticks of heaven before shoving them in her mouth. Both. One might be enough for your run-of-the-mill Jane, but two was what the moment required.

Didn't know what to do about Eli's breakdown in the middle of the church's aisle, both him and Pastor Peter. Panic, is what! Now she had two peeps' emotions to contend with, the pastor's and her partner's. The one she could handle; the latter she could not.

Couldn't even contemplate entering into whatever was going on with him after he'd been the rock in their relationship for half a decade, his stoicism bracing her when the hyper-empath head of hers came rearing up looking for someone to feel all the feels with.

The gum helped. One of the ways she stimmed, or stimulated. The act of chewing two pieces of gum, with the work it took to grind them into a chewy pulp, the fresh spearmint dancing across her taste buds, the smell of minty heaven filling her nostrils—all of it helped focus her attention away from the emotional tinder that threatened to overwhelm and set her ablaze.

The curse of being an autistic person, just like Elijah. She'd managed well enough, her personal spectrum wheel not as complicated as some people she knew similarly challenged with neurodiversity.

But gum helped.

It also reminded her of those silly '90s commercials, the ones featuring twins and that double-your-fun slogan. She could still recall the slogan song, and she began humming it to herself. The one she and her own twin sister Grace had sung together, dancing arm in arm and twirling in their double-wide trailer.

Somehow, the gum reminded her of Grace, and acted as a sort of pathway back to her memory. It grounded her emotions when they threatened to fly off the handle after becoming overwhelmed by empathy—in that case, glimpsing a hole the size of a blackened, rotten apple in the middle of those gray curls and then the emotional meltdown of Pastor Peter and Elijah.

Especially at the sight of Eli.

Seemed to be managing now, her partner busying himself with the authorities. An hour ago, he was heaving desperate breaths and shuddering with wracking cries. Thought he was having a coronary and almost threw her arms around him to make sure he was alright.

But she didn't; she couldn't. They didn't have that sort of relationship and the physical touch could have sent him spiraling further. Figured he needed space, anyhow, to work through it all.

Soon enough, he was mumbling a prayer, then crossing himself before standing on shaking feet and tending to the pastor.

Coming to Peter now, microwaved coffee in hand, Gina wondered what that was all about, wondered how Eli was faring now after exploding with his own geyser of emotion.

That could wait. Would have to, given the turn of their *inexplicitus* case.

Once she'd phoned the Mill Creek authorities, didn't take long before the place was swarming with Mill Creek's finest, the Chief of Police, a one Gerald Roller, heading up securing the scene personally while four EMTs worked at recovering the body and handling it with care. Another eight law enforcement officers secured the scene and kept pesky rubberneckers away— from both the evidence of the crime (suicide was illegal, after all) and the grieving pastor.

She and Elijah had run through the details of the incident with Chief Roller and his boys, what little they knew. Which was pretty much bupkis.

Elijah explained how he'd heard the popping sound, turning a switch on in his brain that something was off. Which sent him searching for it, Gina and Peter in tow, until they came to the narthex where he spotted someone seated in the front row all catawampus (later he'd said he hadn't seen her, but rather felt guided by the Holy Spirit himself; Gina believed him). Then all went in to confirm what had happened.

Death by a single gunshot wound to the face, an old Smith & Wesson revolver still wedged in Katrina's hand and a bullet hole out the back of her head, skull shattered. Apparently, she owned an antique gun collection, and knew how to use them.

The front of the face…somethings were better left unsaid.

Now Peter was sitting hunched and hushed in that pew along the aisle, while Elijah conferred with the law enforcement. Had been that way when Mill Creek PD showed up an hour ago. Eyes closed, still, silent. Bending in on himself as if crushed by the incident.

The *suicide*, she corrected.

Incident. Funny how something so gruesome, so final, so dastardly and despairing and dark can be sanitized with such a word.

Wasn't an incident in the slightest. It was monstrous! Seven of them now. In one town, from one church.

Under the shepherding care of one pastor.

Peter wasn't just crushed; he was undone. Catatonic, really. Who could blame him after his assistant had just blown a hole through her face? After six others had gone through a similar—

Not incident. *Suicide.*

She and Elijah would have to keep their eyes on him…

Coming up from behind, she side-shuffled into the pew to his rear, giving a bright yellow gurney room to rumble down the aisle on toward destiny.

With Katrina lying on top, zipped inside a black coroner bag.

Trailing it was Chief of Police Roller. Looked like a Gerald Roller, too. Big and boxy and bald, but eyes and nose betraying themselves. His brown eyes and nostrils running over with almost as much emotion as Peter. The woman must have been loved.

The man rested a meaty palm on Peter's shoulder, giving it a squeeze, then a rub.

He didn't flinch. Just sat there, folded in on himself in silence. Hunched and hushed. Like he'd been since the chief and his crew had shown up.

Chief Roller cleared his throat. "We'll need a statement later, Reverend. When you're ready," he added softly.

Hunched and hushed, Peter remained. Not a nod, not a grunt of acknowledgment. Just hunched and hushed.

Gina understood him completely.

The chief sighed and withdrew his hand, turning toward Gina to leave.

"Take care of him, will you?"

She nodded, and he left.

Watching him leave, her mouth began to salivate, and that little sensor in her brain seeking relief from the moment flipped on.

Could really go for an Arnold Palmer right about now. The real kind. Not those virgin, off-the-shelves tin cans with that golfer's grin. She was talking hard tea and hard lemonade. Her drink of choice, and Mama's. The day sure called for one after the mess the Holy Spirit had brought their way.

Or rather, the Evil One…

And she had not a cotton pickin' clue what to do about it. What to do with Peter, how to comfort him and tell him it would be alright.

Was never any good at that sort of thing. It's why she was an analyst, for Pete's sake! Sitting with stacks of books and journal articles, case files and evidence analysis sheets going over numbers and chemical compounds and witness testimony, interviewing said witnesses and suspects in order to get inside their heads and figure out what the hey-ho day had happened in the basement of some Victorian-era home in Schenectady or the desert sands of Amarillo, or under the overpasses of any number of highways and byways across America—analyzing bodies and rituals and abuses that needed solving.

No more desk work for her.

All she could do was pray about it. The Lord's Prayer seemed like as good a place as any to start:

> *Our Father in heaven, hallowed be your name.*
> *Your kingdom come. Your will be done, on earth as it is*
> *   in heaven.*
> *Give us this day our daily bread.*
> *And forgive us our debts, as we also have forgiven our*
> *   debtors.*
> *And do not bring us to the time of trial, but rescue us*
> *   from the Evil One.*
> *For yours is the kingdom and the power and the glory*
> *   forever.*

"Amen," she mumbled, returning back to that one line.

'Do not bring us to the time of trial but rescue us from the Evil One...'

Indeed.

Crossing herself, she stepped back out into the aisle and took a breath, then went to offer the gifts she'd been bearing to the good pastor.

When he started mumbling something to himself. Intoning, really, without any rise or fall in pitch, neither rhythm nor rhyme. It was like a chant.

And also familiar.

She caught the tail-end of the first stanza of a very familiar psalm: "'...I shall not want.'"

Psalm 23. One of King David's Hebrew poems about the Divine Shepherd.

"'He makes me lie down in green pastures,'" he went on, "'he leads me beside still waters; he restores my soul. He leads me in right paths for his name's sake.'"

Joining him now, Gina added her voice to the psalm that was really a prayer: "'Even though I walk through the darkest valley, I fear no evil; for you are with me; your rod and your staff—they comfort me.'"

Elijah walked up, sliding into the pew in front of Peter. He didn't startle, didn't move. Remained hunched, but no longer hushed. Supposed that was a start.

"'You prepare a table before me,'" Peter went on, rising some now in tenor and tone, "'in the presence of my enemies; you anoint my head with oil; my cup overflows.'"

Elijah quoted the psalm now, too, along with Gina, joining Peter and his growing resolve: "'Surely goodness and mercy shall follow me all the days of my life, and I shall dwell in the house of the Lord my whole life long.'"

Ending, the trio went silent.

The darkest valley…

Pretty well summed up where they stood right about then.

The minutes ticked by, Gina and Elijah letting Peter take the lead on the conversation.

Then he did: "Must have been the darkest of valleys Kat was walking through to go out like that."

Gina nodded, saying quietly, "Must have been…"

Peter suddenly stiffened, and he glared at Elijah, then moved his gaze to Gina. Eyes wide and skin still blotchy with grief. Yet face now set as flint, his jaw tight with locked resolve.

"I want to know why this happened," he said, voice hoarse and strained. "It doesn't make sense. It's inexplicable."

"That's why we're here," Elijah said, but without his usual snark. It was matter-of-fact, but gentler. As if in solidarity with the pastor's own searching desires.

Peter snapped his attention to Eli, adding, "There has to be a reason. And I want to know the truth of it."

A part of Gina broke inside for the man. Because she knew what was what: there was always a reason; someone's truth always lay somewhere inside—often buried, usually waiting to surface in a way that would dumbfound those closest to the dearly departed.

Now, whether that truth wants to surface, whether it *should* surface—well…that's a whole other ball of ugly.

After all, Gina should know best.

"We'll get to the bottom of it," Elijah said with resolve. "We'll discover the truth. About all these—incidents. By golly, we'll uncover the truth."

There was that word again. *Incidents.* And also *truth.* Felt like Pontius Pilate before Jesus, questioning *'What is truth?'* Gina was questioning the same.

What was the truth of these—let's call it straight—*suicides?* What would drive someone to this sort of brink, to the point of taking their own life? Why would someone think that was their only option, one so final, so totalizing? And why would they want to put those left behind through answering such questions, through picking up the shattered pieces of their beshadowed life —questioning every cross word they'd had or argument, wondering what they could have done differently to show the dearly departed a better way, to offer a ray of hope through the darkened sky?

Like she had done for months, years, after her own sister's —incident…

She wasn't sure she wanted to find out, wasn't sure she wanted to know the truth to those deaths—those seven, that one.

Footfalls broke her concentration from behind, as well as the clearing of a throat.

Gina turned to find a tall man with broad shoulders approaching. Guy was older, but fit, with a bald eight-ball head flanked by ears shaped sort of like a gremlin, oversized and jutting out. Was dressed in a black trench coat and with a matching fedora planted on his noggin. Looked like something out of a comic book. A cross between the Sandman and the Green Hornet.

Looked like serious business.

Perhaps their business.

She sighed. Now what…

CHAPTER 7

Elijah was on edge, his very soul seeming to want to explode again from the freighted weight of all that had happened that morning.

And he wasn't just talking about the dead woman with a hole between the eyes.

It was the emotion of it all. What he had felt from seeing that deceased woman Katrina propped against the pew with that gun lodged in her hand, then seeing Peter doubled over in grief at the sight of it all. What had erupted from him in a way he hadn't felt in ages—probably thirty years.

It wasn't just the cry of dereliction he had shouted for Katrina and Peter, joining with the Hebrew psalmist in wondering where God had run off to, why he had forsaken them. Wasn't all the slobbery, slushy tears and snot he'd shed, either. Not even the wracking sobs that had left his voice hoarse, his chest aching.

Empathy, that's what it was. Like a valve had suddenly sprung wide open, something long rusted shut, the torrent of emotion a physical manifestation of the internal overwhelm that had mentally (spiritually, even) welled within. Something long forgotten, long shut up, long denied.

He'd gotten so good at denying himself a basic part of his

nature, the intense identification with suffering people. The other orphans had beaten it out of him, as did the guardians. So he'd transferred the intensity of his feelings to animals, caretaking God's creatures with a passion that burned bright and strong, eventually earning him the nickname Doc Doolittle at the FBI.

Had shooed worms away from the boys who'd break 'em in half. Had fed emaciated stray cats bowls of milk and greedy chipmunks scraps of bread. Had even nursed a baby bird back to health after it had fallen from its nest, a goldfinch left for dead by its mother.

Oh, how he had understood that bird, all the animals trapped and trampled by the world.

So, animals, they were his emotional jam, not so much people.

Which had served him well in the FBI, being able to sever himself emotionally from every one of their cases that should have sent him over the edge.

Like the Group X one that had unleashed the torrent of bottled-up and pressurized emotions.

Didn't understand in the slightest why now, why that case. Bet Gina could psychoanalyze him; might need a session or twelve. Had a hunch it started with the last one, connected to Dad's death at the hands of a rising evil that had gunned for the man—literally, one of his recovery addicts having a psychotic breakdown and shooting him square between the eyes.

Like that woman Katrina.

Regardless, he had to pull it together. Had to stuff his emotions back inside that bottle and store it away for safekeeping. Because he had a job to do.

Figuring out what the hot Hades was going on in that small town, in that small Baptist church.

Standing against the darkness that had sparked it—whatever that might be.

So when the caped crusader showed up, all Johnny on the

spot and all, waltzing down the center aisle with that swaggery gait of his, and that black trench coat and black fedora of his, with those hazy, hard eyes and set jaw and gremlin ears—all of it looked like trouble.

Actually, flat looked like one of those hard-boiled PIs from the '60s-era pulp writers he'd read at the orphanage, the discards charities plopped on their doorstep. The Ed McBains and James Cains and Lawrence Blocks, their cliché investigators with feet propped on the desk, shrouded in a cloud of cigarette smoke (when that was still a thing), newspaper in one hand and glass of scotch in the other, when a broad in a red silky, slinky something came bursting in wanting someone to kick the keister of their lying, cheating, no-good sonuvagun husband (still unfortunately a thing).

Except in their case, it was Fedora Dude waltzing their way— not in a red silky, slinky something (thank Yeshua Almighty for that!), but black leather that spelled trouble.

So with that, the edge that Elijah was on just narrowed to a tightrope. He worried he'd slip and fall and do something he regretted.

He threw up a prayer to Yeshua Almighty, that Christ would help him not do or say anything stupid.

Was self-aware enough that he could definitely step in the doo-doo if he wasn't careful.

And yet…

This was his case. He was the one fighting for Katrina's and Peter's justice—along with the rest of those girls and women who had taken a wrong turn in the middle of the darkest valley.

So, he took a breath, then took a beat—added another prayer for good measure—and stepped up to the plate to see what was what.

"Can we help you?" Elijah asked in an irritated rush, voice matching the edge he was tightroping.

Don't do or say anything stupid, huh? That didn't last long.

Peter glanced over his shoulders at Fedora Dude, then nodded. "Hey, Johnny P."

"Hey yourself, kid," the mystery man grunted. "What happened here? Did somebody keel over?"

He added a grunting chuckle and glanced around the joint, the trio's silence giving him his answer.

"Umm, someone didn't die, did they?"

"Nope," Elijah said. "Suicide."

"Cripes…" Fedora Dude said, twisting behind before craning toward the front. "Who—"

"It was Kat," Peter said flatly, without emotion.

Now the man's eyes bugged out, his forehead creasing with flat disbelief and neck sticking out like an ostrich. Removing his fedora, respectfully and reverently placing it against his chest, he said lowly, "Katrina Hanson?"

Peter nodded, eyes misting over again and a hand swatting at his nose. He took a swig of his coffee—a first swing since Gina had brought it to him—the silent seconds ticking by like a metronome.

Taking another swig, finally the pastor asked, "What can I help you with, JP?"

Fedora Dude stiffened (some Johnny P character, apparently), placing his hat back on his head. "It's what I'd wanted to help you with, Pete."

The pastor stared at him with confused eyes, giving his head a little shake.

"You know, the thing." He eyed Gina, then Elijah, as if to confirm whether it was safe to spill the tea.

Which irritated the snot out of Elijah.

"About the others who…" Mystery Man gestured toward the front, making a reference to the *incident*, and perhaps the others who'd walked their own green mile toward some fate from hell.

Peter sighed knowingly, running a hand through his hair. "That's right! I totally forgot, JP. I'm sorry…"

"Not a problem. You've clearly been tied up."

"And...who are you?" Gina asked. "Hopefully, some help with this case straight from Mars!"

Elijah gave Gina The Look. The one with pursed lips and furrowed brow and cocked head she'd know was what. Telling her to ixnay the asking-ay for elp-hay!

Hey, he didn't want to spill the tea either with no mystery man! Especially didn't want to share the tea when fighting for justice was concerned.

Except...

Something Gina mentioned last case surfaced. A verse, from the Book of Ecclesiastes.

'Two are better than one, because they have a good reward for their toil. For if they fall, one will lift up the other; but woe to one who is alone and falls and does not have another to help....A threefold cord is not quickly broken.'

Elijah let his face slump with resignation—and recognition. Was doing it again. Getting all possessive over the opportunity to set the world to rights. One of his fatal flaws, thinking he had to do it alone; thinking he could only do it alone, and was the only one to do it.

He was also reminded that *'Pride goes before destruction, and a haughty spirit before a fall.'* More Jewish wisdom from the Hebrew Scriptures, the Book of Proverbs.

There it was: Pride. The mother of all his flaws. Like the Ring of Mordor, ruling and binding his others.

Now Elijah sighed and crossed his arms in a huff. Point well taken, Holy Spirit!

Peter stood, taking another swig before grimacing and setting the mug down on the carpeted floor. Probably went cold. Good man. Lukewarm coffee was major *blech!*

"So," Elijah said, "about that thing you were here for, Mister..."

"Johnny Pope," the newcomer announced.

Gina asked, "What are you, a detective with Mill Creek Junction or something?"

"A priest, actually," Peter explained.

"*Former* priest," Johnny corrected. "That was a long time ago."

"My bad. Sorry."

Elijah asked, "Anglican or Catholic?"

"The latter."

"My dad was a Baptist minister. He was murdered."

Johnny frowned. "Sorry to hear that."

Gina threw Eli a furrowed brow, registering uncertainty.

That feeling was back, the one when he was in the Bureau and the fellas were looking on with besmirked faces. Wondering if he'd fall flat on his keister and mess it all up. Wondered now if he would, if he really would get the justice Peter and Katrina and the others needed.

His heart was racing and lungs were searching for air. Knew his voice was a bit rushed, and he was oversharing in a way that would throw up red flares for Gina. Telling Fedora Dude or Johnny or JP, or whatever, that his father was murdered—what was that about? Felt his fingers automatically start running through the wringer that would set things right. His stimming tick.

Thumb to index finger, thumb to middle, thumb to ring finger, thumb to pinkie. Then rinse and repeat.

His tell that anxiety and apprehension was rising.

Gina cleared her throat and gave the newcomer a smile. "Nice to meet you, Johnny."

Peter went on, "They're with the Order of Thaddeus, JP. You remember them, right?"

Johnny snorted a laugh. "After all the crazy that went down last year? Don't I ever. They're that ecumenical religious order protecting the Church, a real SEAL Team Six, ain't that right?"

"Something like that."

Seemed to be a theme of the Order, the…*kinetic* nature of the faith-defending beast. Was never interested in such a thing, having come of age during the 9/11 heyday when religious wackadoodles leveraged their religion to offer their own kinetic response to Western imperialism. If this was the reputation of the mother ship, then—

Elijah wondered what he'd gotten himself into…

"After all that's gone down the past few months," Peter continued, "especially after Gloria Warner's…incident." Emotion caught in his throat, welling in his eyes again. "I called up Silas Grey and asked for help."

Johnny grunted his understanding. "Probably a good idea, given all the crazy. But who are you folks?"

"Gina Anderson," Elijah's partner offered. "And this is my partner, Elijah Fox."

He threw them a squinting, skeptical eye. "Sounds like the men in black type."

"*Men* in black?" Elijah smirked. "What century are you living in, bub?"

"Huh?"

Gina threw him neither-the-time-nor-the-place eyes. Sometimes she did that; sometimes she needed to do that.

He shrugged and looked off toward the ceiling instead.

She said, "What my colleague was trying to say is, both of us are former FBI."

Johnny cocked his head. "The Feds, ehh? Suppose it makes sense bringing in the big guns for this sort of thing."

"*Former*," Elijah said. "Agents, that is. Still the big guns."

Gina rolled her eyes, knowing she could spot his pride a mile away. Whatever. He was right.

"What are you now?" asked Johnny.

Eli replied, "Investigators with Group X."

"Sounds like something from some comic book universe."

"An investigative agency with the Order of Thaddeus, actually."

"What do you investigate?"

Gina explained, "Cases of an unexplainable nature that bedevil the Church. The two of us performed a similar service with the FBI, delving into more supernatural, even paranormal investigations."

Johnny snorted another laugh. "So, what, like the Vatican's version of Mulder and Scully, sussing out the Holy See's x-files?"

"No, silly," Elijah said. "Sussing out the Church's *inexplicitus* cases."

Peter offered, "Thought they could lend a helping hand with what the Junction's been experiencing."

"The more the merrier, I always say," Johnny said. "Although, too many cooks in the kitchen spoil the broth. Either way, if pastorman wants you on board, then I'm good with that."

He stuck out his hand. "Welcome aboard."

Elijah and Gina both just snapped their heads at it, not all that keen on physical touch.

Instead, Elijah waved. Gina slipped her hands inside her pants pockets, offering a smile instead.

Johnny withdrew his hand, scratching the back of his neck and mumbling, "Tough crowd…"

"Your last name's Pope?" Elijah asked with a smirk. "Isn't that a bit too on the nose?"

"Pope is my stage name. Papadopoulos is my last name."

"Ahh. Got it. What is that, Norwegian?"

Johnny frowned. "Greek. Jonathan Aquinas Papadopoulos doesn't roll very well off the tongue. And let's be honest, Jonathan Aquinas Papadopoulos just sounds like a pretentious prick."

Boy, was that too easy! Knew he should let it go, but…

Elijah laughed. "Yeah, like some East Coast yuppy who stepped off a hundred-foot yacht anchored at Martha's Vineyard. Sporting Sperry loafers and loose-fitting Ralph Lauren khaki shorts, wearing a bright pink Izod polo, donning a faded yellow sweater with said Izod logo in navy draped ever-so rightly across his shoulders."

Peter threw up a nervous laugh himself; Gina groaned. "Always the blunt one, Eli…"

For Johnny's part, he just chuckled. "Polo logo, actually. Not Izod. But yeah, you're right. Name also doesn't fit too good on a business card, and most people can't pronounce it to save their life, let alone spell it or remember it. Which ain't too good for the line of work I do."

"Suppose not," Gina said, giving Elijah her own Look. He just shrugged and looked back off into the ceiling.

"So Johnny Pope it's been the past decade since I set off on my own after leaving my previous profession that inspired my *nom de plume* in the first place."

Peter said, "He's the guy you call when a pigeon has swooped down and crapped all over your life."

"Or sprays brain matter all over your pews," Elijah mumbled, "as the case may be…"

Gina closed her eyes and shook her head. Telling him he was doing it again. Oversharing and steeping in it.

"What's this about being a priest?" Gina asked.

"Like I said, *ex*-priest," the man said.

Peter explained, "He's a private investigator now, working freelance gigs."

"Which begs the question, Mr. Pope," Elijah said, crossing his arms with interrogation.

Johnny chuckled. "Mr. Pope was my father. Johnny's just fine."

"Alright…*Johnny*," Elijah said. "This is all very romantic, a meet-cute in the center aisle of a Baptist church and all. Could make for an interesting bargain-bin romance novel, but we're sort of in the middle of it here. What are *you* investigating?"

Peter explained, "After the twelve-year-old's…death, I contacted JP here to lend a hand figuring out what's been going on. Then you two after Gloria passed. Something is going on here. Something deep, something dark."

The pastor took a breath, then a beat, bringing a trembling hand to his forehead. Seven of parishioners, dead by suicide in the past few months. All those grief counseling sessions with distraught, confused family members. Then all the funerals—for kids, which had to be the worst sort of funeral to preside over, on top of the fact they were suicides. How do you thread that theological needle? Then there was his assistant, whom he'd just found with a bullet in her kisser. All of it would flat shake anyone.

And now Elijah felt bad about trying to get into a pissing match with Johnny Pope in the middle of a Baptist church sanctuary. Not what Peter needed after what he'd been through. Certainly not what the newcomer needed after wanting to help make sense of this *inexplicitus* case from hot Hades.

Pride…an ugly klingon, it was.

Clearing his throat, Peter continued, "I just want to know what's happening to my town—to my *church*." He faltered his words, emotion gripping him again. "Will you three help?"

Johnny looked to Elijah, then to Gina. "I'm game if you are."

Elijah looked to her partner, who gave a shrug, then a nod.

He took a beat, then a breath, then nodded himself with a smile.

"Where do we begin?"

CHAPTER 8

Something real strange was going on with Elijah, and it concerned Gina.

Was strange enough to see him break down like that. Understood it herself, with those empathetic desires welling up to almost a physical ache at whatever drove Katrina to the brink, and then to see Peter himself convulsing under the weight of the revelation. But Eli…

That had been real strange.

Always the rock of the two of them, he was. Steady, sure, solid whenever they climbed up on a new-case pony and rode it into all manner of wicked craziness. From serial killers and satanic ritual abuse, to shape-shifting kidnappings and clairvoyant stock traders, to violent perps with the strength of a hundred men—through it all, Elijah hadn't shed a tear, hadn't betrayed a lick of emotion in the face of so much tragedy and chaos.

Not that she necessarily minded; she'd struggled enough for the both of them. But just once would she have wanted him to show a pinkie drop of empathy for those whose children were sold into sex trafficking by possessed pimps, or for the prostitutes who were found dismembered, or for the spouses held for ransom.

Then there was the way he was stepping up to Johnny Pope, their new PI partner in this *inexplicitus* case. Flat made no sense. Something she'd have to circle back around to later.

In the meantime, she was going to enjoy the stroll through small-town America, giving her noggin a break from all the crazy.

They'd decided a walk was in order. Elijah balked, but she won out, insisting it would help them clear their head and get it back on straight after the trauma. A psychologist was always right about that sort of thing. So, off they walked.

Cherry blossom trees anchoring one side of the driveway stretching to Main Street were in full bloom under a cloudless sky, the sun having crested toward the horizon now and cast a golden hue across a sheet of blue that offered the promise of a new day tomorrow.

The sun was warm against her face as they reached the main drag running through town. A mixture of celery and sawdust and grilled meat came gusting along on a breeze sweeping through town—as if putting an exclamation point on the fact that farms and factories and restaurants made Mill Creek Junction what it was.

"*Oof,*" Elijah complained. "Smells like cow poop."

Peter chuckled. "That'd be Warner Farms on the outskirts of town. The historic windmill still sits right alongside the river, giving the Junction its namesake."

"I thought it was a creek…"

Summer was in full swing, the Michigan humidity hanging like a wet blanket, almost suffocating to breathe in, punctuated by celery and onions from the outskirts of town. It was a cloudless sky, which was nice for their walk, the kind that would have beckoned Gina to make the three-hour trek to Lake Michigan when she studied in Ann Arbor, beach chair and Harry Potter's latest in tow.

Never went to the lake growing up, even though she and her sister were only an hour's drive to Lake Erie. Not that you'd necessarily want to swim in Lake Erie to begin with, but still. Was never a regular family thing. In fact, they never had any regular family things. Unless you counted Dad and Mama's weekly fights, which were certainly family affairs and regular.

Gina shook her head, sucking in a steadying breath laced with grilled meat and growing onions. What was past was passed. Needed her head in the present. A jaunt through Small Town, America, should do the trick.

Strolling through shop-lined Main Street, she yanked out her phone and scrolled through her WeShare account. An innocent habit that had morphed the past year into doomscrolling, mindlessly flipping through depressing and despairing content. Wasn't even just the incessant news stories, either, about climate change and inflation and the possibility of World War III. It was stories from fellow WeSharers—friends, family, acquaintances, re-posts from people she didn't even know. Such was life in the digital age, she supposed.

Gina did note several local posts on the recent...incidents. Had to find a better word, less sanitary for the depths of meaning embedded in those acts. Either way, her ShareFeed was filled with posters commenting on the depths of hidden suffering and despair and hopelessness—sparking a tightening rise in her chest, the hyper-empath in her finding her very soul dragged into the depths of despair herself, pushing her to a brink she hadn't felt since that fateful day when her own sister died.

Until a voice broke through, up ahead, snapping her back to the moment.

"Pastorman!" a voice shouted from the alcove of a doorway up ahead. Looked like a bar and grill. Heavenly smells of grilled meat and frying food confirmed it—sending her stomach into a tizzy!

The shout came from a tall, lank man with long dark hair

wrapped up in one of those man buns she found so preposterous. Good enough looking fella, sporting a Pink Floyd t-shirt and ripped jeans running a bit snug for the man looking like he was approaching forty.

Peter looked up, face still gaunt and guarded with trauma. "Hey, Max…" he simply said.

Max frowned as they rolled up. "Why the long face? How about we turn that frown upside down, ehh?"

"It's been a rough afternoon," Johnny explained, then turned to her and Eli. "This here's Max Blade, proprietor of this fine eating establishment, Max's Place."

The pair said hello. Max folded his arms and regarded them with squinting, skeptical eyes. "And who might you be? Look like Feds or something."

"Former Feds," Elijah said.

The man stiffened at that and whistled. "Well, I'll be a monkey's uncle. What're ya now?"

"The Church's investigators."

"For reals?"

"For reals."

"And what are you investigating?"

Johnny explained, "Peter asked them to help with the thing…"

He trailed off, Max's face falling before he nodded with recognition.

"Speaking of churches, what's happening up at your cathedral uptown, pastorman?"

Peter's eyes immediately glistened, and he opened his mouth to reply but no words came out.

"His assistant died," Elijah answered instead.

"Kat?" Max exclaimed. "What, how?"

No one said a word. Which was really the only word that needed to be said. He got the hint.

"Numero siete…" he whispered before pressing a palm against his forehead. "That's messed up. But nothing a little beer can't cure. After all, what does the Good Book remind us?"

Elijah furrowed his brow. "What does the good book remind us?"

Max grinned proudly. "Beer is proof that God loves us and wants us to be happy, that's what! Memorized that one a while ago."

"Nope. Not in the Bible."

"Huh?"

Gina said, "I thought it was Benjamin Franklin."

Eli shook his head. "Nope. That's a myth. Franklin never said it either."

"I stand corrected."

Johnny said, "Max, why don't you get us a table and a round on me."

Eli shook his head again. "Nope. I don't drink beer."

Max scoffed. "What're ya, a teetotaler or something?"

"I prefer wine. Red."

"Uh, we're sort of more a beer and liquor establishment."

Eli frowned. "What's your best bottle?"

"Yellow Tail?"

"Sweet mother of Melchizedek!"

"Is that a yes?"

"What kind of joint is this?"

"Hey, I run a fine dining establishment! Besides, that's a damn fine bottle. An import, it is."

Elijah sputtered his lips. "From Australia!"

"Exactly!"

"Max," Johnny cut in again. "A table, if you please."

"You've already got one, chief. Your chickadee awaits." The man leaned over with a wide grin and ribbed him. "And ooh-wee is she a looker! Way to go, Johnny. A little on the young side, but I ain't judgin'."

The PI frowned and shoved past Max, nailing him in the shoulder, eliciting a yelp and a loud complaint. Peter chuckled (the first all day) and followed after, then Elijah and Gina. Place smacked her in the face, it did!

First it was the crowd, the noise and jumble of conversations fighting for a hearing above the din of some band already jamming it up on stage. Every table was filled, with others milling in the aisles and roaming from table to table, conversations drowning and joy-filled.

Then it was the smell. The air was thick with the staples of American cuisine: fried potatoes and grilled meat; lots of fries and hamburgers, some fish thrown in for good measure; the tang of garlic and pepper, onion and cabbage. Riding alongside it all was a hefty dose of barley and hops and wheat. Which meant lots of booze was already flowing.

The band was striking up another tune now. A black man sweating to beat the band was working a number on an old, boxy, honey-stained organ. The drums kept up a nice *rat-a-tat-tat* rhythm, too, while a young man with long hair strummed his electric guitar with a twisted-up face that said he was feeling what the organ was putting down.

Not opera, but Gina knew Elijah would be digging the tunage. Which, after what they'd all been through, was just what the doctor ordered.

"Not a bad sounding band," Elijah said to Max as he searched the joint.

"Oh, yeah, Marvin and the Gang are lit."

"Sounds like the organist switched from one of Jimmy Smith's earlier bluesy numbers to a later groovier one from his fusion days."

Max perked up at that. "You a jazzman mystery man?"

"You could say that. 'Root Down,' isn't it?"

"Spot on the money!"

"Max!" Johnny cut in again. "The table."

"Hold yer horses, JP! We're jawing it up over a shared love of the greatest music ever invented."

"Well, do it on your time."

"It is my time. I own the joint!"

"Don't let him fool ya," a middle-aged woman with shoulder-length blond curls said coming up from behind. "We're the ones with the real power in this place."

"Whatevs, Sheila. And you better watch it. I sign your paychecks!"

The woman Sheila laughed. "Those things are barely worth the ink they're scrawled with. Hey, JP. Your table awaits. And ooh-wee is she a looker. Not that I'm into that sort of thing, but you get my drift."

"That's what I said!" Max complained.

Johnny frowned. "Lead the way."

She did, Gina smiling at the back and forth and all the hubbub in the place. Reminded her of her favorite college show *Cheers*, where everyone knows your name, and they're always glad you showed up. That'd sure be nice.

Max joined the jaunt, a table of men erupting with boos and curses, no doubt fueled by the three pitchers of booze crowding the table. A mixture of scrawny fellas and big-boned bruisers. Latinos and Caucasians. The whole joint had the same look about it, the town an interesting diversity all coming together to cool off at the local watering hole.

"Quite the crowd," Elijah said, gesturing to the table, a card game by the look of it.

"Ahh, yes. Our seasonal crop of migrant workers at Warner's farm. Mexicans, Canadians, some blokes from the Ukraine."

"Nope. Ukraine," he corrected.

"Yeah, that's what I said, pal."

"Nope, you said *the* Ukraine. It's Ukraine, not the Ukraine."

Gina giggled. Oh, Eli…Blunt, black-and-white, to a fault.

Max threw him a stink eye and muttered a curse as another table threw up a shouting bout of cheer.

He sauntered off toward it, shouting above the din, "Mayor Goodall, you old sonofagun you—you old mucky-muck…"

Sheila took over, leading them to a back circular booth near the stage. A little loud for Gina, and with all the dinner-time yakking—things could get interesting.

Already found herself growing overwhelmed by all the noise. Still had her Doublemint gum, so she really worked it in her mouth, her jaw muscles aching now after going at it the last hour, but also enjoying the painful pleasure of it. Just prayed that pleasure didn't sour before their time was up.

A small woman about her size stood on their approach. A brunette with long curly hair bunched at her shoulders and wearing a bright smile. Was also wearing dark Levis and a red gingham shirt, along with cowboy boots. Heather grey and probably at the expense of some baby goat. Looked like a cowgirl, or some performer out West.

She looked at Johnny, who seemed to brighten a notch in her presence. Interesting partner. Real interesting. Wondered if there was more there, though she could be his daughter. Maybe that was their thing.

"And who are these fine folks?" the mystery woman asked, voice East Coastish with a bit of a Western lilt to it.

Lots of those people lately, one mystery person after another, in the midst of a spiraling mystery that was making Gina's head spin.

Johnny turned to the three. "Peter Young, the reverend who asked for our help. Then—"

"Elijah Xavier Fox," Eli said, eyes all wide and mouth all wider. Then he did a thing Gina had never seen before.

He took a bow, adding, "At your service."

"My my my," the lady said with a giggle, bringing a small hand to her mouth and cheeks reddening a shade. "What a gentleman! Didn't know them type existed anymore."

Heat ran up Gina's neck at the show of things. If she weren't mistaken, her partner looked twitterpated! Now he was fussing with his hair and standing their dumbly, eyes as wide as ever and tongue licking his chops like he'd lost his words.

Yep. Twitterpated.

Which brought about a sudden rise in something she often felt around other women.

Jealousy.

Which in turn made her feel real small, and no small amount of overwhelm started blooming in her head.

"You government-issued, or what?" the woman went on, jolting Gina back to the moment.

Eli laughed. "We get that a lot."

"Hi, I'm Gina Anderson, by the way."

Gina waved, gathering up her wits about her and trying to engage before she shut down completely.

The woman scrunched up her face and threw up a finger. "Wait wait wait. Fox and Anderson? Are you for real? Like that '90s alien show, Fox Mulder and Dana Scully? Well, Jillian Anderson who played the blond, anyway."

"As real as rain."

"Right as rain," Elijah corrected.

"Tomato, potato…" She meant to say that, of course, but instead channeled the mangled turn of phrase from that FBI lady from their last investigation. Brain got all twisted.

She stiffened, brushing off the embarrassment and raising her head high to reengage.

"And you are…"

The woman put out a hand; Gina and Elijah stared at it on cue, not engaging.

She let slip a nervous laugh and slowly stuffed it in her pocket. "Biffed that one, didn't I."

"Why don't we have a seat," Johnny said. "This could take a while."

The five stuffed themselves around the circular booth.

"This here is Jae McCray," he explained. "She's been working security at a hotel out West in Cave Creek, Nevada, investigating some strange Twilight-Zone nonsense."

Gina smirked. "Never heard of a gal named Jay."

"I get that a lot," the woman said. Then she corrected: "By the way, that's Jay with an E. *Jae.*"

Elijah cocked his head to one side. "That your real name, or some sort of superhero name?"

"Do you want it to be?" Jae smiled, throwing Eli a wink and grabbing a lock of those curls. Gina wanted to puke. "It's a nickname. Short for Jael."

"Jaw…eel?" Gina asked.

"No, no, no," she corrected. "*Jael.* Jay. El. Like the letters. J. L."

She twisted up her face as if she'd swallowed a lemon turned inside out. "What the heck is that?"

"It's biblical," Elijah said.

Even more face twisting. "Biblical?"

Jae answered, "Yeah, as in, from the Bible. My father named me. He's a minister. Or, was…"

Elijah sat straighter at the mention of that one, growing interest written all over his face.

Gina slouched at the mention of that one, seeing the pair instantly connect over familial history. And that dang jealousy started growing heads, sprouting from all sorts of places she didn't know she had! Her cheeks flushed, and her belly was twisting itself in knots—all of it compounded by the din of the restaurant's jumbled conversations and crooners on stage now.

Before Eli could inquire himself, she said, "Interesting name. What is it, anyhow?"

"Jewish," Elijah explained.

Jae startled. "I see you're in the know."

"I'm Jewish."

Now she raised a brow of her own. "And what kind of name is *Elijah Fox*, anyhow? Sounds like a Jewish leprechaun."

He chuckled at that. "What difference does it make? But you're not Jewish. Not that there's anything wrong with that if you are or aren't. I'm an equal opportunity friender."

Elijah was speaking in a rush, tongue moving a mile a minute and tripping over itself. Twitterpated for sure.

Gina rolled her eyes at the flirtatious vibes, that jealousy blooming now.

She said, "So, what's it mean, anyhow?"

Jae turned to her. "You ask a lot of questions."

"I like to know who I'm working with."

"I can respect that. But apparently you either screwed off in Sunday School or were never brought up in the Church to begin with."

Gina burned now at that, and there were all the feels from back in the day rushing back to the fore. The insecurity and feeling less-than in the face of high school cheerleaders and the popular girls, with their football player boyfriends and Ford Mustang rides, their perfect hair and teeth. Like this cat must have been…

"Well, if you must know, Gina," Elijah said, "there was a prophetess of the ancient Hebrew people who sent her military commander to mobilize some tribes to do battle against King Jabin of Canaan."

Jae whistled. "You know the story, then, flyboy."

Gina startled at that. It was what she called Eli sometimes.

He went on, "The fella didn't want to go unless Deborah, the prophetess, also went. But she said a woman would take the honor of the battle, not Barak her commander."

Jae clapped. "Don't let me stop you."

Elijah straightened and brightened even more than he was. Thought his face would fall off, it was so wide with delight.

"The head of Jabin's army was led by Sisera. One thing led to another, and before he knew it, the military commander was sleeping in Jael's tent."

"And what's the big deal, anyhow?" Gina asked in a huff.

Jae shrugged. "And my namesake took a wooden mallet and drove a tent peg through the fella's temple, nailing it into the ground while he was sleeping, killing him instantly."

The table fell silent at that revelation. All except Eli.

"Sounds like my kind of gal," he said, wiggling his eyebrows like a junior higher.

"She might be…"

"Now that we're all best buds," Johnny said, "how about we get to it. Jae, you said you found something that might connect all these—incidents together."

Gina cringed at that word again. *Incidents.* Although, she was thankful for it. It re-centered her back to the case after nearly losing it with that chica who brought up all sorts of memories from childhood. All sorts of insecurities and jealousies.

She prayed the Holy Spirit would stay her restless heart…

Jae swallowed and nodded, sitting straighter. "That's right. I did."

Took a breath, then a beat, then: "You're not gonna like it."

CHAPTER 9

roam the small American town streets pissed off as all get out, my breath huffing and puffing behind me in billowing chunks breezing past a toddler on a tricycle.

Who tumbles to the pavement and promptly lets out a delayed screech.

I grin. That'll learn ya.

Ancient boughs from oaks and maples planted generations ago bow overhead under a waning sun, full of greenery and others dappled by bright pinks and purples. Even the craftsman homes standing in dutiful rows with their low-pitched roofs and overhanging eaves and covered front porches, in their muted earth-tone greens and browns and taupes with manicured lawns —all of them seem to bear witness to the blessings of the good life sheeple always want.

Mill Creek Junction certainly seems to fit the bill.

I aim for Main Street, the stretch of shops and bars teeming with the sheeple who'll become my next victims—and I am hopping mad, I tell ya, hopping mad!

It is not supposed to be this way! People keeling over within earshot of others. There are protocols to follow, time schedules to keep, and the numero uno rule above all else to abide by. Something I plucked from the Good Book and twisted for my own purposes.

'Everything exposed by the light becomes visible,' some dead Apostle wrote—a bloke named Paul, I believe, bleating to the Enemy in Ephesus.

So keep the darkness in the dark, for crying out loud! Sheesh, how hard can it be?

I gave explicit instructions to ensure our test subjects were not to keel over within earshot or eyeshot (is that a word? It is now!) of others less fortunate to have been chosen for my purposes.

But no! The help had to go and let the woman keel over in front of her boss and his friends.

And not just any friends, apparently.

Because now, my informants have come bearing grim news: the Order of Thaddeus is involved. Those dastardly, despicable, dimwitted agents of the Church.

Wormwood will not be pleased…

There's a long memory within our ranks of those buffoons, the guardians and defenders of the faith attached to the Nameless One. Which is so ridiculous! You know you're up a creek without a paddle when you're required to muster up forces to guard and defend yourselves.

What's even more ridiculous is that now it appears Christianity's guardians have solicited the help of Caesar's investigators. Group X, they call themselves, a pair of former FBI agents turned private investigators for the Church—sticking their schnozes where they don't belong.

My business!

Passing one of those perfectly pedestrian turn-of-the-century bungalows that are so common in these parts, I puff a raging snort as I pass a geezer watering his wilting petunias. He sets down the hose and scurries inside.

Was it something I said?

But that's not even the worst of it. The Order I can handle.

Even that upstart investigative agency. What are a pair of retards in the grand scheme of things?

It's the others I'm enraged about. The hired hands who should know better by now. After all, my people dispensed our wisdom, made all the arrangements, all so they could get rich and buy their dachas on the Black Sea.

My rage spills over now huffing and puffing toward the main artery running through the small town. A rug rat misses catching the football on my approach, and a dog skitters away after dropping a load on the sidewalk in front of me, its owner seemingly jumping out of the way as I pass. It's as if my movements frighten them.

Interesting…

What's not interesting, and positively maddening, is what was left behind in the bungled test at that church.

I'm not talking about the body and the witnesses, though those are massive headaches as well. I'm talking about the evidence. The connections.

What to do, what to do…

Pulling up to Main Street now, cars are racing past in a blur. Ditto for the shops.

One is Landry Jewelers, with a big fat diamond ring sign hanging above the shop door. A couple walks out arm in arm, tiny bright lights shining from tracks in the ceiling down on cases lining the perimeter of the shop at the edge with an island of the same at the center. It is packed, too. Probably a dozen patrons.

I huff and sneer at the lovely couple looking positively ecstatic. They'll never make it. I'll see to it, bucko.

Now I pass Millie's on Main diner, black-and-white tiles paving the joint. Complete with chrome seats at a counter near the kitchen, baby blue- and pink-patterned booths along with steel tables and chairs.

Taking a deep breath, I wish I could smell the freshly ground and brewed coffee saturating the air inside, compounded by melted cheese and frying beef. But no cigar on that one.

Poor servers are running back and forth taking orders, and runners are balancing trays packed with food. I look at one of them, dead square in the eyes, and he slips and slids to the floor —sending a tray of burgers and fries and soup and sandwiches crashing down in a splattering pile.

I giggle to myself, then off I trot.

Plotting, scheming, and worrying about the evidence.

Yes…evidence.

Then I have it.

Know exactly what to do. What I need to do. Well, not me, but my boys.

Should be enough to stop those Order miscreants in their tracks.

If not, well…

Then I'll get creative.

After all, why not slip them the same poison as the rest?

Despair.

CHAPTER 10

Elijah was floating among the clouds, riding high on cloud nine!

Noggin was light and airy, like he was hiking up Mount Kilimanjaro. Thought he even caught stars twinkling in the periphery of his vision. His palms were slick with sweat. Mouth sure tasted of pennies, and coursing blood made him feel all giddy and energetic and euphoric and hungrier than an ox!

Or was it a moose?

Neither.

Bearded dragon, like his teenage pet. Boy, can those puppies put away the sweet potatoes!

And he knew why. He'd studied these things. Read all about it in his mother's *Cosmo* magazine one afternoon, so he knew the culprit of all the physiological crazy.

Norepinephrine.

One of the hormones released in your body when you're thrown into stressful situations. Also floods your body during attractive situations.

Like the kinds of situations with a smokin' curly haired brunette named after one of his favorite biblical characters.

Jael.

She also looked like one of his favorite *Lost* characters, Kate. The spunky, sassy gal who kicked butt, took names, and took no prisoner.

And she was talking—to him! Joking with him and winking.

At him!

Was that considered flirting? Wouldn't know. Maybe he could ask her!

He went to, but was interrupted by Sheila, a petite woman who reminded him of his grammy—with the curls and all the pancake doing a bad job hiding all her wrinkles and the bright red lipstick slathered on those thin lips of hers. That was the worst, getting a big, wet smoocheroo on the cheek that left behind a Betty Boop special delivery.

Although…wouldn't mind one of those from Jae. Not in the slightest!

"What can I get you fine felines this evening?" Sheila interrupted, voice husky from too many Camels.

"Food!" Elijah said, stomach rumbling something fierce now. "A burger, on the moo side."

"We can do that." She took the rest of the food orders, everyone ordering the same—the evening's special—but at various stages of doneness, with Gina going all the way to well. How anyone could ruin a perfectly fine hamburger patty like that was beyond him. Jae ordered the same moo-ready patty. Had that in common, at least.

"And don't forget a round of beers," Johnny said. "Whatever's on tap is on me."

"Coming right up!"

"I'll just take a Shirley Temple," Jae said. "And not only because I'm an old-fashioned kind of gal at heart."

That was startling. Elijah asked, "Old fashioned? How old are you?"

Johnny leaned over. "Never ask a pretty lady her age, kid."

Jae giggled. "It's fine. I'm not even cresting forty. But Shirley's are my jam because alcohol and me don't mix well."

Heat ran up the back of Elijah's neck. Biffed that one good. What a moron!

"Last time it did," she went on, "was 3,901 days ago. Just over a decade. Got my chip to prove it."

"You were an alcoholic?" he asked.

"*Am* an alcoholic," Jae said with emphasis.

He considered this, nodding. "You said 3,901. Which means there was a Day Zero."

"That's right."

"The inciting incident that sparked the change."

"Remember it like it was yesterday."

Elijah waited a beat, then cocked his head. "Annnnd?"

Gina leaned over. "Sometimes people don't like verbal vomiting their life, Eli."

"Why not?"

"Because sometimes it scalds people."

Jae chuckled. "That's alright. Don't mind…verbal vomiting my life, as you say."

Elijah perked up at that. A chance to dive deeper into her story. "Vomit away! What's Day Zero?"

"The day I found my lyin', cheatin', no-good sonofagun fiancé with my maid of honor the night before our wedding."

His face fell. "Oh…"

"By now, we'da had two-point-five kids, a two-story brick house perched behind a white picket fence. Cadillac on one side of the garage, Ford F-150 on the other side. My side."

She sighed, settling back in her seat and giving a shrug. "But it wasn't meant to be. Knew Grey Goose and me were like the British and Irish: never the twain shall meet. Yet, I insisted. And persisted. Leading to an assault charge that was later dropped. Against me, not to me; dropped by him for me."

He perked up at that. Sounded like an aggressive gal. He liked them kind!

She also sounded available. Another plus.

"This little bit of travelog sure is fascinating," Gina said with interruption, "but can we get on with it?"

Johnny grunted a nod. "You said you found something to do with the case, right Jae?"

"Something we wouldn't like?"

Jae straightened. "I did some digging into the backgrounds of our…victims, I suppose you could call them."

Peter asked, "How did you manage that?"

"Got in touch with the surviving family members and explained I was working for you."

"Suppose that's true."

"And wicked smart," Elijah said, throwing her a wink.

She caught it, and threw one back. "Thanks…"

"Any-*whooo*…" Gina said with a huff that sounded like someone got her goat. "What did you discover?"

"Nothing, that's the problem."

Elijah said, "That wasn't at all anticlimactic."

Gina snorted a dismissive laugh. "Yeah, a real Perry Mason, you are."

"Nope. You're mixing metaphors, Gina colada. Mason was a lawyer, not a detective. I think what you're looking for is something along the lines of Catherine Willows from *CSI*."

"Whatevs…"

"You got nothing?" Johnny said.

Jae sat back and sighed. "A whole pile of it."

"Thought I trained you better than that."

"What can I say. I learned from the best."

"Ha-ha. Very funny."

Elijah asked, "So, what, nobody wanted to spill the tea?"

Jae raised an eyebrow. "Spill the tea?"

"Yeah, like cough the cheese."

"Don't you mean cut the cheese?" she said with a wry grin. "But I get what you're putting down. Nobody really wanted to talk. It's all been such an overwhelming jolt to the town."

"Ain't that the truth," Peter said, lower lip quivering and eyes misting over.

A siren just outside the joint flared up, along with its reds and blues. Police, by the sound of it. Which put an exclamation point to the urgency.

Elijah wanted to get to it, a rising sense that things were really not OK. Had felt it from the start, something unsettled in his very soul about the whole thing. And knowing the seven deaths were all connected to this one town, even the one church —he wanted to hop to it!

But drinks arrived, waylaying that plan for later until after they imbibed. And with food coming, and his stomach doing the cha-cha again, it'd be at least an hour before they could head out.

Elijah chanced a sniff of his red wine—and regretted it! Smelled sour and astringent. Like food-colored Mr. Clean. Wincing, he chanced a sip, sweet red berries, vanilla, and chocolate hitting his taste buds. Not his jam, but not the worst thing he'd drunk. One glass of it would work.

Gina threw back a swig of beer and asked, "What about Katrina's laptop?"

"What about it?" he asked.

"There was this look about the woman when she was engaged with the device. Something…off."

"Now that you mention it…thought she did look a bit cuckoo for Cocoa Puffs myself."

Gina gave him The Look, but didn't press it. He caught what she was putting down. Probably shouldn't call people cuckoo in a conversation about mental illness and suicide.

"I don't think I'd put it like that," she went on, "but I did notice her seeming to fixate on the screen."

Peter added, "She did seem to hide whatever she was looking at."

Elijah snorted a laugh. "You mean *Fifty Shades of Grey*?"

The Look morphed into a solid jab into the ribs; sometimes she had to do that.

Point taken.

He threw up his hands in surrender. "Sorry. I'll stop. But you're right, Gina colada. Before we retired to Peter's office to debrief on the…situation, I saw her fiddling with that laptop again and going all Apple 1984 commercial."

Jae gasped. "The one with Big Brother and all the lemmings lookin' like slack-jawed yokels, all zombie like?"

"Totally!"

Gina cleared her throat. "Can we get back to it? But yeah, a bit of a zombie, right before she hoisted up her purse and peered inside."

"And then…" Elijah trailed off, choosing not to finish his thought. Imagined she'd carted that Smith & Wesson around in that lady bag of hers before yanking it out to take her life. But why?

That was the *inexplicitus* part of this case from hot Hades.

Jae said, "Maybe she saw something that set her off."

"Sounds promising," Johnny said. "We should look into it. Can you give us access, Rev?"

Peter nodded, saying nothing more.

The food arrived now, thank Yeshua Almighty! And Elijah meant every praise to Jesus, too, because his stomach was about to lick his ribs clean.

He tore into his burger and moaned with delight. "Perfection…"

And he wasn't lying! The perfect amount of pink, moist and juicy, with crisp lettuce and a fresh tomato, slathered in brown mustard and ketchup, rubbed with some sort of concoction tasting of paprika and coffee and pepper. He threw some fries down the hatch for good measure—sweet potato, if he wasn't mistaken. The others joined in, the table going silent while the group enjoyed their meal for a few beats of peace.

Chewing, he held his burger and looked off toward the stage, those jammers getting back on the horse and striking up another

Jimmy Smith number. From *Back at the Chicken Shack*, if he weren't mistaken.

Before chomping a bite, Elijah muttered, "Wonder how much the Watchers might be involved in this one?"

"Watchers?" Johnny asked with a full mouth. "What's that?"

Peter said, "Hey, I recall something about that last year."

Oh my cheeps. Elijah didn't want to get into that. Not that second, anyhow. Might down the road, but not now.

He waved his burger in the air, trying to dismiss it. "They're spiritual beings from the Unseen Realm. Not important. Not now, at least."

"Sounds like it is," Jae said. "Like you're fixin' to make a point."

"My point is, all this seems deeply spiritual. That's my point."

"It's medical," Gina countered.

"Nope. Spiritual. But I'll also grant you it's medical."

"Gee, thanks..."

"What do you mean by that?" Jae asked. "That it's spiritual?"

Elijah turned to her, eager to share with the vixen, but also to clarify for himself what had bothered him from the start when Silas Grey had handed over their case.

"Think about it," he said. "Thoughts that tell you your life is not valuable, that it would be better if you were not here, that life's not worth living, that it's time to give up, or there's no hope for the future—whether they are thoughts that come to your head or words others say—you can be a bazillion percent sure that you're under attack by supernatural forces from the Unseen Realm who want nothing more than to destroy your life. Probably seeing it as a threat to their work of darkness."

"You're talking about the Book of Ephesians," Peter said, "chapter 6?"

Elijah nodded, then closed his eyes and intoned: "*For our struggle is not against enemies of blood and flesh, but against the rulers, against the authorities, against the cosmic powers of this present darkness, against the spiritual forces of evil in the heavenly places.'"*

"'Therefore,'" the pastor went on, picking up the next part of the passage, *"'take up the whole armor of God, so that you may be able to withstand on that evil day, and having done everything, to stand firm.'"*

"Bingo. Stand against the darkness. Even when it's calling from deep inside yourself."

"But not everyone can," Gina said. "Sometimes dread and depression and despair, anxiety and hopelessness run so deep that people can't see a way forward. See the green pastures on the other side of the darkest valley."

A siren blared outside Max's Place again, the reds and blues racing by as if putting an exclamation point on it. Then another, two wailing coppers racing by that reminded them of the ever-present threat against the people of Mill Creek Junction.

The group went silent, all heads having snapped toward the interruption and registering the same response. And hoping it wasn't another…incident.

The vehicles faded from a hearing, and the group offered a collective sigh. Not of relief, but as if holding their breaths for the next suicide shoe to drop.

Still might…

"I see what you're saying, Gina colada," Elijah resumed, stuffing his mouth with fries. Throwing back the rest of his wine, he swallowed and continued, "And I don't want to suggest every mental illness is spiritual."

"Why do I sense a but coming on?" said Jae.

"But—"

"Butts are for toilets," Gina said before throwing back a swig of beer.

Elijah frowned at being interrupted, but went on: "But…it's about awareness. An awareness that supernatural actors roam Earth seeking to devour people. To steal, kill, and destroy them."

"Like John's Gospel reveals," said Peter.

"Bingo. And in the Apostle Peter's first letter, warning about our ravenous enemy who *'prowls around, looking for someone to devour.'"*

Gina folded her arms. "Then what would you suggest?"

Her tone and tenor was a bit more challenging than he was used to. Got it, given she was a psychologist and all. So he was basically raining on her sciencey parade.

Elijah answered, "Don't entertain those thoughts for a second, is what. Reach out to someone and feed yourself the truth of God's Word. Believe the story he tells about humanity—that they are uniquely and wonderfully made by a Creator who has a plan for their life and wants to lavish them with his crazy love!"

She smirked. "Easier said than done, Eli. Sometimes medication is the answer."

"Nope. Well, yes. I agree. There is a clinical dimension to it all. Definitely. And with anything medical, the right prescription can work wonders."

"But..."

"But...well, what people need more than Prozac is to know, deep in the depths of their very soul, that Jesus loves them and will walk alongside them through the valley of the shadow of death—carrying them on his back if need be—no matter how dark that valley may seem. They will come into the light again. Life is worth living because Jesus himself lives. Even when it's hard."

"A memo," Jae said, "seven Mill Creek Junction gals didn't get, apparently."

He shrugged. "Touché."

Another siren roared outside, jolting the group and sending their heads spinning back toward the large window overlooking Main Street. It was followed by a livid horn. One of those major honkers on a—

Fire truck.

And not just singular. Two more of those red beasts went barreling down Main Street.

Jae said, "Looks like a four-alarm fire with all that fire-truck power."

"Nope," Elijah replied. "A four-alarm fire has sixteen engine companies, nine ladder companies, six battalion chiefs, one—"

"Yeah yeah yeah. I stand corrected."

"Except there goes one more," Gina said.

Another roaring siren, followed by a livid honker that meant business. Joined now by a few red-and-white SUVs and an ambulance singing its own song.

Which meant nothing good…

Elijah sucked in an uncertain breath. "A first-alarm fire…with all hands and all companies operating."

"What's that, kid?" asked Johnny Pope.

Before he could answer, something came over him. A cold rush of dread, followed by a tingle across his skin and a pressure in his head cluing him into a revelation-insight that was straight from the Holy Spirit.

Elijah had felt that sort of thing before. Began at the orphanage, as a child, being super spiritually sensitive to not only Yahweh's call on his life but also the deeper, supernatural cosmic powers of this present darkness. It's what carried him through the Bureau working on the government's crazy paranormal cases.

And it was carrying him along now.

Something was wrong.

He knew it. He felt it.

"We need to go," Elijah announced, then bolted to his feet and turned to leave.

"Why?" Jae asked.

"Because, we need to go."

"Eli…" Gina said, her voice staying his departure. He snapped his head toward her, meeting her eyes searching for an answer. "What's happened?"

Happened. Did him good to know his partner knew whatever was going on in him wasn't about something being the matter or something bothering him.

Something had happened. *Was* happening. Out in the world, and unveiled to him.

"I think it's the church," he answered.

Peter startled. "Mill Creek Baptist?"

That cold dread returned, compounded now by a blooming anxiety in his head that spilled down into his fingers—strumming up that tick of his.

Thumb to index finger, thumb to middle, thumb to ring finger, thumb to pinkie. Then rinse and repeat.

"We don't have much time."

Elijah bolted for the exit, not waiting for the others. But also knowing by their shuffling bottoms against the booth and scuffing feet against the wood floor they were close behind.

Pushing outside, a cloudless evening sky the color of a bruised peach by the setting sun was lit by a Waxing Gibbous hanging like a growing pearl amidst a sea of emerging stars.

Sure made him rethink city life.

Something else joined those celestial bodies.

Smelled it before he spotted it, the faint whispers of a burning building—pine wood rafters and gypsum-based walls and asphalt shingles, along with honey wood pews and copy paper and office furniture.

A faint orange and red glow down and across Main Street— at about eight blocks, the sight blooming from behind a beautiful gauntlet of cherry blossom trees—confirmed what he had felt. What he'd been told.

They'd best hightail it down to Mill Creek Baptist!

"No, no, no…" Peter moaned, rushing past in a sprint.

"Pete!" Johnny called out after him, but it was no use. Man was much younger and quicker on the twinkle-toes than Fedora Dude.

Elijah chased after him, the others falling in behind.

Looked like the rest of Mill Creek Junction had the same idea, clumps of rubberneckers trotting on uncertain feet toward the blaze that was coming into sharper focus now that they were a few blocks away.

There were those four fire engines, along with the battalion chief units and squad company and rescue vehicle—

And the source of all the first-alarm panic.

The back half of the small-town Baptist church was belching acrid black smoke, fingering flames rising high into the evening sky. The main sanctuary looked untouched, for now, but the offices were sure ablaze with a fire and fury that definitely closed one of their open investigative doors.

"Welp, there goes the laptop," Elijah said, shaking his head.

"There goes my church!" Peter shouted, hands thrown against the sides of his head.

"That too."

Johnny slung an arm around the pastor's shoulder, giving it a squeeze. "Doesn't look like a total loss, Pete, but sorry just the same."

Peter buried his face in his hands, a rise of emotion seizing Elijah at the sight of more loss. Not the same as Katrina, by a mile-long bridge. But how much more loss should one man carry?

He swallowed hard, his throat dry and sandpapery and that lump of clay returning.

"I'd say the worm has definitely turned."

CHAPTER 11

Gina brought her arms around herself, the blazing furnace actually sending a chill ratcheting through her every bone, throwing a blanket of itchy goose flesh across her skin at the horrifying sight.

The ironic part was it was the middle of a Midwest summer, and the heat from the engulfed building overwhelmed, even at their distance behind the fire trucks doing their darnedest to keep the inferno under control. Her forehead was beading with sweat, and she felt faint. Yet she was chilled, to the bone, even while orange and crimson flames cast eerie shadows across the property looking like a horde of demonic observers.

The thought ratcheted another bout of goose flesh skittering across Gina's skin, her eyes darting around for signs of the Enemy's presence, beyond the wicked intent on display inside the office wing of the sacred space. She didn't doubt for a minute the cosmic powers of this present supernatural darkness were involved. Someway, somehow.

But in what way…that was the haunting question.

The quintet stood in stunned silence—amazed, horrified, disbelieving the scene splayed out across the parish property. Pastor Peter burst out into another blubbering cry, the freighted emotional weight too much to bear after losing his assistant like that, compounded by losing his ministry—on top of six other parishioners.

The Church certainly isn't a building. And yet the local manifestations of Christ's Body on Earth in such spaces certainly carries long memories of those local sacred moments—confessions of belief and baptisms, infant or believer; the celebration of the memory markers of Christ's broken body and shed blood, whether through Communion or the Eucharist; the preached Word of God and weekly dose of encouragement to stay the course; weddings, celebrations, funerals, the whole nine yards.

And look at it now…threatened to become ash and soot in the heap of small-town history.

A gusting breeze whipped through the property, fanning the flames into hungry tendrils reaching for more destruction, reaching toward the heavens, even, with wicked intent. The putrid stench of burning materials joined the gust, compounded by the heat—wooden pews, Styrofoam cups and plates, copy machines and computers, hundreds of books and Bibles.

Gina's stomach clenched tight. Wanted to retch from its stench. Reminded her of the factories that belched toxins and a similar stench across her Toledo hometown, an every-present miasma of burning detritus and acrid smoke hovering for most of her childhood.

At least the sanctuary was untouched—for now. But still…to see this church belching smoke to beat the band and flowers of fire still blooming with mangling intent—all of it brought a sudden rise in emotion, her throat choking and lungs searching for breath.

Someone had set this blaze with deliberation. On purpose and with purpose. Gina had been around the investigative block enough to know that when something like a blazing furnace consumed a crime scene just hours after the start of an investigation—well, foul play was close at hand.

Elijah broke the silence: "I'd say the worm has definitely turned."

Johnny grunted. "You can say that again, kid."

Eli repeated, "I'd say the worm has definitely turned."

Gina giggled at her partner, the familiarity of his quirky personality lightening the mood.

"Now what?" Jae said.

Gina answered, "There goes a solid piece of evidence for our investigation, is what. Probably deliberately destroyed."

She turned to Gina. "You think?"

Gina raised an eyebrow. "You don't? Because unless this is ruled some mechanical, electrical, whatever mishap—this is flat arson in my book."

"Maybe it was the AC?" Elijah said. "Peter said it was on the fritz."

"Naw—" Peter said with a choking sniffle, poor guy trying to engage but still overcome with emotion from it all. "We'd shut it down while waiting for a replacement. To avoid this exact sort of thing."

Gina said, "There you go. Arson."

"But who, why?" Jae asked, turning toward the blaze with no end in sight, even with the four fire trucks.

"Sorry to put you on the spot, Reverend," Johnny said to Peter, "but know of anyone who had a beef with you or the ministry?"

Peter hung his head and squeezed his eyes, then shook it. "None. Can't imagine in the slightest."

"So the who is certainly a mystery—*if* there is a who. And I'm not a hundred percent sure on that front of things."

Gina folded her arms. "Well, I am. I know what I saw, what Katrina looked like with that laptop. Something on it connects all of it. All of this—" She gestured at the continued blaze "—to her death. Maybe even the others."

Johnny shrugged a grunt, then went silent, casting his gaze back to the blaze himself.

"If what you say is true," Jae said, "and I believe you—what you saw in that latest victim, her and that laptop—what's next on the docket?"

Elijah answered, "I think it's time we pay the victims' surviving family a visit."

"Probably a good idea," Johnny said. "But at this hour?"

"Yuppers."

"Suppose that could be arranged."

Gina asked, "Who should we see?"

Jae explained, "The only victim's next of kin I hadn't yet had a chance to connect with is Herb Warner."

"Gloria's husband, is that right?"

"Right. As well as…."

She trailed off, gesturing toward the building that looked less a raging inferno and more like one of those backyard pizza ovens Gina had wanted to spring for. But the point was well taken.

"Kat was single," Peter said lowly, voice choking off any further reply.

Elijah said, "Maybe we can swing by her house later. Lift a key from under some garden gnome and have a look around."

Johnny nodded. "Good idea."

"Sounds like Herb's the word, then."

Gina let herself smile at that, her partner mirroring her own rhyming all the timing shtick.

Johnny asked, "Reverend—"

"Peter, please," the man said with a bit of bite. Made sense. Nerves were fraying on them all at that point.

He nodded. "Sorry, Pete. But you know Herb Warner, right? A member of your parish congregation?"

"Yeah. Man only owns the largest industrial farming operation in the Great Lakes. Just south of town. But it was Gloria, not Herb, that had attended."

"Right. Care to make a call?"

"I know him well enough…" Peter took a breath, then a beat. "I'll make the call."

"Nope," Eli said, shaking his head. "We go, now, unannounced."

"Why?" asked Jae.

He turned to her, then eyed the others. "Because the darkness is lurking."

Spinning back to the blazing fire, he added, "And tonight we stand against it with surprise."

"Agreed," Gina said. "No telling what measure of darkness is creeping in the shadows."

The others agreed, and the five muscled through the fire fighters to retrieve their vehicles—thankfully unscathed.

Retrieving their Cadillac Escalade—Gina piloting the beast after Elijah balked—the quintet set off for Warner Farms, with Peter riding with Johnny and Jae in the PI's vintage F-150 pickup truck.

Twenty minutes later Gina was throwing the Escalade into *Park* on a freshly paved driveway in front of a beautiful two-story white farmhouse with black trim and sloping, peaked roofs, a large wrap-around front porch to die for lit with a dim-yellow glow. Oaks and maples older than the house itself towered above it. A weather-worn swing was anchored out front with a nice bed of flowers. Probably planted by Gloria herself, just a few months ago.

A GMC Denali flatbed was parked inside the open garage. One of those weird cars that made not a lick of sense. A luxury pickup? Who in their right mind would haul lumber or a cement mixer or bails of hay in one of those nonsense puff vehicles?

Gina was a car gal. That was Daddy's doing, before he ran off. Had read every *Car and Driver* issue cover to cover through the '90s, and then kept on keeping up when he up and left. Was probably subconsciously a way for her to keep on keeping touch with him in some small mystical way, keeping his car hobby close and personal.

Regardless, it meant Gina knew her cars. Which was funny, because her car of choice was a Honda Odyssey!

Figured the guy would be more a Chevy or Ford kind of fella, peddling around his farm in something like Johnny Pope's F-150 or a Silverado, given his professional persuasion. Would have thought the Denali was the missus's car, but the BMW sitting next to it was most likely the one Gloria had tooled around town in before her untimely demise.

To each their own and all that jazz.

The five climbed out of their rides and made for the generous front porch, the sun having sunk behind the horizon in a fiery blaze of glory that rivaled the blazing church building. Night-time creatures were out in force now, the crickets and katydids playing their tunes. They walked across a nice green lawn smelling of fresh-cut grass, a strong whiff of celery and onion crops gusting in on a hot breezy breath from somewhere in the distance.

Gina smiled, that impulse to buy an alpaca farm flaring up at the sights and smells of the country, especially given all the stressful crazy. Why put up with the stress, the heartache, the horror?

Then her smile sank, because she knew why.

She had a calling on her life to bring some measure of justice in the world. To fight for *shalom*, as Eli had called it, a deeply Jewish understanding of the way God meant for things to be at the foundation of the world when he breathed it all into existence. When things were whole, at peace, very good. When brother didn't kill brother, or dads didn't run out on their family, or kids didn't hang themselves because of brutal bullies.

Her sister. That's why Gina did what she did. Why she continued to do what she did, now for the Church.

For those girls, for that woman, Gloria, and the husband she'd left behind.

After all, what did the prophet Micah say? *'He has told you, O mortal, what is good; and what does the Lord require of you but to do justice, and to love kindness, and to walk humbly with your God?'*

Wasn't so sure about her performance of the latter, knowing how prideful she could be, even when it came to her relationship with the good Lord above. But about the other two, doing justice and loving kindness—well, she'd be darned if she didn't throw herself fully into pursuing both. And for her and her profession, both as former FBI and a psychologist, doing justice and loving kindness meant taking on the bad guys.

Standing against the darkness, as Eli had said. Both back in her Bureau days and now these Group X ones.

Taking a breath, she nodded, swishing across the grass to make sense of the crazy, the *inexplicitus*.

When the snarling sound of some ankle-biter came into a hearing. And she didn't mean the kiddo kind.

Dog!

Was hollering something fierce as they sauntered toward the front door. Thing must've had a real set of ears on that head, it was going at it so much. Probably more bark than bite, an itty-bitty thing that was ten pounds wet. Definitely didn't sound like your typical farm dog, that's for sure. Would've expected more a Golden Retriever, maybe a German Shepherd. Probably woke the long-dead Warner ancestors buried in the family plots hanging off to the side, it was going at it so fierce!

Hated dogs with a passion that burned bright and strong. Especially the yip-yappy kind, like the one coming at them from behind a screen door.

"Shut your yapper, Cupcake!" said Herb Warner from inside.

The five of them turned to one another, mouthing the obvious.

Cupcake?

The man stopped cold when he saw the group approach, throwing up a nervous laugh. "Oh, hey, Father. Didn't know it was you who'd driven up."

"Herb," Johnny said, clomping up the wood stairs painted

forest green, "you know darn well I've been retired for a decade now. Johnny's fine."

A large man greeted them, a tiny white furball with a stumpy tail firmly clenched in his large arms and nestled against his blue overalls. Yip-yapping to beat the band! Cupcake, Gina presumed. As long as the thing didn't leave those arms, she would be fine.

Gina grabbed her hair for good measure, though, twisting it with rising anxiety before plucking a single strand of hair to calm her nerves. Wish she had some of that Doublemint gum, her mouth salivating at the thought, but she'd left it in the Escalade. She did grab Gloria's diary, however, carting it along in hopes that Herb might offer some insight.

Herb himself looked like he'd taken a frying pan to the face, his skin all leathery and creased with age and stress, surprisingly pale for a farmer; bags the size of fertilizer propping up watery, blood-shot eyes; what little greasy silver hair he had sticking up all askew, like he'd stuck his finger in an electrical socket.

Elijah approached Cupcake, eyes all wide and mouth hanging open with love. "Hey there, cutie-pie. You're a good doggie, yes you are."

In one quick motion, he scratched the furball's little white head, humming and smiling and connecting with her wide, brown eyes.

Cupcake looked like a deer caught in headlights, it didn't know what to do. Actually, the dog was caught in Eli's nemawashi tractor beam, her partner having a surprising way with animals. Which earned him the nickname Doc Doolittle at the Bureau, among other names.

"Well, I'll be..." Herb said, mouth hanging open with wonderment, eyes misting over. "The dang thing hasn't shut up in days! Not since Gloria..."

The man trailed off, face pinching and eyes running over now.

The five stood quietly, letting the man have his moment.

A few beats went by until it passed.

"Sorry…" Herb wiped his face on Cupcake, the little furball still mesmerized by Eli. Then the man slapped a meaty palm on her head, nearly taking the thing off before stroking it gently, endearingly. "The little doggie is my wife's. She's been lookin' for her the past few days. Surely wondering where she's run off to. When she's comin' back…"

Gina noted the use of the present tense. *Is* my wife's little doggie. Poor guy.

"I understand, Herb," Johnny said. "That's why we're here."

He gestured to the group before landing on Peter. "You know Pastor Young, I presume."

Herb nodded. "Sure do. Gloria was part of your congregation, wasn't she?"

Peter managed a smile. "Sure was. A lovely woman. Terribly sorry for your loss."

"She loved your church. Loved your sermons most of all. Always put a skip in her step, they did."

"Thank you," he said quietly.

"Peter here," Johnny went on, "asked if I and Jae McCray—" he gestured to the petite brunette "—along with these two other investigators, Gina Anderson and Elijah Fox—" another gesture to the Group X agents "—would have a look at what's been going on in Mill Creek the past few months. We wondered if we might ask you some questions about your wife's…well, death."

Herb took a deep breath. Looked like he was about to object. Would understand if he did, still needing time to process, not wanting to get into it after the authorities probably put him through the wringer.

But then he nodded and gestured with his head inside, sauntering back in with his dog.

Gina clenched the diary tight and followed the others inside.

Through the investigative portal for some answers…

CHAPTER 12

Elijah felt a growing sadness the farther he walked into the darkened farmhouse. Deep, in his belly.

Something he hadn't truly felt until that day Dad was shot square between the eyes in their country church. Something he hadn't really expressed until a hot minute ago when he was face to face with Katrina—or at last face to the back of her blown out head.

Either way, it was like the woman's dread and depression and despair, anxiety and hopelessness had manifested itself at the front of that church. Like her dead body was exuding a deep darkness that had driven her to the brink—and then over the cliff with the Smith & Wesson.

And he'd felt it, deep down.

Which had triggered a long-buried empathy and emotional side that had lain buried for decades.

No, not buried.

Bludgeoned to death, stuffed away in a hole deep in his soul, encased in lead, and sealed with a blast hatch armed with a ABUS Granit lock, arguably the world's most secure of padlocks sporting a tensile resistance of over six tonnes.

Yeah, that.

And now, clomping across scuffed hardwood walnut floors still smelling of lemon polish through the narrow farmhouse hallway entrance crammed with three or four dozen family pictures lining one wall opposite the staircase leading to the second floor—small school pictures of the grown-up Warner kids, twin boys and a girl; large portraits of Gloria and Herb, faces smiling and bright and young; various sizes memorializing family fishing trips and outings to the zoo, vacations to Disney World and the Eiffel Tower and Giza pyramids—all of it threatened to open up the floodgates again that had sent him reeling with empathy back at Mill Creek Baptist.

Which shouldn't have, given his place on the spectrum, his Autism Spectrum Disorder supposedly making him some heartless robot, like the Tin Man from *The Wizard of Oz*, his favorite childhood television movie. But a funny thing about autism is that not all autistic people are alike.

That was sure lost on Hollywood, which portrays them all as a monolith of unemotional, feckless, socially detached zombies who can't handle anything physical invading their space and fly off the handle when they don't get their way.

Sure, there was some of that in Elijah's own experience; he was self-aware enough about that, mostly thanks to the love and care of his adoptive parents. But as Gina colada had always insisted: autistic people will confound you.

He'd confounded himself, actually! For one, Elijah discovered that, while he sucked at one-on-one interactions, becoming super self-conscious about what he said and what he didn't know in the midst of a personal conversation, he was a master at public speaking. Could work a room as well as a street-corner prostitute could work—well, a street corner!

Which he knew wasn't kosher, but it was true. Surprised him as much as anyone, but as a professor it was the social separation between him and his students that had allowed him to excel. Helped he had an eidetic memory, too, being able to recall almost anything he read or saw with photographic precision. All of it was what had helped him excel as a professor where he couldn't at the FBI.

And yet…Elijah's emotional detachment from circumstances, from people even, had been a thorn. Couldn't recall the last time he'd shed a tear—even when his own adoptive father died in front of his very eyes. And there were times he hated himself for his differences, for the thorn that paralyzed him in moments like that when every neurally normal person would offer a comforting word or reassuring touch.

Nope, not him. No words came, no impulse to reassure he was present. At least, up until that hot minute ago back at the Baptist church!

Had pleaded with Yahweh to change him more times than he could remember. To make him whole, to put him back together again and repair his damaged mind and body. Because Lord knew that's how the rest of the world viewed him, as damaged goods. As disordered, as a problem.

No bananas on that one. Yahweh instead used him in ways that confounded allistic people. His ability to detach from highly emotive situations had been a superpower that had served him well at the Bureau.

Lucky for him, and for Group X, Gina's emotional spidey senses had been more tuned toward offering comfort. Probably her estrogen.

Then it all broke earlier that day, in a small-town Baptist sanctuary. Something inside he had shoved deep into his inner being had been unleashed. And now, taking in the memory markers of another suicide victim—pictures of Gloria and her family, a purple shawl with a gold dog pinned to its breast slung on the railing, a tea cup collection filled with sweet-smelling rose petal potpourri—all of it ratcheted up the overwhelm.

His heart rate spiked, his lungs searched for air, his under-shirt was starting to soak with sweat, his head felt light, his throat tumbled over itself with dryness.

Before he knew it, he was strumming up his stimming tick to

cope: thumb to index finger, thumb to middle, thumb to ring finger, thumb to pinkie. Then rinse and repeat.

He needed air; almost said so, too, his watchword for an impending meltdown from overwhelming stimulation and anxiety.

But pushing through to the other side of the hallway helped, a sort of valve releasing from stimming and from escaping the pictures that had ratcheted up his emotional overwhelm in the first place, compounded by the claustrophobia from the cramped space. It also helped the house opened into a brighter, cooler, larger open floor plan.

A well-appointed kitchen anchored the right side—light gray quartz countertops, white shaker cabinets, stainless steel appliances with one of those brushed-metal hoods over the stove, a generous island dividing it from the rest of the floor—opening up into a dining area and large living room. Bright recessed lighting shone from above, and a 75-inch television had some football game running on mute (*bo*-ring!) in front of a bank of leather wrap-around couches and recliners.

Joint spanned three of his row houses, it was so large! Apparently, he'd gotten into the wrong line of work.

Herb motioned toward the collection of seats, sauntering over and slumping into a leather loveseat looking about right for his girth. He was a comical contrast to his itty-bitty Bichon Frise that looked like the name sounded: snow-covered white. It was a curious, playful, peppy breed that reminded him of his teenage pet, Doggy. Named the little guy himself, a West Highland White Terrier that was his best friend, his only friend.

Until he got hit by a school bus, that is. Another loss, another hatch encasing his emotional core.

Was never one for small talk, so Elijah got to it: "We're sorry for your loss, Mr. Warner. I can only imagine what it was like. To find your wife...dead. Like that."

The man stroked Cupcake's head, saying nothing more but nodding.

"Can you tell us about that…incident?"

"I already went over this with the authorities," Herb said.

"If I understand it," Johnny piped in, "Gloria was in the bath-tub, wrists…"

He trailed off, making a cutting motion and saying all he needed to say.

Another nod from Herb; more saying nothing.

Couldn't blame him, with that memory of the bathwater colored somewhere between Kool-Aid Tropical Punch and Sharkleberry Fin seared into his memory.

Johnny added, "An empty bottle of sleeping pills had been found on the bathroom floor next to the tub."

Gina cleared her throat and shifted, taking over. "Do you know why she might have done this?"

"No idea," Herb said, voice thick and husky and eyes mist-ing. "Makes not a heap of cotton pickin' sense! We were living the life, her and me, now that we were empty nesters. Were fixin' to do some traveling, now that I'd hired some fine executive types to help run the farm. So I don't…"

He trailed off, burrowing his face in Cupcake a bit, using her back to wipe his face and soak in the memory of Gloria, no doubt.

"What about the diary?" Elijah said, moving it along.

"What about it?"

"Gina—" He turned to her and took the leather-bound note-book from her. He opened it and turned to the back, showing the demon-like illustration to Herb, who cringed, along with the others.

"Golly…" Jae said, with Johnny and Peter expressing about the same shock.

Herb returned to the land of the living, explaining, "She'd all these thoughts racing through her head."

"What kind of thoughts?"

"Voices, really."

Elijah noticed Gina sitting straighter, no doubt her

psychology training kicking into high gear at hearing that bit of revelation. Knew the most common type of hallucination in people with mental health conditions such as schizophrenia are voices in the head. Which could be true…

But he had other ideas.

Gina asked, "Had she been diagnosed with schizophrenia in years past?"

Herb shook his head. "Not that I was aware."

"Any other mental health issues?"

"None. Was fit as a fiddle."

Johnny leaned over to Gina. "Sounded back at Max's Place like you've got some sort of background in psychology."

She nodded. "Ph.D. from the University of Michigan."

Herb whistled at that. "Nothing to shake a stick at, that's for sure."

She smiled, a hand going for her ginger locks and beginning to twist them at the attention.

"What's your assessment, doc?" Johnny asked. "Sound like schizophrenia to you?"

She let her hair go and shook her head. "One might think that, but no. It's exceedingly uncommon for someone older than 40 to be diagnosed with schizophrenia."

Jae asked, "What sorts of voices had Mrs. Warner expressed hearing?"

Herb shrugged. "Lots of 'em, telling her her life wasn't valuable, that the world would be better off if she were not walkin' around, that her life wasn't worth living anymore, that it was time to throw in the towel, no hope for the future…"

The man trailed off, voice running hoarse and growing thick, his eyes misting again until they spilled over with emotion.

He brought Cupcake in closer, to his face, as if his wife's dog were an echo of her memory he wanted to soak up into his skin.

Elijah's gut twisted with recognition. "What did I tell you? Sounds like a massive attack by supernatural forces from the Unseen Realm to me."

"Perhaps…" Gina acknowledged.

Elijah rolled his eyes. "It's the Watchers, I tell ya. The Watchers!"

"Eli…" she said, voice laden with skepticism. "I don't think this is the place or time."

"Watchers?" Johnny said, brow furrowed. "What are they?"

"The Watchers are the sons of God in 1 Enoch," Elijah explained.

Jae said, "You spoke about these Watcher characters at Max's Place. But what about these…sons of God ones?"

He cleared his throat and sat straighter, heat running up his neck at her inquiry, but also delight. Time to bring it.

"They concern the other gods in Psalm 82 called the sons of the Most High. Elsewhere they're called the *beney ha-elohim*."

Jae snorted a laugh. "Oh, is that all…"

Johnny nodded. "I'm with her, kid. I was a priest for three decades, and even I don't know what you're talking about."

"Not a very good priest, apparently."

Gina jabbed him in his ribs; he yelped.

Elijah frowned, his tongue getting the best of him. "Sorry. That wasn't called for."

He waved a dismissive hand. "Don't mention it, kid. I've been called worse. Trust me. But what of this Psalm 82 business?"

"Right, verse 6. Most Bible translations read: *'I say, 'You are gods, children of the Most High, all of you; nevertheless, you shall die like mortals, and fall like any prince.'*"

He twisted up his face and shook his head. *Children of the Most High* felt like sucking on a lemon, it was so sour! "Not a fan of that translation, because 'children of the Most High' is *beney ha-elohim*, and the original Hebrew is—"

"Right right right," Gina said with interruption. "*'The sons of God.'* I've heard this before."

Peter added, "Yeah, I recall some of that insight last year with that crazy alien conspiracy."

"Alien conspiracy?" Herb exclaimed.

Elijah waved a dismissive hand. "Not important. What is, is that Yahweh, the Most High God, is surrounded by a divine council of lesser gods."

Jae furrowed her brow. "Don't you mean angels?"

"Nope. They are what the text says they are. Gods. They outrank angels. The Hebrew word for *angel* is entirely different."

Johnny said, "But this verse in Psalm 82 says they fell, that they would die like mortals."

"That's right. These are the supernatural beings who rebelled."

"Are they demons then?" asked Jae.

"Not exactly. Some are indeed fallen spiritual beings, but they outrank demons as well. The details aren't important. What is, is that there is a deeply Jewish understanding that these fallen ones, and the disembodied souls of their offspring, are the demonic forces that continue to roam Earth and haunt humanity."

"I'll be damned…" Herb said, before correcting: "Oops, sorry about that, Father, Pastor."

Both Johnny and Peter chuckled and waved him away.

Herb's face fell, and it suddenly darkened, his eyes narrowing and growing serious, the caterpillars chilling above his eyes slumping with worry.

He said lowly, "I don't know nothing about no sons of God or Watchers or whatever. All I know is, something came over my Gloria. It's why I urged her to get help."

"Help?"

"That's right. Up at that doc at Mill Creek Community."

Jae sat straighter at that one. "A psychiatrist?"

"Something like that. A shrink, whatever."

"His name didn't happen to be Cain Vaughn, did it?"

Herb cocked his head with recognition. "Sure was. A young fella we came across through an ad posted on WeShare. Was the one who encouraged Gloria to write down her thoughts in that journal of hers."

Elijah startled at that. "Your wife answered a shrink's WeShare ad for mental health help?"

He shrugged. "Didn't know where to turn when her thoughts started going dark. And it turned out alright."

"If you call Kool-Aid bathwater turning out alright."

Gina jabbed him in his ribs again; he yelped. Point taken.

"Sorry. He'll be numero uno on our to-do list."

"Most def," Jae said.

Johnny asked Jae, "Sounded like you're familiar with Gloria's shrink."

She nodded. "One of the other victims, the fourteen-year-old—"

"Abby Peterson," Peter clarified.

"That's right—well, her mother mentioned she'd been seeing a shrink by the same name."

Gina said, "Doctor Cain Vaughn."

"Up at Mill Creek Community?" asked Peter.

"That's right."

"You know him?" asked Johnny.

"Not really *know*, per se. Know of him. But now that you mention it…"

He looked off toward the gargantuan flatscreen TV, face draining of color some.

"What do you got, Reverend?"

He sucked in a breath and shook his head. "Just that…I think Kat mentioned seeing someone up at MCC."

"Doctor Vaughn?" Gina said.

"I think so, the man offering pro bono counsel."

Elijah grinned. "Looks like we got ourselves a hot lead. No way that's a coinkydink!"

Gina nodded. "I'd say. Perhaps the other victims sought his help as well. Can't imagine a town this size has very many mental health practitioners."

Jae said, "Or very many practitioners heading up clinical trials for the NIH."

"NIH?" Peter said.

Elijah explained. "National Institutes of Health."

"Right on, hot shot!" Jae said.

Heat raced to his cheeks. Sure liked the sound of that.

"Good find," Johnny said. "What's the clinical trial for?"

Gina added, "And how did you manage to discover that one?"

Jae held up her phone with a grin, giving it a shake. "I've got my ways."

Elijah scooted to the edge of his seat. "I like the sound of those ways…"

Gina colada cleared her throat and threw up one of those huffs she'd been throwing up all evening, whipping out her own phone and flipping through it.

"According to the grant proposal," Jae explained, "he was spearheading a clinical trial examining the effects of social media."

"Worthy cause," Johnny said.

"Yuppers." Elijah pulled out his new digital pal. "Dumb phones are the way I roll now."

"Me too!" Jae exclaimed, yanking out her own Jitterbug Flip2. Apparently, it wasn't only for grannies! In his opinion, its manufacturer was missing out on the whole hot babes demographic. Just think how many of those hot puppies they'd sell if they slapped Jae McCray on their packaging instead of a *Golden Girls* leftover.

"Any results yet from the trial?" Gina asked.

She shook her head. "Nothing published yet."

"Definitely something to look into," Johnny said. "Pronto."

"Especially," Gina added, "with two of our vics, maybe a third apparently seeing the lead clinician. Maybe they were even involved in his clinical trial."

Jae addressed Herb: "Know if your wife was a trial participant?"

He scrunched up his brow. "Can't say. All I know is, she spent a good amount of time with the fella, then took to writing her thoughts down in that diary. And then…"

He trailed off, the rest being history.

Didn't sound like Doc Vaughn was any help, but he was the best lead they had.

"Any reason we can't leave now?" he asked, bolting to his feet. "Maybe look around, get the shrink to spill the tea?"

Jae glanced at Johnny, who shrugged and looked to Gina, then to Elijah.

"I'm game if you are," he said. "Maybe he has a night class."

Elijah headed to the door.

"Onward ho!"

CHAPTER 13

nd onward they went, Elijah at the wheel this time driving down a country road darkened by towering trees and stretching limbs, flanked by rows of onions dotting black soil while Gina enjoyed a break in the passenger's seat. He balked, of course, but she wasn't having anything of it. Had a needling headache in the middle of her forehead and needed a breather from the crazy.

Could really use some sleep after the day they'd had. But the show must go on, as they say. Especially when you've got an *inexplicitus* case involving a suicide cluster that seemed to be spinning out of control into a suicide contagion.

So she settled for quiet contemplation with her head resting against her window.

As her partner drove, some trumpeter doing his jazzy thing from the radio instead of her favorite soprano doing her operatic thing, Gina pulled out her phone for a scroll. Funny how that sort of thing was so automatic. Like a bodily appendage begging for attention, her fingers tingling for a pop of dopamine at a like or share or morsel of newsy gossip. Or was it gossipy news?

Either way, she understood the psychology behind social media engagement, with the fear of missing out and all baked into the product. Even felt the device buzzing at her leg some-times when nothing was there. Phantom buzzing, they called it. The mistaken feeling a notification was begging for attention. Reminiscent of the psychological condition of amputees, actually, who sometimes struggle with phantom limbs after they are removed, the feeling they are still attached and begging to be itched or scratched or used.

Sounded about right.

Yet, scroll away she did, the familiar WeShare digital sharing space offering a surprising dose of community, as false as it was. Old college friends shared about promotions and newly published journal articles (an unfulfilled personal dream of hers). Former FBI colleagues shared photos from ski resorts in Switzerland or Alaskan cruises (she hadn't had a vacation in a decade). Others posted ironic jokes and witty memes she didn't understand (her autism tripping her up with those sorts of things).

The more she scrolled as Eli drove on, the more Gina's anxiety about her own unfulfilled dreams and miss-outs, the in-joking and in-crowding, the window into lives more interesting and clever than her own bloomed into the feeling she was a big, fat zero—capital Z.

Driving her to start twirling her hair even as she popped two sticks of Doublemint in her mouth, the phone on her lap glowing with invitation to further her descent into the rabbit hole.

The intense spearmint flooding her taste buds and nostrils helped bring some measure of calm to the rising overwhelm, as did using her jaw to grind the polymers, plasticizers, and resins of the gum base that made up her stimming technique into a pulp.

Gina knew she should stop, knew she should shove the device back into her pocket—of all people, knowing the harmful psychology behind the social feedback loops WeShare engenders to fuel self-esteem and share self-referential thoughts to garner likes and shares that further the loop. But she couldn't—especially with the new posts coming into view.

Ones that mirrored her own doubts about her recently chosen profession (*"OMG, did I make the biggest mistake of my life taking this job!"* from a friend of a friend), and fears about nearing the Big Four-Oh without any romantic prospects on the horizon (*"Just me and my four cats on a Friday night, with a pizza, watching Gilmore Girls. Nope, not a nun. Just a 39-year-old doomed to socially imposed celibacy!"* from another shared post), and general feelings of malaise (*"Why did no one tell me life would suck this bad??? I would have slit my wrists a decade ago. LOL! JK!! <3 <3 <3"*)

For a split second, she agreed with Mandy Fosdick's self-confession, whoever she was—just some random acquaintance connection from a friend. But there she was, verbal vomiting on her ShareFeed. It was as if the darkness Gina had been surrounded by with this *inexplicitus* case had seeped down inside, stirring up her own dark, despairing, desperate thoughts.

The self-defeating ones that told her she was still that double-wide trailer-park trash that would amount to nothing but her stoned mama.

The self-doubting ones that said she'd made the biggest mistake of her life joining Group X, wasting her life in service of the Church instead of catching the real bad guys, the flesh and blood ones terrorizing the country.

The despairing ones that kept her attention on the headlines shouting about rising inflationary indexes and stock market corrections, tension in Eastern Europe and suicide bombers in the Middle East, police shootings and urban lootings, the next variant leading to the next pandemic.

The anxious ones that feared she'd missed her chance to marry and have 2.5 kids and find the Happily Ever After she and her sister had giggled about as girls, then early teens, until...

Now her mind slumped fully into the darkness, those haunting memories of Grace swinging from the carved-out ceiling, the cloying smell of deathly rot already blooming in the stuffy, stifling double-wide.

She tried to climb back out, but it was no use. Tendrils of despair had wrapped themselves around Gina's very soul—the more she scrolled, the more her memories surfaced of all the darkness from her life, past and present.

Until a dot of light spoke through it. Just a pinprick, really. A ray of truth slicing through the swamp and climbing toward the surface of her consciousness. A set of verses, from the Apostle Paul's second letter to the Corinthians:

> *Indeed, we live as human beings, but we do not wage*
> *war according to human standards; for the weapons*
> *of our warfare are not merely human, but they have*
> *divine power to destroy strongholds. We destroy*
> *arguments and every proud obstacle raised up*
> *against the knowledge of God, and we take every*
> *thought captive to obey Christ.*

The verse jostled her from doomscrolling through her Share-Feed, awakening her from the mindless enslavement to her thoughts—the dark ones, the despairing ones, the hopeless ones.

Take every thought captive to obey Christ…

Indeed.

Gina stuffed the phone in her pocket and cracked the window, the blessed scents of onions and celery from the farms racing by grounding her in this reality—not the fake one crafted in the digital nether. Those dueling scents were joined by woodsmoke and manure. Heaven…

The jazzy trumpeter switched to a bluesy organ and tenor saxophone. Not her style, but the change in sound helped unwind those tendrils the darkness had wrapped around her heart and mind, the aural shift re-centering.

She considered those weapons of our warfare the Apostle Paul spoke about. Ones he goes on about in our journey with

Christ to remain victorious against the Devil—our quest as citizens of the Kingdom of Heaven to stand against the Darkness as the Book of Ephesians speaks about, wearing the whole armor supplied by the good Lord himself: the belt of truth, the breastplate of righteousness, the shoes of the gospel of peace, the shield of faith, the helmet of salvation, the sword of the Spirit.

All of it is given to empower God's children with the strength of Christ to take their stand against the darkness, their own *personal* darkness during the evil day when the Devil and his minions rise with menacing purpose.

Like in that moment, in that Escalade barreling down a country road, the trees parting some now to show forth a bright moon spraying soft silverlight across Warner's fields and the small town assaulted by this present supernatural darkness.

Buildings from that town were coming into view as well, another mile down the way. Houses with husbands and wives trying to hold their marriages together in the face of those assaults. Children nestled in beds and dreaming dreams too wicked for words.

A shiver ratcheted up and down Gina's spine at the thought, knowing the truth of that wicked assault. The personal truth of that wicked assault.

The Apostle James exhorts believers to resist the Devil, promising he will flee from those who stand against the darkness.

So she joined that promise with a prayer:

> *Dear Lord and Savior Jesus Christ: I hold up all my*
> *weakness to your strength, my failure to your faith-*
> *fulness, my sinfulness to your perfection, my loneli-*
> *ness to your compassion, my little pains to your*
> *great agony on the Cross. I pray that you will*
> *cleanse me, strengthen me, guide me, so that in all*
> *ways my life may be lived as you would have it lived,*
> *without cowardice and for you alone. Show me how*

> *to live in true humility, true contrition, and true*
> *love.*

"Amen," she muttered, crossing herself.

That tension eased some inside her chest now, and light slowly faded into a strong hearing, the Word of God and Spirit of Christ chasing away the darkness.

For now.

She did feel lighter, though, like she could breathe again.

Sniffling and batting at her eyes, she thanked the good Lord above for his—

Something suddenly came into view out front.

On the road.

The headlights slicing through the nighttime darkness dowsing white beams against—

A woman. Blond and young.

Stepping out from the shadows.

Arms crossed against her chest.

Facing them with eyes closed.

Standing dead-center in their lane.

With only seconds to react.

"LOOK OUT!!!" she screamed.

Her partner joined her with a high-pitched scream of his own, joined by squawking brakes and squealing tires and a spinning world as Eli tried to avoid running the woman over.

Didn't work.

Gina glimpsed the woman's face just before it smacked against her window with a hideous slapping thud that would stay with her for days.

Right before a rumble underneath the car, the body crunching under the front tires and thudding against the undercarriage.

Brakes squawked, tires squealed, the world went twirling as Elijah sought to right the ship and keep from capsizing.

Then it all stopped. The rumbling, the crunching, the thudding, the squawking, the squealing. Only sound left was the echo of their cries and a mournful, haunting sax.

"Did I just hit someone?" Elijah asked in a rush on a horrified breath, the sound of his hyperventilating breaths joining that damn sax. "Did I just ram this Caddy into some poor soul out for an evening stroll?"

He was heaving desperate breaths, mouth open as if in a question and eyes just as wide.

"I believe so," Gina said. She startled at her answer, then she spun to him. "I mean *no!* This was not your fault. She stepped out into your path. You didn't do anything wrong. There wasn't anything you could—"

Eli threw back his head in a primal scream that sent an electric charge of horror skating across her skin and belly slumping to the fine leather seat beneath.

Then he threw open his door and bolted from the SUV, tearing across the road and into one of Herb Warner's fields.

"Eli!" Gina called after him, head pulsing with wicked pain and confusion and indecision—and paralyzed with what to do.

Could things get any worse?

Actually…watching Eli scramble over a downed portion of a fence butting the road, Gina knew they could.

And would, if she didn't go after him.

She had a hunch what was coming.

And it would be no good for anyone.

CHAPTER 14

Gina threw off her seatbelt and threw open her door, a heavy summer humidity joined by onions cloying and clawing at her. Slamming her door shut, she raced after Eli.

But not before catching a glimpse of the victim. Number Eight, if her gut told her right.

What she saw was unrecognizably human.

She was pretty sure it was a woman, the victim wearing a tight-fighting white blouse over a buxom chest and an hourglass figure. But other than those obvious tells, it would have been hard to know for sure.

Limbs were wrenched around a mangled figure sprawled on the cracked pavement, bent and broken, going this way and that. Face was a pulpy mess, the bridge of her nose smashed clear inside, along with her eyes and upper jaw. Her mug puckered like a donut at the forehead and chin, the inside a pool of raspberry jelly.

Blood shimmered black across her arms and legs in the silverlight of the moon. Soaking her clothes, streaking her hair and skin, pooling on the pavement.

It was a horrifying sight. Made sense why Eli had run.

Gina couldn't worry about that now. Worry what had led this woman to end her life in such a way—involving them, even!

Especially Eli…

Tearing herself away from the sight, she followed after her partner, scrambling over the same downed fence portion—

And landing on her face.

Thick, wet earth shoved up her nose and in her mouth, tasting of worms and wet newspaper and those onions pushing through the soil.

Blech!

She spat it out and swatted at her face, taking a stumbling step forward.

When the sound of slamming car doors and a shout drew her attention: "Gina! What's happened, what's going on?"

She spun back around, glimpsing two shapes silhouetted in a pair of pickup truck headlights, a low-lying fog rolling in on a cool breeze now. The sight sent a frigid chill skating up her spine, the mangled body of that woman streaked by dark crimson shimmering in the moonlight several yards away.

Gina yelled back, "Going after Eli! There was an accident, and…"

She trailed off, her throat tripping over itself and running sandpaper dry.

"Is he alright?" Jae yelled in reply.

Her breath seized in her chest, along with any words. She didn't have any, because she wasn't sure.

She flat wasn't sure.

But Gina prayed to the good Lord he was, because if not…

Well, then she and the Almighty would exchange a few choice words when all was said and done.

Spinning back toward her partner, Gina called back, "Stay there. We'll be back!"

Then took off across the field, her partner several yards ahead and screaming now, with flapping arms and head thrown back with another primal scream that told her all she needed to know about what was happening.

Meltdown.

The kind she herself had had more times than she'd care to recall growing up. The kind autistic people sometimes struggle to keep at bay, but nothing like what she was witnessing.

Not a tantrum, as allistic people are prone to finger-wag. Meltdowns were the last leg in a slow burn when the overwhelm bloomed into an explosive outlet.

Understood completely what was happening, Elijah's inner emotions boiling into a fierce frenzy. A physical welling inside that needed to escape. Like a vomiting sensation that found relief when one expelled the contents of their stomach.

Gina caught up to him as he fell to the hard soil, hyperventilating between screams and desperate cries to the good Lord above why this had to happen, combined with a few choice words that would make a sailor blush.

She wanted to put a hand to his back, let him know she was there, give him a small measure of comfort through human touch. Knew that would be the wrong move; would be for her, as well.

Instead, she went with: "This wasn't your fault, Eli!"

"B-B-B-But I—" He heaved a breath, eyes bugging out and lips curled back in horror. "*I. RAN. OVER. HER!*"

"No, you—"

"*YUUUU-PPEEEERS!*" he screamed. Something primal, something that sounded not of this world.

He rocked back and forth, sobbing and blubbering like a child.

Had never seen her partner act like this before. Was the stoic, solid one between them. To a fault. Figured it had something to do with his childhood, and what had unfolded in the Baptist church was the floodgates opening from decades of bottled-up emotion.

But this…

This was a whole other level.

What was she going to do?

"The s-s-s-*SOUND!*" Eli said, a shudder racing through him.

"Sound? What—"

"*SMACK!*" he shouted with sudden surprise.

Then again: "*SMACK, SMACK, SMACK!*"

More rocking, more sobbing.

"Like the birds used to *SMACK* into the big picture window at my orphanage. Robins and cardinals."

Gina's head was reeling, a horrifying fright gripping her at the sight.

Elijah grabbed his hair, clenching it and twisting up his face. "Just keeps ringing, ringing, ringing in my head, *head, HEAD!*"

He let go and smacked a hand against his forehead.

SMACK!

Then again: *SMACK!*

The sound eerily like what she recalled from the woman's face *SMACKING* into her window.

Now he was going at it with both hands, all over his head.

SMACK, SMACK, SMACK!

"Eli!" Gina cried out before grabbing his arm and wrestling him down to the ground.

Which jolted him from his self-abuse, the touch neither of them tolerated much resetting him. He recoiled from her but relented, doubling in on himself in the dirt and wailing.

Gina's heart was rending in two at the sight of her partner, her friend, unraveling. She wanted to pull him into an embrace and tell him it would be alright—that *he* would be alright, *was* alright.

Because that victim, whoever she was, was just that. A victim —and of suicide, by the way it all went down. Probably their eighth.

Instead, she quoted Scripture, using Psalm 23 as a prayer—as a weapon against whatever manner of dark, supernatural wickedness was coming against them.

And manner of despair was rising in Elijah.

She cleared her throat, quoting: *"'The Lord is my shepherd, I shall not want. He makes me lie down in green pastures.'"*

It was exactly what Peter had quoted earlier in the day—or yesterday, who knew what time it was—in the middle of his own dark night of the soul after Katrina had shot herself in the head.

Whether it would work now, with Eli, helping bring him back from the brink…

She didn't know. Prayed to the good Lord it did. But flat didn't know.

"'He makes me lie down in green pastures,'" she went on, willing the Word of God to act as a healing, comforting, calming balm for Eli's meltdown, his pain. *"'He leads me beside still waters; he restores my soul. He leads me in right paths for his name's sake.'"*

Her voice faltered, squeaking out the final words through a tightening throat thick with emotion. She didn't know if she could finish.

Gina went for the second stanza, when a small voice cut in through the noisy field fauna.

"'Even though I walk through the darkest valley, I fear no evil…'"

The words sounded barely above a whisper with all the racket around from crickets and tree frogs, but they were there.

And they were Eli's!

Which loosened her throat enough to join him: *"'for you are with me; your rod and your staff—they comfort me.'"*

Remained hunched, but no longer hushed. Supposed that was a start!

But now he was sitting straighter, voice more sure of itself, more determined. Resolute even: *"'You prepare a table before me.'"*

Gina went silent as Elijah went on, rising some now in tenor and tone, *"'in the presence of my enemies; you anoint my head with oil; my cup overflows.'"*

Her heart burst with compassionate empathy for the man who was her partner, but it quickly turned into admiration for his courage to face the darkness—his own darkness that he had been carrying, and that had been unleashed through this case.

Their voices joined together for the final stanza, in a lament as much as into growing resolve: "*'Surely goodness and mercy shall follow me all the days of my life, and I shall dwell in the house of the Lord my whole life long.'*"

The darkest valley was right…

Always loved that Hebrew poem, and its honest assessment of the sour end of life's stick along with the promise of the Lord's goodness and mercy.

Lord Jesus Christ, Son of God, where's the promised goodness and mercy?

They were drowning, she and Eli, though he was the first one to break. She wasn't close behind, with all the dark thoughts rising within and the threat of random people jumping in front of their car!

Eli heaved a breath, and Gina wiped a stream of tears she hadn't noticed brimming at her eyes. The seconds ticked by, counted off by the creaking and crowing katydids and tree frogs in the near distant, the pair still and silent in the middle of onions that smelled about as sour as life had turned.

Elijah finally stood, edging to his partner, though the two didn't embrace. Instead, he put up his hand. She instantly put up hers as well, edging it to his own but not touching.

Almost, but not quite.

They both waved their hands, the motion synchronized, one that had been honed from their days at the Bureau as a greeting for the pair who loathed touching, but also as a way to comfort in the middle of the crazy.

Gina smiled. Eli was back.

One end of his mouth curled upward as well. "Thanks, Gina colada."

"Don't mention it."

"The shiznit has sure hit the fan."

"And our Escalade…"

Gina caught her careless tongue, heat racing up her neck. But any embarrassment was intercepted by a loud laugh from Eli, deep and from his belly.

"Good one." Another laugh, his head thrown back and his guffaw echoing across the field. "Shiznit hit our car is right…"

He heaved another breath, Eli going silent and the weight of it all aging him in the silverlight of the moon, stress lines across his baby face deepening at his eyes and brow and chin.

"You guys alive out there?" bellowed Johnny from the road.

Eli turned to leave and sighed. "Suppose we better get back to it."

Gina added, "Take our stand against the darkness."

He turned back, with a grin. "Together."

She grinned back. Yes, together.

She liked that.

CHAPTER 15

Elijah felt like he'd been run over by a Mack truck. One of those honking, two-ton beasts with tires as big as a T-Rex and an attitude to match.

Which was ironic, because he'd just run over a woman.

Not funny, he knew that. But it was the truth of it.

Ached something fierce, from top of the head to his tippy toes. A wicked pain lanced from ear to ear. Throat was rawer than sandpaper, and his lungs burned like he'd run a marathon. Surprised his eyeballs hadn't popped out of his sockets and were still moist with all he'd cried.

Worst of all, though, was the embarrassment of it all, his head blooming with anxious dread returning to Johnny and Jae. Could manage well enough with Gina, knowing she understood their kind did that from time to time.

Melted down.

And by meltdown, Elijah meant full-on Chernobyl out there in the middle of Herb Warner's onions. Didn't even have time to rumble, to get worked up and build up the typical head of steam like Mount St. Helen, the tremors foretelling what was to come.

Nope. Blew right past the foreplay and straight to the Big Kahuna.

Was just flat completely overwhelmed by what had happened.

Not only that he had hit some poor soul—the *whacking* of her face against Gina's glass window, the *thwapping* of her body against the aluminum sheet-metal door, the *rumbling* and *rattling* of her head and torso and limbs against the undercarriage and exhaust piping still clattering in his head (was a bell that would not be unrung for quite some time).

But that the poor soul had stepped out from the shadows in the first place—on purpose and with purpose. One singular purpose.

To kill herself.

To end her life.

To pull the plug on whatever gloom and depression and despair, anxiety and hopelessness—whatever darkness had gripped her so much that she thought the only way out was stepping in front of a Cadillac Escalade barreling through a country farm road, making her the eighth victim of whatever cosmic power of this present supernatural darkness had its hold on this small town.

No way around it, this was a hostage takeover by a maniacal Power not of this world—one so gripping and totalizing that women and girls as young as twelve couldn't resist, couldn't find release.

Because mark Elijah Xavier Fox's words: It *was* not of this world. No doubt about it.

And it was dragging Image Bearers of the Creator of the universe himself into the darkest valley, strangling and striping the life out of them—mawing and mangling and destroying!

He'd be damned if he let it happen to anyone else.

The gentle swish of boots across soil changed to crunching gravel, then the soft settling of his boots on pavement, yanking Elijah out from his contemplation and back to the moment, back to the investigation at hand.

"You got this, Eli," Gina whispered from behind, the scent of lavender and vanilla from her perfume suddenly giving him resolve. Her presence, standing beside him in the Ford's head-lights, gave him all the confidence he needed, more than even her words.

Wanted to believe her, but Elijah could see it written all over their faces, the pair of them glancing at one another with wide eyes and licking lips and furrowed brows and shifting feet. Not knowing worth a lick what to do with what had gone down in the field.

His heart was pounding in his ears, that lancing pain return-ing. Lungs burned something fierce again, too, his ratcheting ticker searching for more air with the spike in anxiety.

But he knew what he needed to do.

Address the ginormous, smelly hippo on the road.

"I had a meltdown," Elijah announced matter-of-factly.

"Uh, yeah, you sort of did…" Jae said, taking a step back that smacked of self-defense. She quickly added: "But anyone of us would have, given what'd happened to—"

"Nope. Not like that," he said with interruption. "I'm autistic. That's why."

The word landed hard. He could see it. Hated those looks. The uncertain ones that quickly morphed into pity before painting him as broken, disabled, disordered.

Less than.

"Meltdowns," Gina explained, clearing her throat, "are a way for autistic people—" she turned to him, one end of her mouth edging upward "—for people like the two of us to cope with overwhelming conditions that can be difficult to express in other ways."

Johnny and Jae stood in silence, listening without response.

She went on, "It happens when someone becomes completely overwhelmed by some situation and temporarily loses control of their behavior, expressing this overwhelm verbally or physically—"

"Or both, as you heard," Elijah explained.

Gina nodded. "I understand it may look like a temper tantrum, something bad and naughty."

"Nutty, even," he added again, discomfort growing with the silence and being put on display like some frog to dissect.

"So, what," Jae was the first to say, "you've got Asperger's or something? One of those high-functioning types?"

Elijah shook his head. "Nope. That's not what it's called. Not anymore. At least, not after revelations about Herr Asperger's experiments on children for the Nazi Great Cause. Society switched things up real quick after that little nugget of revelation, making a switcheroo to the Autism Spectrum Disorder lingo."

"I see…"

Earlier in his life, he had simply been called a retard. And a difficult, out-of-control retard at that. The kind who drove his birth parents to the brink, and then made the guardians at the Commonwealth of Virginia's orphanage and his eleven foster parents want to pull their hair out.

And beat him with the backs of their hands, and their belts, even copper pipes and coat hangers when they were within arm's reach.

It wasn't until a psychologist and her pastor husband adopted him that the world finally got him. An Evangelical Baptist minister and a practicing Catholic adopted an ethnic Jew. Only in America.

Johnny said, "Alright, so you're a person with autism—"

"Autistic person," Elijah corrected.

"Isn't that what I said?"

"Nope."

"Umm, alright…"

"So, what are you," asked Jae, "some sort of savant or something?"

"Nope. That's a common misconception. Only point five percent of autistic people are savant. I'm not one of them. I suck at math. And playing the piano."

Gina chuckled. "Eli's being modest. He does have an eidetic memory, so he might as well be a savant."

Johnny said, "Bet you were a real asset to the FBI, I reckon."

Elijah nodded. "I was…"

"Well, you're certainly an asset to us, to this investigation. And I don't care if you're a one-legged purple people eater, so long as you put it all on the line to get the justice these women —*that* woman deserves."

Elijah eased in a measured breath, his heart settling and a sort of calming hope washing over him at Johnny's apparent acceptance.

He glanced at Jae, who had clasped her hands behind her and widened her stance, nodding and throwing him a reassuring smile.

They had his back. He saw it; he knew it.

What a great feeling that was.

Elijah said, "It's one-eyed, one-horned purple people eater, but I'm picking up what you're putting down. So, thanks."

Took a beat, but Johnny snorted a laugh that rolled into a full-on belly one. Same for Jae, the tension from the last half an hour melting.

"You're alright, kid," the man said. "How about we get to it?"

He took a breath and nodded, following Johnny's lead.

They all did, the four taking careful steps over to the remains of the mystery woman still sprawled out like a rag doll on the cracked pavement. Understood why Pastor Peter had remained inside Johnny's pickup. He wanted to join him…

Looked like something out of a nasty Stephen King fever dream—the broad's face crunched into a bloody, black-crimson pulp; hair matted with the same sticky fluids crusted on the rest of her body, her arms and legs; those same limbs jutting this way and that at odd angles and bent in places Yahweh never intended when he created the human body.

Almost retched at the sight, adrenaline flooding his veins and hitting his stomach hard, compounded by that lancing headache again. But he held it together. Had to. For the mystery woman's sake.

Johnny bent to one knee beside her, pulling out something from the inside of his shirt.

A gold cross attached to a string of beads.

Then the man started muttering something under his breath, a prayer.

"Lord Jesus, holy and compassionate," Johnny intoned, "forgive this woman of her sins. By dying you unlocked the gates of life for those who believe in you: do not let our sister be parted from you, but by your glorious power give her light, joy and peace in heaven where you live and reign forever and ever. Amen."

"Amen," Elijah whispered, joined by Gina and Jae. Supposed it made sense a former priest would find his first impulse to pray for the dearly departed.

"Do you recognize her, Johnny?" asked Jae, voice betraying a tremble.

He stuffed the cross and beads back in his shirt and gave his head a rapid shake. "Been here forty years and I can't make sense of her."

Elijah replied, "Perhaps if her head weren't smashed like a Halloween jack-o-lantern you could."

Gina said, "Maybe she has some identification on here."

"Good call."

Elijah and the others got to it, searching the road in the dim moonlight augmented by the vehicles' headlights.

Bupkis on his end, and it seemed like the same sad result for the rest.

The four paced several feet up and down the road in search of a purse or wallet. Again, bupkis.

Hustling back to the body, he had an idea.

"Maybe she's got ID on her, in a pocket."

"Could be," Johnny said.

"Watch the crime scene," Gina advised. "Gotta be careful we

don't mess with anything the authorities would want to use for their own investigation."

"Yeah yeah yeah…" he said, carefully easing the broken, bloodied body around for a better—

The woman flopped to her back, giving Johnny a start that sent him skittering backward.

Elijah flinched, his heart soaring through his throat and into his eyeballs! Expected her to rise to her knees, then feet, then come lumbering after him to exact her revenge.

But there was no more movement.

Swallowing, he caught sight of a bulge at her front right pocket. Had to reach across her to fish it out. Averted his eyes from her face, that smashed jack-o-lantern looking more like Mason Verger from that crazy Hannibal movie—all puckered and swelling and bulbous; one eye punched clear through, the other hanging by an optic-nerve thread.

Elijah sucked in a stabilizing breath and got to it, slipping his hand inside the tight pants and pulling with *one, two, three* yanks until it popped out.

Yuppers. A wallet.

"Bingo!"

A smile raced across his face at the good get.

It was a pink little thing with a gold zipper and a loop handle. Large enough for a driver's license, a credit card or two, some cash, but not much else.

"Let me see it, kid," Johnny said.

Elijah stood and handed it off, knowing the man who had lived there most of his life would know who she was.

Johnny unzipped the thing and flipped it open, fishing for the mystery woman's ID.

And muttering a curse.

"Sonofa—"

He dropped it with a start, as if a scorpion had crawled out. It flopped face down with a thud, some coins clattering out onto the cracked pavement.

Confused, Elijah picked it up.

Jae said, "Did you recognize her?"

Johnny nodded, grabbing his chin without a word.

"Who is it?" asked Gina.

He didn't answer, his hand covering his mouth now and clearly too stunned for words at the revelation.

Elijah squinted in the faint moonlight, finding a New York address, both the city and the state.

"Name is Rebecca Lynn Goodall."

"Goodall?" Gina looked at Johnny, walking up to him now, almost getting in his face. "Who is this? What aren't you saying? Why aren't you—"

"The Mayor's daughter," Johnny interrupted. He took a breath, then a beat, clarifying: "Chet Goodall. His daughter is Rebecca."

Elijah said, "But the license says she lives in New York."

"She does!"

"Then why the hot Hades did she step out in front of our Escalade?"

"I don't know!"

"This breaks the pattern…" Jae said.

Elijah turned to her, confused. "What pattern?"

"Victims one through seven were from Mill Creek Junction. Every one of them."

"That's right," Gina said. "And from Peter Young's church, amiright?"

"Exactly."

It dawned on Elijah. He turned to Johnny. "You're saying Rebecca ain't from around here?"

He swallowed and nodded, eyes returning to the twisted body.

"Then presumably," Jae continued, "she's not part of Peter's Baptist parish. Doesn't attend his church."

"Presumably…" Gina agreed.

"Bingo. Breaks the pattern," Elijah announced. "Just like Jae said."

"But what does it mean?" Jae asked.

"The worm has turned, that's what."

"The worm hasn't only turned—"

"It's gone belly up!" Gina said, swallowing hard. "If I were British, I'd say it's gone bloody belly up!"

"Bingo…" Elijah whispered. Then: "We need to pray!"

"Pray?" Jae said with skepticism.

He turned to her. "The shiznit that just hit the fan—or, well the Escalade—it's straight out of the Unseen Realm, I just know it. If we're to have any hope of standing against the darkness, then—well…we need to pray!"

Johnny said, "Not the worst idea in the world."

"You got one for us, Father?" Jae said.

"As a matter of fact…"

Johnny Pope (which was too awesome for words) closed his eyes, Elijah and the others joining. He intoned:

> *Most loving Father, you will us to give thanks for all*
> *things, to dread nothing but the loss of you, and to*
> *cast all our cares on the One who cares for us.*
> *Preserve us from faithless fears and worldly anxi-*
> *eties, and grant that no clouds of this mortal life may*
> *hide from us the light of that love which is immortal,*
> *and which you have manifested unto us in your Son,*
> *Jesus Christ our Lord.*

"Amen," Elijah said, crossing himself, feeling the weight pressing in against him lifting. Head even felt better, too, and so were his lungs, the ache seeming to evaporate from the prayer.

Amen, the other three muttered in agreement.

"Now what?" Jae said.

Gina replied, "We follow our lead."

"The doc?" Johnny said.

"Still," Jae added, "after all that just happened, what we discovered about the pattern break?"

Gina said, "We don't know what we discovered."

"Technically, we didn't discover anything," Elijah clarified. "She popped out of the shadows at us!"

"I mean about the pattern break. You're on to something, Jae, for sure. The suicide cluster isn't looking as clustery with this outsider."

"Who's also an insider," Johnny added, "given the connection with the mayor."

Elijah said, "Suppose it's about time we call the police."

"I'll call Chet. Let him know his daughter..." He gestured toward the mangled woman and pulled out his phone.

Gina said, "In the meantime, we should get some shuteye."

Elijah protested, "I don't want to get some shuteye. I want to find this woman her justice—all eight of them!"

Johnny shook his head. "Too bad, kid. We've all just been through it—you both twice over now, with what happened to Katrina."

"But—"

"Butts are for toilets, Eli," Gina said, "you know that."

Elijah went to bite back but took a breath instead, running an irritated hand through his hair. Now that the ex-priest mentioned it, he did feel tired, knackered, bushwhacked, a sudden weariness coming over him.

So he said, "Meet at Mill Creek Community tomorrow morning?"

"First thing," Johnny agreed.

First thing. Because the darkness will not slumber tonight.

But tomorrow...

Tomorrow it will meet its Maker.

Elijah would make certain of it.

Dead certain.

CHAPTER 16

Gina slept like crap, hadn't showered in a day, and seriously wanted her money back from Happy Camper Inn.

Was false advertising, as far as she was concerned. Because she was the farthest thing from a happy camper.

Room smelled like an ashtray and bed was lumpier than Mama's mashed potatoes (hence, sleeping like crap). Shower was streaked by mold and had the pressure of a pinched garden hose (hence, no shower in a day). And the promised continental breakfast was a box of stale Cheerios and milk a day past its use-by date; browned, mushy bananas; and curdled yogurt that had sat out too long.

Yep. Definitely wasn't a happy camper. Hopping mad, was she—hopping! On top of being sleepy, hungry, and moody. Didn't help none she'd had nightmares all through the night while jostling for the perfect combination of lumps to support her body just right. Dreams about driving long-haul trucks (a once career aspiration during junior high) through Nevada's deserted Highway 50, the Loneliest Road in America, while women kept jumping out in front of her path!

Spent near well the entire night avoiding the leaping

zombies, their white faces and darkened eyes and crimson-streaked blond hair a reminder of what had happened during the night. The conscious part of her brain knew it was all just dreams conjured from the horrifying run-in with the Goodall woman. The subconscious brain wouldn't let her out of it though, nightmare compounding nightmare in a death grip that wouldn't let her awaken.

When she finally did manage to slip back to reality—her big rig cascading over a cliff and the barely conscious part of her mind yanking her through the looking glass during her free-fall before ending up in a mangled pile of steel and limbs—Eli had been knocking at her door to leave for Mill Creek Community College. Might have been relegated to permanent vegetative unconscious state, too, having died from the zombie apocalypse fright had Eli not intervened.

Didn't help matters she had been doomscrolling again just before bed, WeShare serving her a double-portion of gloom, depression, despair, anxiety, and hopelessness on top of the horrifying accident. Nothing different than any of the other times she'd scrolled through WeShare, the perfectly manicured pictures of people's lives clubbing and bar hopping, vacationing and sightseeing, marrying and babying—all of it reminding her how lonely and isolated, uninteresting and unaccomplished her life was.

So, yeah. Gina was in a mood. And the world better watch out.

For Elijah's part, he sat still. The only part of him moving were his fingers, running through his stimming routine that helped center him when the shiznit hit the fan.

Or in his case, he ran over a blond in the middle of a country road.

The technique was a way of dealing with stressful situations or a burst of excitement for people like him and her.

People on the autism spectrum.

He wound his stimming tick back to the beginning: Thumb to

index finger, thumb to middle, thumb to ring finger, thumb to pinkie. Then rinse and repeat.

Could only imagine what he was dealing with, having run over that woman and endured the rapid-fire questions from that blowhard Chief of Police Roller fella. Man really went after Eli, questioning everything about the accident—from whether Eli had been drinking (no) to speeding (double no!) to falling asleep at the late hour (no, no, and triple no!). She nearly blew her lid defending her partner, but he let the police do their own investigative thing.

Didn't know how he'd been able to hold it together through it all. Gina thought she would've wilted under the interrogation, but no meltdown or outburst from him. Perfectly calm, cool, and collected, her partner the perfect professional. A real champ, Eli was.

After an hour of that, and when Gina began pitching a fit about their treatment of her partner and how she knew from here to Sunday that they had an eighth victim on their hands, Mill Creek PD finally let them go.

Now they were arriving at destiny, Mill Creek Community College, to get answers to the *inexplicitus* case from nightmares.

Or so she hoped…

"Oh my cheeps," Elijah said, sitting straight and craning this way and that as she entered through a grand wrought-iron gate emblazoned with the school's name.

Gina understood him perfectly.

When Jae and Johnny said Gloria and Abby had seen a psychology professor at a local community college, she'd expected a boring, unadorned campus on unwanted property next to the highway, filled with buildings straight from the Cold War—cinder block eyesores passing for academia teaching tech-school basics for small-town teenagers without any ambition or prospects for life beyond Midwest onion fields and factories.

Boy, was she flat wrong.

Instead, the campus rivaled anything she had seen while

living on the East Coast the past decade. Like a mini Princeton University up in New Jersey or Georgetown University down in Washington.

"I'll admit it," Elijah said. "I pretty much expected something along the lines of Homer Simpson going to college to brush up on his physics after a near nuclear meltdown than something more along the lines of *A Beautiful Mind* or *Good Will Hunting*."

"Ditto…" Gina said, still marveling.

Baseball and football fields sat farther out beyond a massive lake shimmering under the rising sun, adorned by a large central fountain spraying with delight. A long student center and outdoor eateries sat alongside the lake closer toward the main campus, as did bike paths and even an outdoor amphitheater.

Five main buildings, a few stories tall and made of red brick, were arrayed around a generous quad of towering oaks and maples. They were styled in the traditional collegiate gothic architecture that had marked the building boom on campuses in the early 20th century. Places like those East Coast universities had positioned themselves as America's answer to Cambridge and Oxford universities, and their buildings reflected such intellectual rigor and aspirational ambitions.

Same for Mill Creek Community, which struck a dissonant chord in Gina, the gothic vibe of those elite universities planted at the edge of a small farming town in West Michigan. Did not compute.

Johnny's vintage F-150 was waiting for them in a visitor's parking spot when they arrived. Gina slid next to it, and the ex-priest and Jae got out.

"Welcome to Mill Creek Community College," Johnny said, wearing the familiar black trench coat and fedora and gesturing widely.

"This place is amazeballs!" Gina marveled.

Johnny grunted a chuckle. "Suppose you could say that. The college was established by one of the founders about a century ago who had made it big feeding furniture factories wood milled from acres of forests that used to dot these lands. A real gold-rush era, that time was."

"Don't you mean timber-rush era?" Elijah said.

"Suppose so. Anyway, the man, Jedediah Walker, established a trust fund for any Junction high school graduate to receive a complete college education for free. Needed to maintain a 3.0 and stay out of the clink."

"Not bad requirements," Jae said. "And a generous offer."

"Over the years, it's built up into a modest private liberal arts college with some noteworthy professors helping Mill Creek's youth become doctors and accountants, even tradesmen like mechanics and builders."

"Speaking of which," Gina said. "How about we find a one Cain Vaughn, see if he can't help us make sense of all the crazy."

Johnny led them across the quad, a well-manicured lawn with those towering trees, the sidewalk flanked by square-cut hedgerows. Alcoves in the bushes housed benches with summer students dutifully reading and clattering out some term paper and studying for some test.

"Any news on our mystery woman?" Gina asked Johnny. "What's her name?"

"Rebecca Lynn Goodall," Elijah promptly replied.

Supposed it made sense he'd memorized the name of the woman he'd hit—and killed. Her heart sank for him.

"Right, Rebecca," she said softly. "Any further word?"

Johnny pulled off his fedora, his countenance darkening in the bright morning sun. "Chet and Millie are a mess, as you can imagine. Their only child. To add insult to injury, she'd just gotten engaged. That's why she'd come to visit, to share the good news, as well as…"

He trailed off with a catch in his throat. Heaving a breath, then a sniff, he tried again: "She'd also come with the news she was—"

There was that catch again, joined by a mournful shudder that stopped him cold along the red-brick pathway. He swallowed, then again, as if searching to grasp words that were lodged down deep.

"Pregnant," Elijah said flatly. "She was pregnant, wasn't she?"

Jae offered a weak, muffled cry, batting at her eyes.

Johnny nodded, hanging his head. "That's right, kid…"

Gina gasped. "For real?"

He said nothing more, pinching his eyes and putting that hat back on his shiny eight-ball head.

"For the love…"

"Sweet mother of Melchizedek…" Elijah said lowly, the normal exclamation point on his exclamatory phrase missing.

Her heart threatened to rend in two now—both for this woman and her parents, and also for her partner, her friend.

"That means," Gina said, more to herself than the others listening in, "that this woman, this victim, had every reason to live. Plenty of hope for the future—with her fiancé and each other, with their future family and kid on the way."

"The pair had been Mill Creek high school sweethearts," Johnny confirmed. "Went to college together down South. Lived together on the Upper East Side in New York. Both in finance working in Manhattan with stable jobs and plenty of income."

"Certainly not a despairing, hopeless life."

He heaved another breath and sighed.

Jae asked, "Any sign of…well, depression?"

"You mean," Elijah clarified, "was she cuckoo for Cocoa Puffs?"

She shrugged. "Suppose anyone who steps out in front of—"

"No, she wasn't," Johnny said emphatically, as if shutting down that line of inquiry. "None whatsoever. Interviewed both Chet and Millie myself after breaking the news to them, along with Rebecca's fiancé. Nothing of that sort."

"That they knew of…" Elijah said lowly again.

Johnny didn't fight that one, because there was an obvious truth to it.

And yet…

Gina couldn't make sense of it. Defied any clinical explanation. Anyone with that level of motivational stability, her Maslowian needs from the famous psychologist's hierarchy clearly met—from physiological to safety to love and belonging to esteem; from her income level, professional pursuits, and recent familial developments all fulfilling those in spades—anyone in her shoes would surely have been the least likely candidate for the sort of self-exit she chose just hours ago.

Flat didn't make any sense; none of it did. And it pissed her off.

Pissed her off these women were following in the footsteps of Gracey, without a rhyme or reason, without any psychological pattern—she could make sense of anyway. Which probably pissed her off the most, that she couldn't work it out, that the resolution to this inexplicable case eluded her.

Not for long.

"Maybe our lead can help," she said, nodding toward an imposing building bathed in the morning's orange sunlight.

Johnny grunted. "Hope so. By golly, I hope so…"

He sauntered onward, retaking the lead. Looked like each of the academic departments had their own building, organized into schools. The School of Science and Mathematics; the School of Business Administration and Communication; the School of Human Literature, Language, and Education; and the School of Social Sciences and History.

Johnny made for that last one, a three-level stately affair that looked like it rivaled the others. Good for Jedediah for investing in the bedrock of all other disciplines, as far as Gina was concerned. Though she was a bit biased, given her own attachment to the social sciences through her psychology degree.

Wood and carpet and fresh paint greeted them upon entrance, a hallway of walnut hardwood floors painted moss and lit by yellow lighting in sconces—not the dreadful fluorescent lighting typical of colleges. She liked this place already.

Looked like offices were on the third floor, so they made for that, Elijah taking the lead up a set of stairs and bypassing the elevators. Gina smiled at the gesture, knowing he did it for her with her aerophobia compounded by claustrophobia that made riding those things a nightmare.

Reaching the top, a receptionist counter was anchored between two closed doors, presumably leading to offices for the social science professors.

"Let me do the talking," Elijah said over Johnny's shoulder. "I have a way with older women."

Johnny gestured. "Have at it, kid."

He made for the desk, where an older woman was buried in a hardcover. A Jeffrey Archer book, titled *Twelve Red Herrings*. Gina joined him.

"Hi, there," Elijah said to the short, pudgy woman with grey hair swept into a bun that meant business.

She startled violently, clutching her chest and throwing up a squeak. Apparently, she was so engrossed in the mystery author's yarn. She hadn't noticed them.

But Eli plowed ahead anyway: "We're looking for Professor Cain Vaughn. Can you direct us to his office?"

She peered over a set of narrow raven glasses, black with up-swept corners, resting on the bridge of her nose, one eye twitching with suspicion between him and Gina.

The woman crowed, "And why do you need to see the professor?"

"Is he here, in his office?" he replied, side-stepping her question. "I understood this to be his office hours."

The twitch was growing faster with skepticism. "He is. But what is the nature of your visit?"

"Forgive me, ma'am," Eli chuckled. "Where are my manners? I'm a professor from up the road, at Grand River Theological Seminary. Or rather, was, until it was blown to kingdom come last year. But that's a long story."

He seemed to be playing the part of the absentminded

professor—or rather, in his case, former absentminded professor. Gina wasn't sure the woman was buying it.

"Grand Rivers you say? Professor…of what?"

"Biblical studies. Well, former professor, if I'm to be completely on the up and up with you. Long story, involving aliens and UAPs and government conspiracies."

The woman's eyes narrowed further. "Did you say aliens, UFOs?"

"Nope. Not UFOs. UAPs. Unidentified Aerial Phenomenon. The government updated its language when—"

"What Eli's trying to say…" Gina said with interruption, noting her partner's ramblings and wanting to get on with it. "We have an urgent, academic matter we believe the professor can help us with."

Now she threw those narrowed eyes at Gina. "Really? In what way?"

Nosy little busybody, she was. Far too nosy for her own good.

"It's a private matter but concerns the professor's academic interests, as well as an investigation involving the deaths of his patients."

Her eyes went wide. That sure got her attention!

"So, if you wouldn't mind directing my colleagues and me to his office, we would be much appreciative."

Her face sagged, having been denied some juicy institutional gossip. But she rose from her chair without a word and waddled toward a doorway. "Follow me."

Gina glanced at Eli, then back to Johnny and Jae, who smiled and nodded toward the woman. She followed after, joined by her crew.

The woman stopped at a door and held up her hand, instructing them to wait at a distance from the entrance while she announced them to the professor. After a few minutes, she returned. "He's meeting with a student, but will see you when he is finished."

Elijah smiled. "Thank you, ma'am. Appreciate your help."

She smiled curtly, then waddled back to her desk. A few minutes ticked by before a young man emerged clutching a paper and wearing a disappointed scowl. Apparently, his appeal hadn't gone very well.

But the door was open, and a dashing young man in a tweed jacket around Gina and Elijah's age was sitting behind a generous wood desk in a well-appointed office, motioning them to enter.

Gina obliged, stepping inside, joined closely by Elijah, the pair giving one another a familiar nodding glance with a wink and a weak smile from back in their Bureau days. The one from when they stepped into the investigative portal for a good interrogation.

Good-cop, bad-cop style.

Time for answers.

CHAPTER 17

've been summoned, by the Chief himself.

No, no, no. Not *that* chief. The Grand Poobah. The Supreme Leader. The Highest Potentate in the universe, Apollyon. At least *our* universe, the realm that goes unseen by those sheeple hustling and bustling about on Earth where I and my cohort make our abode.

No, I'm talking about Wormwood—aka Bitterness, as the sheeple might know him best. He's the one who orchestrates all of our affairs in this neck of the universe. Who keeps the trains running on time and the machinery humming and orders straight. Who dishes said orders at the drop of a hat, sending me and my kind out to do the Shining One's bidding.

But…why the summons? What could he want?

Probably just a status update. Yeah yeah yeah, right right right. That has to be it. Making sure my designs are fit as a fiddle, that the crazy train is running on schedule, the plans to entrap and ensnare are humming right along, that I've got my own orders straight to put the finishing touches on the plan before it's rolled out across America.

Then the world.

These things take time, after all. They always do when

sheeple are involved, even the ones who willingly partner with us to do our bidding.

Especially the ones who willingly partner with us to do our bidding. Because as I've discovered in all my years on this Third Rock from the Sun, those partners usually have their own motivations for accepting our help, ones that are often ulterior to our own.

To Wormwood's.

Of course, it was my idea to begin with, this new plan of ours. Didn't take a genius to know what would be the end of humanity, if we truly wanted it. My kind have been pining for such a thing from the very beginning.

And by beginning, I mean since that dreadful Garden. Little did we know the Adversary's (I swallow hard before spitting the word out like a hairy ostrich fetus) *love* would prove more powerful than our offer. The one that gave the sheeple the chance to be like us. To be gods, literally, taking matters into their own hands to decide for themselves what was right and wrong.

What was good and evil…

At any rate, if the last few years have taught us anything, it's that humanity is feeble, frail, fragile. A year of plagues and pandemics, economic uncertainty, the threat of nuclear annihilation from old enemies, dotty old men ruling the world whose use-by date was expired long ago—all of it would have clued anyone who had eyes to see and ears to hear on that reality.

Boy, did I see the window of opportunity yawning wide open! Had been for generations, but it took just the right amount of exhaustion and isolation, fear and frustration to ratchet up the perfect storm for me to make magic.

For Despair to rain despair upon the sheeple's parade…

You see, I'm a watcher—literally, yes, a spirit of those ancient beings—but more an observer. A student of behaviors and nature, impulses and drives. Sort of have to in my line of work. Yet most of my fellow conspirators are impulsive and rash, leaving their enticements to chance, to the whims of fickle sheeple.

No, no, no. Not me. My operation, the one I've been waiting a long time to unfold, has been going swimmingly! Look at all that has unfolded in my little playground the past few months. Death, destruction, dearly departed souls.

Despair...

Sure sure sure, there have been setbacks. No thanks to that new upstart agency with that wretched religious order, the Order of Thaddeus!

Why can't those *Believers* be more like their monkish brethren —contenting themselves with washing the soiled bottoms of gutter-trash orphans and dementia-addled octogenarians, delivering food baskets and sacks of used clothes to the less fortunate?

No, no, no! They have to go and defend the faith using muscle and moxie more reserved for military special forces than anything the Church has seen since those dreadful Knights Templar!

And now, I and my brethren have to contend with an investigative agency poking its schnoz into our business—this Group X affair that brought down Chaos's operation months ago.

That certainly did not go unnoticed among the Deadly Seven, I can tell you that! And this latest setback is only that: a setback. So a quartet are flittering about Mill Creek Junction with notepads and pockets full of questions. Nothing I can't handle. Nothing I won't handle, I can tell ya that, bucko!

And yet...

What if he is unhappy? What if Wormwood thinks that the mess Chaos made is what is unfolding now, in my playground?

I must confess, the reports coming from that small town are worrisome. The Church's investigators are skating awfully close to the project meant to sow the seeds of despair across the globe. This was meant to be my coming out moment. The grand gesture to show the Deadly Seven I'm worthy of joining their ranks.

And yet…

What if it all falls apart? What if the source of the project's power is discovered?

And shut down—by the Order, by that new Group X nonsense?

What if Wormwood declares me unfit to lead?

No, no, no. Surely not. We get along fine enough. Have always had a mutual respect for one another, for what he and I both bring to the table. Though I could certainly do his job better than him, yessiree. My operation is proving it!

Was *meant* to prove it at least—to the Deadly Seven, the council of our kind that stands in the way of my full manifestation as leader of the Unseen Realm. When I win, sowing despair across Earth, no way will they be able to deny me my rightful seat at the table.

The Deadly Eight they will be!

We will be…

Now all that is threatened—and by a pair of retard investigative agents, no less, along with their Wild West cowboys, the ex-priest and Vegas showgirl. Amusing really, their pluck. Thinking they can stand against the darkness, the despair, the distress.

To stand against me!

But they've got another thing coming, bucko! Because I've got an ace up my sleeve that will send one of them reeling.

Joining the others who have slit their wrists, blown their brains, and leaped in front of SUVs barreling down back country roads.

Yes…that's what I'll do! Rally the troops to target Group X.

Surely that will satisfy Wormwood. A sacrifice, from the Church's investigative agency.

I only hope it's enough to save my hide.

Because if not…

Surely it's off with my head for me! Wormwood is not forgiving.

Neither am I. My next victim will find that out in short order.

When they do, it'll be lights out.

For them, for the case, for Group X.

For good.

CHAPTER 18

Elijah's old stomping grounds at Grand River Theological Seminary were a far cry from this one.

And it made him jealous.

Correction: *envious.*

Because as Merriam-Webster explains, envy means discontented longing for someone else's advantages, while jealousy means unpleasant suspicion, or apprehension of rivalry.

So it wasn't so much that he was angry that Vaughn had what he didn't have, and so then didn't want the professor to have it. It was that some covetous feeling toward the man's attributes, possessions, and stature suddenly seized Elijah—something deep and gripping.

And he wasn't sure why.

Sort of had an inkling, given the man was working on a campus that was much plusher and cushier than the one he'd been at before joining Group X. The university building where he had worked was as functional on the inside as it was on the outside—gray cinder block walls endemic of your typical '70s-era utilitarian box. Smelled like it too—old wood and the dampness of a basement with wet newspaper was masked only by the dueling scents of new carpet and coffee and couches.

Then there was his former office, a cramped space that barely fit him and his desk, let alone any visitors and students. It did—or rather, *had* overlooked a large pond, but it all went kablooey last year. Loved watching the sun cast a waning palette of burnt oranges and brilliant pinks across its waters as it set while he worked late into the evening.

Had poured himself into his work, laboring at a fevered pace to write that next journal article and make those next connections between the Bible and the Unseen Realm, noodling on what those truths meant for the *seen* realm, for our daily lives standing against the darkness in all of the personal ways with his students and with their future church ministries.

And where had it gotten him?

"Margaret is telling me you are having an urgent matter to be discussing?"

The voice with a curious lilt snapped Elijah out of his funk, then snapped his head over to the professor.

Cain Vaughn, professor of clinical psychology, an unfortunate name given its deeply biblical connections to the fratricidal account from the Book of Genesis. Not sure who would want to name their child after someone who'd murdered their brother! Elijah was just thankful his own birth parents had given him at least a passable given name. "Yahweh is my God" isn't a half bad meaning, named after the prophet who defeated Baal and the god's priests. Supposed Baal Crusher wasn't half bad either, but that didn't roll off the tongue as easily as Eli.

Gina answered, "Yes, thank you for seeing us, professor. We have a few questions to ask you about two of your patients."

Busying himself at his desk with papers, the man scrunched up his brow. Which was a bit too well-manicured for Elijah's taste, the dark lines seemingly plucked into twin lines of perfection. Between those and his cleanly shaven face, joined by a mane of curly blond hair and a perfectly cliché professorial tan tweed jacket and pressed brown pleated pants—all of it made him look a bit dandy to be a professor.

"Patients, you say?" Vaughn replied, having stopped his rummaging.

Johnny pushed past, responding: "Gloria Warner and Abby Johnson. Recently deceased from a set of…unfortunate incidents."

The professors flashed wide hazel eyes before casting them down and to the right.

A tell, indicating he was searching for the right words to respond. Had learned to read people, to a T. Mostly from his orphanage days, the daily beatings and bullying forcing him to rewire his brain that was more interested in facial avoidance than facial reading. But he'd adapted, had to in order to survive. So he'd hammered and honed his ability to work out what a person was thinking—or not saying, as was the case with most of the perps he'd interviewed at the FBI, and now this dandy searching for the right set of words to navigate his sticky wicket.

Although it's almost universally accepted that autistic peeps can't read emotion, the amount of scientific evidence to back it up is exactly bupkis. Not all autistic people are socially inept robots.

Put that in your neurotypical pipe and smoke it, as Gina says!

"I see…" the man finally said, sitting down with care.

Gina said, "Your online schedule says you're free for the next hour, so can we have a few moments of your time?"

The man sighed and nodded, gesturing to a set of leather wrapped wooden chairs in front of his desk.

Elijah hustled to one of them, joined by Gina.

The office was orderly, no piles of books or folders spilling papers strewn about, much like the way he'd tended his own professorial domain. Smelled of juniper and cedar as well, the familiar piney, earthy scents of his own former study filling the room from a lit candle at the center of a generous meeting table in the corner. Far larger than his had been, which was stuffed in a corner. Same for the office generally, something rivaling a two-stall suburban garage than the rentable storage unit that had been his office.

Maybe that's where the rising envy was coming from. Something about status and unfulfilled expectations from his former career choice, perhaps. A comparisonitis that had plagued him from the orphanage, where he would constantly size himself up against the other boys—noticing straight away how weak and stupid and ugly and uncoordinated he was compared to the stronger, smarter, handsomer, athleticer orphans. Something he carried with himself like a gangrenous leg well into adulthood, a demon that haunted him still.

Music played softly from a black turntable mounted on a stand behind Vaughn's desk, a violin screeching some classical tune from ELAC hi-fidelity speakers on either side. Nothing at all like the all-in-one wood contraption with built-in speakers he'd had in his office. The one his dad had gotten him for his sixteenth birthday. And definitely not playing *classical* music. *Blech!* Jazz for him, all the way. New Orleans and Chicago style Dixieland to swing and big band. Bop, cool, and hard bop. Then straight into the free jazz and avant-garde of the 1960s through to the fusion jazz of the 1970s and the eclecticism that rounded out last century.

So, yeah, jazz.

The Nespresso machine nestled on a shelf between massive mahogany bookcases that ran around the room was a nice touch. A clean mug was perched beneath its nozzle, ready to go at a moment's notice. Eyeing it, Elijah noticed a crimson and gray logo, thinking it was from Harvard.

But wait…

It sported some odd initials: SPbU.

If he wasn't mistaken, it was for Saint Petersburg State University, the oldest and one of the largest research universities in Russia. Interesting school of choice for an American.

But, wait again…

Something caught Elijah's attention in the corner. A small

picture, the size of a MacBook, hanging above a brown leather reading chair.

A tri-color square border of black, yellow, and red ran around the rectangular print. Running from top to bottom on the left third was thick, black Sanskrit script. The right two-thirds was taken by a river scene, the blue water winding through a reedy marsh behind a small, gold-platted carriage pulled by white horses adorned in gold rigging, punctuated by rubies. The gilded carriage was similarly adorned by crimson and white ornaments. Inside, sat a finely dressed man in the same gold-crimson pattern, hands folded as if praying. A bluish man sat at the front, twisted toward him with pedagogical intent.

Elijah's eidetic memory was working overtime, having seen such folios before at an exhibit in London. If he wasn't mistaken, it was from the Bhagavad Gita, a 700-verse Hindu scripture, with blue Krishna offering the spiritual revelation to prince Arjuna.

"Interesting choice of art, professor," Elijah said, gesturing toward the print.

Cain Vaughn craned for a look and smiled. "Well, it is bearing an interesting message, an eternal message of spiritual wisdom."

"And what is that?"

"The necessity of freeing one's mind, one's very soul, from the attachments of this life in order to attain the supreme perfection of freedom from Karma through renouncing life."

Elijah mumbled to himself with recognition, "I am become death, destroyer of worlds…"

The Gita words Gloria had scrawled in her journal. The professor and his print had certainly made an impression on his patients…

"At any rate," the professor said, waving a dismissive had, "how am able to be helping you? And who are you being?"

"Elijah Xavier Fox," he jumped in, waving a hand. "Former FBI."

"FBI?" Vaughn startled, eyes flashing wide again. "What is the American government wanting with me?"

"*Former*," Gina added with emphasis, taking over, "as Eli said, him and me both. The pair of us had been part of a specialized subunit within the Bureau. We're now investigative agents with the Church, trying to get to the bottom of the raft of suicides that have plagued this small town."

Vaughn nodded and *tsk*ed, those hazel eyes of his flittering down and to the right. He was searching for something—to say, to not say and hide, perhaps…

"Dastardly business it is being," he acknowledged. "But I am not being sure how I am being able to help."

"You saw at least two of the patients, Abby Johnson and Gloria Warner, as my colleague Johnny Pope mentioned."

"That is being correct."

"My background is in psychology myself, having studied in the University of Michigan's doctoral program."

"Interesting…But what does this matter?"

Elijah frowned. Rude. Gina smiled and crossed a leg, then got back into the ring. Made sense, given her background. He'd let her play her good-cop part before he swooped in for the bad-cop kill.

She went on, "What can you tell us about these patients of yours, especially their treatment for suicidal ideation and the kind of acute psychosis that might have led to them taking their lives?"

An annoying, nasally, screechy laugh skittered from the man. "I am not able to be speaking about their treatment, surely you are knowing that! Patient confidentiality and all. I am sure you are understanding, especially one with a distinguished background in psychology, such as yourself."

"Which both families waived," Johnny revealed, reaching inside that black trench coat of his. He withdrew folded pieces of paper and handed them over.

Vaughn's eyes flashed wide again before his face fell. Went a little white, too, if Elijah weren't mistaken. Go, go, Johnny Pope, go!

"You'll also see waivers from two others who were seeing you, Trisha Lyndon and Jessica Briggs."

Elijah started. That was new. The two teenagers, which made at least four.

"There you go, professor," Gina said. "So, what can you tell us about their treatment?"

Vaughn finished scanning the waivers with a huff and sat back, elbows on his armrests and fingers propped against one another like a tent.

He answered, "Abby Johnson started seeing me when she developed an eating disorder."

"Body dysmorphia?"

He nodded.

"Not all that untypical for this age. Was it acute?"

"Very. And she seemed to have a clear idea where it came from."

"Which was?" asked Elijah.

"Her attachment to WeShare."

"The social media platform. But why?"

"The incessant comparisonitis and the glamorized images of skinny girls from class. What girls catch on WeShare are their peers with slim waists and well-endowed chests. Not to be crude about it. This can lead them to have body image issues during a very critical time of development as they are trying to figure out themselves and everything around them."

Made perfect sense to Elijah. Didn't know what he would've done had there been a WeShare back in his day—with all the comparing and cyberbullying, the sizing up and posturing and posing for likes and shares and hearts. Didn't know what his head would've done…

He asked, "This was the case for Abby?"

"It was. But she wasn't the only one."

Gina said, "Trisha Lyndon and Jessica Briggs?"

Vaughn nodded. "That's right."

Jae asked, "Is this what your clinical trial was about?"

The professor nearly jumped out of his saddle at that bit of revelation, the man jerking straight and eyes flashing wide before he licked his lips. Go, Jae!

"How did you know about that?" Vaughn said lowly, voice gravelly, almost growly.

She shrugged. "The interwebs."

Gina added, "Jae saw your grant application with the National Institutes of Health."

The professor sucked in a measured breath, color returning to his face and it softened some. He smiled now and nodded. "Ahh, that's right. Studying the effects of social media use for Uncle Sam."

Elijah asked, "What was it about, exactly?"

Running a hand through that mane of his, Vaughn answered, "Studying the effects of WeShare on broader psychological phenomenon."

"And what did you find?"

"Well, for one, thirty-two percent of teen girls said that when they felt bad about their bodies, WeShare made them feel worse. So far, the research indicates WeShare is harmful for most notably teenage girls. The platform makes the issues of body image worse for one in three teen girls. The teens also blame WeShare for increases in their anxiety and depression. In fact, among teens who reported suicidal thoughts, 13% of British users and 6% of American users traced the desire to kill them-selves to WeShare."

That little tidbit seemed to jolt the entire room to attention.

"And these girls," Elijah said, "Abby, Trish, Jessica…they were part of this program?"

"Now *that* I cannot divulge. Uncle Sam's confidentiality agreements for such clinical trials are strict and exacting."

Elijah pounded an angry fist on the man's desk, sending the professor back against his chair.

"To hot Hades with your confidentiality agreements! Lives are at stake—"

"Explain these findings," Gina said with interruption, putting out a staying hand.

Vaughn threw Elijah narrowed, irritated eyes—hateful, even, his cheeks going red. But he relented.

"Social comparison is heightened on WeShare because it is grounded in performance with its heavy focus on the body and lifestyle—features that appear to be most harmful to teens."

"Suppose the tendency to share only the best moments, combined with a pressure to look perfect, can leave anyone reeling."

"Especially sending teens spiraling into eating disorders and an unhealthy sense of their own bodies. Depression, even."

"So, if I understand it," Johnny said, "Aspects of WeShare exacerbate whatever's going on inside a person, creating a perfect storm."

Vaughn nodded.

"Sounds like what you're saying is," Gina said, "just as Big Tobacco should have been more truthful about the link between smoking and lung cancer back in the day, WeShare should be more upfront about links to depression among teen girls."

"Now, now," Vaughn said with a chuckle. "Correlation does not prove causation. So far, the trial hasn't established any causal connection."

Elijah scoffed. "Sure sounds like it, doc!"

Gina nodded. "What other alternative explanation can you offer for such a massive, sudden deterioration among teenage mental health during this period?"

Vaughn leaned back, bringing those tented fingers back. "WeShare will claim that while it may not be nicotine, it is closer to sugar—which is delicious and has a place in our daily nutritional life, but must be consumed in moderation."

Elijah furrowed his brow with anger. "So, what, blame it on the victims, is that right? Just a lack of self-control?"

He went to respond when Jae intercepted: "Besides, WeShare is not like sugar, affecting only people who overindulge. When teens went from texting on flip phones to posting carefully curated photographs and awaiting comments, their social life was entirely re-wired."

Gina added, "I have to imagine this is especially true for girls—like Abby and Trish and Jessica, whom you saw. Where the wrong photo can lead to school-wide ridicule or even national attention if it goes viral, resulting in cyberbullying from strangers, and a permanent scarlet letter."

She cast her gaze to the floor, her chest rising with a heavy breath before a sigh.

Elijah felt for her, knowing what had happened to her own twin sister a few decades ago. The bullying, the taunting, the name-calling. That was all before these newest digital monsters chewed up and spat out unsuspecting teenagers! Back in the day, it was all face-to-face. Didn't know which was worse, the cyber-stalking from anonymous trolls or the physical kind from ghoul-ish, teenage brats.

He'd certainly had his own fair share of such bullying abuse. Even thought about ending it all a time or two when it got real bad, mostly in a handful of foster homes, which never lasted all that long. Was remarkable he'd endured. By the good graces and loving mercy of Yeshua Almighty, it was!

Now, looking at Gina, and imagining these suicide cases from teenagers who were similarly harassed might have triggered something inside of her—a dreadful sadness from the memories of her own sister from the familiarity of such cases—he wondered how she was doing, how she was holding up. Hadn't thought about it until that moment. He'd have to check in on her.

"My, my. Would you look at the time." Vaughn sat up, then stood. "Happy to have been of service, but I must get going."

"Hold the cheese stick," Elijah said, rising to his feet as well.

"You were seeing not just teenagers but adults. Twentysome-things and even retirees."

He frowned and clenched his jaw, then smiled. "Gloria Warner, yes."

"One of the other suicide victims."

His face fell now, and those irritated eyes returned. "Suppose so. But if I were you I would be speaking with one of my colleagues about your investigation, if causation is what you seek."

"Who's that?"

Vaughn opened his mouth, then snapped it shut, eyes flittering up and to the left. Like he was hiding something, or wanted to hide something. Maybe deliberating whether he should spill the tea.

Elijah knew darn straight he should.

"Spill the tea, professor," he said, jolting the man from his upward gaze.

He hesitated, but slumped back in his chair and said, "Gretchen Dolf, that's who."

Elijah joined him, settling back down. "Why her?"

"Are you familiar with synesthesia?"

"Nope."

"I am," Gina said. "The term for a peculiar neurological phenomenon where stimulating one part of the brain activates another part."

"More that neural pathway stimulation also stimulates a secondary, but you get the idea."

Elijah shifted. He didn't get it, which he didn't like.

"Maybe you can spell it out," Johnny said, "for us back-of-the-room kiddos."

Gina turned to him. "It means tasting color or seeing sounds."

"That's a thing?" Jae asked with a start.

"There was a lot of interest in the research a century ago, and actually many autistic people experience such a phenomenon, where words can feel a certain way in their mouth, for example."

Elijah rolled his eyes, feeling like this was a massive rabbit trail. "Can we get on with it, doc? What's this got to do with anything?"

Vaughn frowned. "I was getting to that." He scuttled to his desk and leaned in now, whispering, "Dolf has restarted this research, only this time using infrasonic, high-frequency sounds to stimulate certain parts of the brain."

Now Elijah scooted to the edge of his seat. "And?"

"And…" Vaughn bit the bottom of his lip, eyes glancing to the right. More hiding, more obfuscating.

Irritation was rising, so he clapped his hands together. *Once.* Then: *again* and *again.*

Making everyone jump.

"And?" Elijah said, not giving a lick except for the answer.

"And," Vaughn answered, "there was an accident."

"What sort of accident?" asked Gina.

The professor ran a hand through that blond mane of his. "I really shouldn't be telling you this…"

"Spill the tea, doc," Elijah said. "What happened?"

"Well, she made a discovery that certain sound frequencies could trigger shadowy, ghostly visions."

Gina said, "So unusual sensory manifestations, like synesthesia."

Vaughn nodded. "That's right. Along with odd, unpredictable behaviors—including dissociation from reality itself."

"Dissociation? Like, what, manic, schizophrenic episodes?"

Jae added, "The kind that might drive someone to…"

She trailed off, clearly not wanting to voice the truth of the matter. Johnny finished it for her: "Driving them to kill themselves, you're saying? To take their life?"

Vaughn licked his lips and sighed, nodding but saying nothing more.

"Oh my cheeps!" Elijah exclaimed, hope rising. "Sounds exactly like what might be happening with the others."

Johnny nodded with a grin. "Sure does!"

Elijah stood, ready to go at this doc. "Where can we find this Dolf character?"

"I'm afraid you can't," Vaughn answered. "At least, not on campus."

Gina asked, "Why, what happened?"

"She's been put on administrative leave."

Johnny said, "Probably at home, I'd reckon. Can't imagine she has much to do without her teaching gig."

Elijah pulled out a pen and notepad, flipping it open and handing both to Vaughn.

"Give us her address. Now."

The professor hesitated, but took it and scribbled the goods.

Elijah smiled. Just the lead they needed for their *inexplicitus* case.

Things were finally looking up.

CHAPTER 19

Gina colada was going to give Gretchen Dolf a piece of her Ohio-bred mind. Forget any sort of good-cop method to her investigative madness.

She was going in with both guns blazing.

Experimenting on live human subjects by resurrecting early twentieth-century tech that left them crazier than a one-legged mule? Driving them crazy enough to take their lives—just like these latest victims?

What was she thinking?

Forget the noble pursuits of curing schizophrenia. Leave that up to the docs at real universities. Like her alma mater. The University of Michigan would never put up with a rogue professor trying to make a name for herself in the annals of psychological history. Not some two-bit, small-town, corn-fed-and-bred schoolmarm like Gretchen Dolf.

No way, no how!

Gina gripped the steering wheel to the Order-issued Cadillac Escalade, grateful for the baby goat that gave its life to wrap her steering wheel in its soft, black-dyed hide. She sighed and chided herself for her immaturity.

Now she was just being snooty. She knew it, and it wouldn't help her interrogate the woman.

So she cranked a SiriusXM channel dedicated to the late Luciano Pavarotti. A little pedestrian for her tastes, but there was something about the man's operatic lyric tenor that was able to yank her back to Earth and ground her in the moment.

Soon, she was parking their ride across from a three-story Victorian home. A far cry from her Navy Yard condo that sat just south of the U.S. Capitol Building. Was a vibrant neighborhood on the Anacostia River within walking—and hearing—distance of the Washington Nationals baseball stadium. But this…

What commoners call a "Victorian house" is actually an architectural style for a broad category of houses, looking similar but bearing varying elements depending on the architectural subcategory. Mama taught her that, the woman constantly fantasizing about escaping their Presidential Estate double-wide and buying one of those houses featured on the cover of the *Victoria* bimonthly women's lifestyle magazine that cycled through their mobile home.

The most common of those cover photos was what Gina was staring at now, sending her envy soaring to heights that would do nobody any good.

The Queen Anne home, with the familiar elaborate architectural features and spare-no-decorative-expense additions.

This one fit the model to a T. A generous porch with an as-generous overhang swooped across the front and wrapped around the side, appointed by white wicker chairs and rockers. Ivy wound up the supports and white and purple hydrangea bushes bent in a bow with weighted flower heads at its base. Bay windows covered in lace curtains stared out toward their position, with two turret towers running up three floors at both front corners.

A red-bricked chimney rose from the center, and Gina imagined what falls and winters were like, the woodsmoke curling upward and lacing the inside with a spicy scent. Perhaps argyle stockings trimming the mantle, with a tall, fat Christmas tree nestled in the corner, engorged by presents galore all wrapped in tasteful paper and gold ribbon.

Queen Anne homes were usually painted in bright colors, and this one was robin's egg blue with white trim that screamed cliché.

And it made her want to puke. All of it.

Mostly because it was the home her mama had always wanted but had never been able to afford—no thanks to an Oxy habit that drove her daddy away and left her and Grace high and dry. It also symbolized a lifestyle she'd always wanted, but had remained out of her grasp. Especially since foregoing a professorial gig for the FBI, one that hadn't materialized into much—and the ecclesial investigative one pretty well kicking all prospects of a cush life to the curb.

She grabbed for her ginger locks and started to twirl, finding a single strand of hair and plucking it—envy winding through her even as she continued winding her hair into a rope.

"You alright, Gina colada?"

Elijah's voice startled her.

"I'm fine," she answered in a rush, dropping her locks and reaching into her pocket.

Which was a lie. She wasn't. Hadn't been since this whole dang case started. The whole thing had been plucking her nerves something fierce.

And now a freakin' Queen Anne home—bought and paid for by grant money that fiddled with peeps' brains, thanks to Nurse Ratched?

Gina's heart was pounding, so she pulled out her security blanket: a pack of Doublemint gum. Sliding two sticks out, she fumbled with their aluminum wrapping, then promptly popped them into her mouth.

The minty rush and pleasurable ache in her jaw from pulping up the two sticks was a heavenly grounding to her rising anxiety —about the nature of the case, yes, but also her role in solving it.

Her role in wrestling the unwieldy, unexplainable, open-ended elements of the case still flapping their kimono in the breeze to a finalizing close.

Her role in bringing a measure of justice to the women who had been driven to the brink. To their families and friends who were holding the smelly bag of crap and left wondering what they'd missed, what they'd done wrong, what they could have done right to avoid such a horrifying, gut-wrenching, finalizing and totalizing end to their loved one.

Her role in bringing a measure of justice to Grace…

Gina threw open her door and slid out, then slammed it shut.

Showtime.

Three more shutting doors and the quartet was assembling across the street.

Johnny sauntered over, eyeing the looming white house of horrors, joined by Jae. They met Gina and Elijah at their ride.

"How do you want to approach this?" the ex-priest asked.

"Both guns blazing," Gina said, blowing a massive bubble with a pop. "Metaphorically, of course."

"Of course."

"I'd wager," Jae said, "this is the connection we've been waiting for."

Elijah smirked. "You think? Some shrink finds a wavelength that fiddles with people's noggins, triggering schizoid behavior, even leading to slitting their wrists—naw, sister magister, I'd say this is *definitely* the connection we've been waiting for!"

"Then let's do this," Gina said. "Before the next shoe drops."

"Or body…" he added grimly.

Or that.

On her way toward the front door, she pulled out her phone, flipping to the WeShare app for a look-see. Had become a bad habit, a mindless one she went to as a default when things got hairy. A sort of adult pacifier, as well as a new tick she'd added to her arsenal when the anxiety rose and overwhelm threatened to overtake.

Which was odd, because all the scrolling never actually relieved her of anything—and actually ratcheted the anxiety higher. The pithy comments showcasing someone's humor and intelligence; air-brushed, coiffed images of perfect bodies; the proud moments and braggadocios accomplishments—all of it played on her insecurities that she didn't measure up. That she had no pithy, intelligent bone in her body; that the mole on her upper lip was an eyesore, not a Cindy Crawford beauty mark; that she'd done nothing noteworthy, had no accomplishments to her name, leaving her high and dry at the twentieth reunion dinner table with nothing more to talk about than her cats and Honda Odyssey minivan.

But she couldn't take her eyes off of the screen. Scrolling, then scrolling some more, until—

She scrolled upon a curious advertisement…

A pastoral scene with gently waving switchgrass and doves flying through a beautiful sunset, the horizon blazing orange. The Fields of Elysium, it was, the ancient Roman afterlife. A woman dressed in a white smock, smile wide with an outstretched hand waving her toward a path running through the tall grass, offered a curious invitation:

"On your own terms, Gina…"

Should've startled at the mention of her name, but something about the woman's lulling, powerful tone kept that part of her brain at bay. Figured it was some WeShare algorithm on their ad platform. What's the saying? If a product is free, you're the product? Pretty much the case for all of social media, the entire WeNet platform slicing and dicing her data to serve up ready-made ads for consumption.

But this…

Couldn't help but be intrigued.

Stepping over a curb, Gina jabbed her thumb at the image. It took her to an online checkout page. A fuchsia box (her favorite color; not purple, fuchsia) greeted her with a smile, literally. On it was a bag with a drawstring and a smiley face was on its face, along with a tube labeled HeN2.

"An exit kit…"

"What was that?" Elijah asked.

Jolting her from the image.

She quickly shoved it in her pocket and quickened her pace. "Nothing. Ready, Freddy?"

"You know it."

The pair took the stairs, Johnny and Jae close behind.

Elijah went to ring the doorbell when Gina gave a startling shout.

"Egads! What are you doing?"

He jumped and threw her a furrowed brow. "Uhh, ringing the door bell?"

She shoved past. "I've got this."

Surprisingly, Elijah didn't protest, instead stepping aside while the other two clomped up the stairs and stood on her other side.

"Suit up, buttercup," she muttered to herself before heaving a steadying breath and giving the heavy black door a rapping knock.

A beat ticked by, then another, the sounds of some muffled shuffling about sounding beyond the door, but nothing else.

Irritation bloomed, as well as impatience.

So, she rapped it again: *knock, knock, knock!*

More shuffling until a voice finally called from beyond: "Hello? Can I help you?"

"FBI, ma'am." Gina chided herself at the tongue-slip. Broke 18 U.S. Code section 912 making illegal any *'whoever falsely assumes or pretends to be an officer or employee acting under the authority of the United States or any department, agency or officer thereof…'* Major fineage and hard prison time for such offenders.

"I mean, *former* FBI," she corrected. "We're with a…private investigative agency, and we'd like to have a word."

A deadbolt slid to the unlocked position, and the heavy black door whooshed open—until catching fast on a heavy brushed steel security chain. A single eye on a long pale face peered through the crack, the house darkened beyond.

"Did you say FBI?" the woman said.

Elijah answered, "Nope. Former."

"What is it you want?"

Gina scrunched up her brow. Was that an English accent she heard?

She shook her head. No way was that going to blind her to the woman's nincompoopery! Any first-level psych student knew about ingrained linguistic prejudices. How studies have shown that people, especially Americans, judge those with 'prestige' accents like Queen's English as being more competent and intelligent, more effective at communication and persuasion, and far better suited for high status professional jobs—like professors, whether at U of M or MCC.

No way, no how, was she gonna pull the wool over Gina colada's eyes with a posh accent!

"Gretchen Dolf, I presume?" Gina said without any foreplay. Might as well get on with it; no use pussyfooting about when lives were at stake.

A quick intake of air and rapid blinking indicated surprise, and maybe a certain level of fear.

Perfecto.

"Yes, I am she. What's this about?"

"We're here regarding an investigative matter. Something that concerns several suicides that have—"

"I've already spoken to the authorities concerning this matter!" Dolf spat out in her defense, clearly getting ready to shut the door on the inquiry—and on them.

That was unexpected. Gina asked, "The recent ones, from this past day and week? The teenagers?"

"No…the ones from—" she stopped short, inching the door closed.

Gina shoved the toe of her boot inside, wedging it open.

"The ones from your clinical study concerning schizophrenia, you mean?"

Another intake of air, more rapid eye movement. "How did you...That was supposed to have been sealed under the confidentiality agreement!"

Her voice was shaking now, and Gina feared she would lose the woman.

Donning her toothy, good-cop grin, she said, "Gretchen, we're here on a different matter, unrelated to that one. Please. Just a few moments of your time, then we'll go."

That eye peered back, unblinking and with clear uncertainty. A grandfather clock literally ticked off the seconds from somewhere deep inside the house. A gong sounded, chiming the hour, which seemed to snap the woman into a decision.

Here we go...

The door slammed shut with a whoosh of that flowery air, ruffling Gina's bangs.

Her heart plummeted to that fancy Queen Anne porch. That was it. She'd failed. Spooked the woman and floundered her one job getting justice for those—

A sound, at the door, gave her renewed hope.

Elijah sighed. "Welp, there goes—"

Gina shushed him as a scraping, a clanging, a clattering sounded from beyond the door.

Then it opened and out stepped a petite woman in her late-50s with a silver pixie cut dressed in hot pink yoga pants and a matching zip up. Gretchen Dolf.

The woman closed the door, locked it, then turned around and said, "You've got fifteen minutes before I need to get off to my pilates class."

Gina nodded, but thought about a comment Eli had made from their last investigation: Never trust a woman with short hair. Especially a pixie cut.

She thought that was bunk, but it did make her wonder.

Regardless, she was desperate for answers, and she was sure this woman could help.

"Absolutely," Gina answered, and Dolf ushered them to the wicker furniture.

They settled, and she got on with it.

"We understand you were engaged in an important clinical trial, something about curing schizophrenia."

Dolf settled back into her chair. "Right. The National Institutes of Health granted me funds, millions of dollars, to research the possibility of curing schizophrenia using sound-wave technology."

Heat raced up Gina's neck at the mention of the figure. Millions of dollars. Of course. Joining it was a worm of envy at the woman's accomplishments, hers paling in comparison.

"What happened," Elijah said, continuing the interrogation, "during the course of the trial, to the participants? Did you discover anything of use?"

Dolf explained, "The participants spoke of a terribly noxious stench and a feeling that something was pressing in against them. Then there was the feeling of a maleficent presence, something hostile and foreboding. During the middle of the test, they collapsed and then began shouting incomprehensible gibberish. Had to be restrained, they did. Even spoke of voices in their heads."

"Voices?"

"What did they say?" asked Johnny.

"The participants just went on about wanting to get voices out of their heads," Dolf explained. "No more voices, please, they insisted, adding with complaint: It follows me wherever I go. The darkness, the Presence!"

"In other words," Gina said, "they experienced a schizophrenic fit. Classic symptoms, along with what you described earlier."

Dolf nodded. "That is true. When the research began last century, of course it wasn't called that."

"Dementia praecox."

"Correct. The goal was to cure schizophrenia, with the basic idea that if you could induce it, then you could also reverse it."

Elijah said, "So, if some sound waves could influence the brain to send someone into such a state, then there could be other, more harmonic ones to pull them out from it?"

"Precisely. The disease is a wretched one, baffling and plaguing humanity for generations. Including my late husband."

Dolf went silent, casting her eyes down toward the porch floor.

"At any rate," she said, heaving a breath, "I tried everything, every frequency range. Different tones and different amplitudes. Masking the sound with synthetic filters and introducing interference to bend the waves that might influence the change."

"Nothing?" asked Gina.

"Nothing. The hallucinations grew more intense and bizarre, with the behavior of the subjects flying off the handle until—"

Elijah said, "One of them blew their brains out?"

Dolf nodded, saying nothing.

Silence followed for a long stretch until Dolf continued: "All I was able to achieve was the influence of schizoid behavior, discovering that a certain high-frequency range of sound waves stimulates serotonin receptors in the frontal cortex of the brain. There is some indication that they act upon the raphe nuclei as well, but the project was shuttered before I could confirm any of it. The only fruits of my labor was what we learned about synesthesia itself, as well as what might trigger schizophrenia."

"But not a cure," Jae said.

"Much to my disappointment."

Gina asked, "Were any of these seven victims—"

"Eight," Elijah corrected with interruption.

"Right, the eight recent victims of suicide—were they part of your study?"

"Not at all. We had very narrow requirements for the trial,

including only those who were already beginning to experience the earlier onset of dementia and schizophrenia."

Eli asked, "Then why do you think Cain Vaughn believed you might have answers for our investigation?"

Dolf smirked. "Cain Vaughn…"

The woman spat the name out like a sour lemon.

Gina said, "Sounds like a story behind that tone."

The professor crossed her arms. "A competitive little git, he is. And I had always wondered whether he had sabotaged the trial somehow."

"Why?"

"Because he lost out on the gig, that's why! There was major funding from NIH, lots of prestige if it were to be successful." Now she grinned, arms falling to her lap. "But I was the better scientist. I was chosen, he wasn't."

"Which set him off," Johnny said.

Dolf nodded. "And eventually derailed the trial, resulting in a series of…unfortunate deaths."

Elijah said, "By unfortunate deaths, you mean…"

"Suicides."

He flashed Gina eyes that told her what was what.

She asked, "Did any of the subjects express suicidal ideation?"

"None. Either before or during the trial." She folded her arms again, sighing and adding with a mutter, "Unless you count that ridiculous Oppenheimer nonsense."

Elijah perked up at that. "What ridiculous Oppenheimer nonsense?"

"Each of them, toward the end of the trial, before their untimely demise, had expressed that infamous quotation of his. *'I am become death, destroyer of worlds.'*"

"Oh my cheeps!"

"Egads!" Gina echoed. "That's what Gloria had written in her journal."

"Nope. Well, yuppers on that detail, but it's more than that."

"What do you have, Eli?"

He turned to her. "Vaughn had a folio of that exact phrase in his office."

Johnny said, "The one hanging above the reading chair."

"Bingo."

Heat raced up Gina's neck. That bozo wasn't being straight with them.

And she aimed to find out why.

She stood and waved at the professor. "Thank you for your time, Dr. Dolf. You've been most helpful."

Then she hustled down the porch stairs on toward the Escalade.

Elijah caught up, along with Johnny and Jae.

Her partner said, "Knew that Vaughn character was a rat. Just knew it!"

"What're you thinking?" asked Johnny. "That he sabotaged his colleague, the doc was holding out on us and maybe had his own side project that went sideways, contributing to more deaths?"

"All of the above." Gina reached the Escalade and threw open the door. "Only one way to find out."

CHAPTER 20

Didn't take long before Gina was sliding back into a visitor parking spot and the quartet was hustling across the quad. Man, that woman could drive. A real speed demon, she was.

Elijah's kind of lady.

Especially because of her spunk and spit when she was fully invested in a case, going to the mat to bring resolution and justice. Was the reason why he liked her so much, why they got along so well, the pair of them giving it their all.

And yet…

He wondered whether this case was beginning to wear on her, given her close connection to its details. The personal details, with her sister's suicide. Not that he was judging or anything. The last case had nearly sent him over the edge, with its eerie connections to his father's death. Thanks to his partner, he'd pulled through to the other side, and they'd solved the case.

Then there was the other thing: She'd been glued to that phone of hers on the drive over—scrolling, scrolling, scrolling until he thought either her thumb would fall off or his own head would from her crashing their ride. Had noticed every time she whipped that thing out, she got more irritable, more anxious, more depressed. Was why he chucked his smartphone a month ago and sprang for the granny phone. Life was sure better for it!

And there Gina was, huffing irritated breaths while hoofing it across the quad. Like a bee out of hot Hades making for the academic building—ready to whip out a can of Gina colada on our boy Cain Vaughn.

Another worry.

So Elijah hustled up to her, asking, "How you holding up?"

"I'm fine," she snapped.

"Are you sure? Because I know how personal this case—"

"Personal? What personal? What's personal about it?"

"Well, your sister Grace—"

She pulled up to a quick stop and put up an index finger that meant business.

"This has nothing to do with my sister!" Gina said, wagging it in front of Elijah's face.

Johnny and Jae stood off to the side, throwing confused eyes at Elijah.

Gina sighed, then put her finger away. "Sorry, but I just want to put this bleepin' puzzle together. I can't make sense of it. Why anyone would want to just end things. Why these women, these girls…"

She choked on her words, her eyes glistening and face turning red with a sudden rise of emotion. She looked away, then turned away, batting at her eyes and nose.

Elijah's heart raced at the sight of his friend. He knew that it was more than just the women she was confused about. Wouldn't admit it—to Elijah, to herself—but she wondered why her sister Grace had ended things.

Flat knew the answers she was looking for weren't in this case. Although, might be the next best thing, putting this *inexplicitus* puzzle mystery together to make sense of the unexplainable from years past.

And he wanted to help her do it. Help her gain some small measure of justice for these women, for those they'd left behind.

For Grace.

"Come on," he said. "Let's go ask Vaughn what the hot Hades he's up to, what he's hiding."

A smile edged upward at one corner of Gina's mouth, and she nodded.

Then she and him took off toward Vaughn's office building, Johnny and Jae at their heels.

Where they found the same short, squat secretary reading a mass-market paperback. One of those romance yarns this time, with a beefcake hugging a Corinthian column and a half-naked woman wrapped in vines clutching his ripped chest.

She startled on their approach and sighed. "Oh, you're back..."

"We need to see Doc Vaughn," Gina said.

"Can't."

"I won't take no for an answer!"

Elijah put out a staying hand. "What my esteemed colleague means to say is, we have some follow-up questions for the doc."

The woman threw those narrowed, twitching eyes at Gina before settling back on Eli. "Although, with reluctance, I might send you to his office, unfortunately he's gone for the day."

"Gone?" Gina exclaimed.

"Gone."

"Is there an echo in here?" Elijah said.

Gina slapped her palms down on the desk. "Where is he?"

The woman clutched her chest with a squeaking gasp. Drama queen.

"Home!" she offered. "Felt faint and canceled his day of classes."

"When was this?" Johnny asked.

She looked at him. "Shortly after you all left, actually." Now she threw those familiar twitching, skeptical eyes at Gina. "What was your meeting about?"

"We need access to his office," Gina demanded.

"Are you mad, woman?"

"Yes, actually. I am. Hopping mad, I tell you!"

"Gina…" Elijah said.

"I'm calling security!" the woman crowed.

She picked up the telephone. Johnny reached out a hand and pressed the switchhook receiver, cutting her off from the cavalry.

He said, "That's not necessary, ma'am. We're going."

Gina huffed a sigh. "But—"

"Gina!" Elijah exclaimed. "We're done here. Move on."

"For the love…"

She threw up her hands and spun around, stomping off down the hallway.

"What's up with her?" Jae asked.

"Yeah, she alright, kid?" Johnny asked.

Elijah didn't look their way. Instead, he took off after his partner.

"Gina, wait up!" he called down the stairwell.

"Why, what's the point?" Gina yelled back.

Elijah caught up with her just as she pushed outside.

"Where are you going?" he asked, his partner hustling across the quad.

"To bed."

"To bed?"

"Is there an echo in here?"

"Hey, that's my line…"

Worry mounted with each step, wondering if the case was too much for her. Seemed like it'd set her over the edge, or near the edge—and he worried she'd take a flying leap herself soon.

Elijah sighed. "Would you just hold up! I've got an idea."

She didn't stop. "What idea?"

"We bust into Vaughn's office, have a look around."

She didn't slow. "I'm out."

"Why?"

"Because, that's why! And besides, I need a nap. Pronto."

Elijah slowed now, but she kept going, Gina throwing up her watchword for the rising anxiety that could bloom into a meltdown at any minute. He was right. The case was getting to her.

Had gotten to her…

But he let her go. Just watched her hustle on toward their Escalade, worried for his friend but also wanting to get inside that office. There was still an *inexplicitus* case that needed solving.

Friendship or investigation, which should he choose?

Wasn't even a choice. Because ultimately, all of this was about something bigger.

A little thing called justice, throwing up some public love those victims' way.

Heart broke for Gina, feeling it deep in his bones. An empathetic ache, a jittery queasiness knowing how much pain she was in. But he knew he needed to let her go and sort herself out.

And they had an office to bust into.

Johnny came up to him. "She gonna be alright?"

"Should I go after her?" Jae asked. "Have a chat, woman to woman?"

"Nope. She'll be fine," Elijah said. He turned to the pair with an announcement: "And I've got a plan."

Which was a bit devious, and frankly a bit knuckle-headed. Involved Johnny impersonating law enforcement informing the secretary that her house had burned down. Thought about having him claim her husband had been in an accident, but didn't notice a wedding ring. Then wondered about invoking the woman's mother, but didn't want to give her a heart attack and wondered if her mom was still alive. So, char-broiled house it was.

At least it was for a good cause.

Johnny hemmed and hawed but eventually agreed. Elijah positioned himself inside the alcove at the men's and women's restrooms just down the hall. Listened to the whole sad episode unfold from there. Her screams, her cries, her near-heart attack experience, but she'd pulled through the conversation just fine and scurried down the hallway on toward destiny.

While Elijah promptly hustled down the hallway, through the glass door leading to the professor's offices, and on toward his own destiny.

Lock pick in hand.

Johnny and Jae hustled to his side just as the final key pins clicked into place, and he pushed through into the office.

Easy peasy.

Indeed, it was empty, Cain Vaughn having left the building—wherever he himself had scurried off to.

Johnny pushed past. "Fan out. I don't want to spend any more time than we need to."

Elijah went straight to the doc's desk. There was a desktop computer, and Jae sidled up to it, withdrawing some USB stick.

"What's that?" he asked.

She threw him a grin as she shoved it in the computer's backside. "Help."

"Some help."

"There's an algorithmic bot that'll download all the contents of his hard drive."

"Sounds sexy."

Jae threw him a wink. "Don't you know it…"

Heat raced up his neck at that one. Flirtatious gal. Which he didn't mind in the slightest.

Spent the next several minutes rifling through his file drawers. Nothing but receipts, class schedules, lecture notes. Nothing worth nothing that'd help their cause.

Johnny looked like he was having about as much luck.

Elijah heaved a sigh. There had to be something. Somewhere.

He glanced at the desktop and at Jae's proctological doohickey. Probably something stuffed deep inside the Dell's bowels. Some paper, some set of notes—something that would make the picture clearer.

Picture…

Sucking in a startled breath, Elijah whipped toward the Gita folio.

Then raced over to it.

Heaving it off the wall and tossing it to the ground. A bit sacrilegious, but whatever.

Nothing but nothing behind it. No safe, no hidey-hole.

Wanted to cuss, but didn't. Shook his head instead.

"Nice job, kid!"

Elijah glanced behind at Johnny Pope. Who was kneeling down on the floor and wrenching something off from the backside of the print. A manilla envelope!

"Sweet mother of Melchizedek!" he exclaimed as the man stood.

Johnny grunted a chuckle. "That's one way of putting it."

Jae hustled over. "Don't count your eggs before the golden goose lays 'em, partner."

Elijah frowned. "Mixing metaphors a bit there, but I'll take it."

Johnny opened a flap and pulled out a stack of papers. Research, charts, a whole lot of numbers.

The man handed Elijah half the stack. "Look through these, we'll take this half."

And they did, the trio combing through the papers.

Until Elijah announced, "I've got something."

He held it up for their viewing. The pair huddled over his shoulder, and they read it in silence:

As teenage girls increase their use of WeShare and WeGram, so does the long-term risk for suicide increase among females—most markedly among teenagers, but young adults and middle-age women are also not immune.

Girls who started using WeShare at two to three hours a day or more at thirteen, and increased use over time, had the highest levels of suicide risk into adulthood. Not so much boys, as the primary driver for WeShare interaction is relationships, which is generally a typical characteristic of females.

Feeling and internalizing relationship distress at different levels is a type of psychological distress present in social media interactions for many girls and women. They also have higher levels of social comparison, fear of missing out, and anxiety about social presentation, resulting in strong effects among females versus males.

Recent research suggests that as their screen time increases over the years, so does their risk for suicide by the time they hit their early- to mid-20s. Does such teenage depression increase WeShare use, and ultimately suicidal risk? Or is it the other way around, WeShare use triggering depression that leads to suicide? This classic chicken-and-egg question remains open to debate, though the data suggests it is likely a two-way street.

Researchers did not look at how depression symptoms changed over time. So it is uncertain whether girls and women become more depressed, resulting in increased use of WeShare, or whether using WeNet platforms causes an increase in depression and suicidality.

As such, screen time is likely a small contributing factor to suicide risk, alongside other issues—such as feelings of exclusion and invisibility—that could impact risk outside of a WeShare context. However, there is a substantial enough correlation between suicidal ideation within a matrix of anxiety, despair, and depression brought on through WeShare use to warrant further study.

Johnny growled, "The doc wasn't telling us the complete picture. Not by a long shot."

"Got that right!" Elijah said.

"I've got something else."

He handed it off, and Elijah read the document:

More than 40% of WeShare's users are 24 years old and younger, and about 50 million teens log onto WeShare in the U.S. each day, compared with 12 million teens logging onto the rest of WeNet platform offerings, where young users have been shrinking for a decade, our studies suggest.

On average, teens in the U.S. spend 40% more time on WeGram than they do on the rest of the WeNet platforms proper, while 50% of adults are on WeShare.

Researchers conducted a "mental health deep dive" and follow-up among teen girls, stratified upward with adult women. The conclusion drawn is that some of the mental health problems are specific to WeGram compared to other parts of WeNet, such as WeVid. That is especially true concerning so-called social comparison, personal assessment of their own value in relation to the attractiveness, wealth, and success of others.

WeGram can be thought of as the online equivalent of the high-school cafeteria: a place for teens to post their best photos, find friends, size each other up, brag and bully. However, there seems to be a corollary effect among adults on WeShare: similar symptoms of anxiety, comparisonitis, despair, and depression manifested.

"Oh my cheeps!" Elijah said, feeling like they'd found something close to a smoking gun. "That's the whole taco, right there…"

Johnny grunted. "Don't you mean enchilada, kid?"

"Nope. Taco."

"Listen to this," Jae said, then quoted: *"'It's the ones who are most vulnerable or are already developing a problem that WeGram and WeShare can escalate.'* The language of *'mounting public-health epidemic'* is used, referring to both WeShare and WeGram as drugs. Get this: many docs are seeing their female patients learn tips for restricting food intake or purging, estimating that half of patients have eating disorders because of WeGram."

Johnny said, "If WeShare or WeGram or whatever can influence gals in such a powerful way, to despair over their body image, maybe it could influence them to despair over life itself."

Jae nodded. "Exactly."

"Maybe suicide."

She nodded. "It's clear doc Vaughn wasn't…"

The voice faded from Elijah's hearing, a sudden feeling coming over him that blotted out reality—the world spinning, the light in his head dimming and sparkling with starlight until something…not of this world came into focus.

It was vivid, it was cinematic. It was a vision—of Gina!

She was walking down a darkened hallway lined by mirrors. All shapes, all sizes. Bent and angular, like a funhouse he recalled from childhood. She recoiled from them. Hid her face, shielded her eyes. Wept, screamed.

Roary, snorty, skittering, screeching voices of an unknown origin and tongue now raged around her. Didn't know in the slightest what they were saying, but Gina looked like she did— her hands thrown against her ears, her face pained and pinched with agony until she took off running.

And running…

And running…

It was an endless gauntlet of haunting mirrors, malicious and monstrous from the way she looked and sounded.

Elijah was following, floating from behind and could see—

The hallway at the end came to an abrupt drop, cascading down into an endless, mawing darkness that was all consuming.

Which Gina didn't seem to see.

He shouted for her, but there was no sound.

He wrenched his mouth and heaved his lungs.

But nothing came.

He couldn't warn her!

Panic flooded his veins, and a helplessness bloomed in his head—even as his partner, his friend, his soulmate barreled toward no uncertain doom.

Until…

Relief sprang into an eternal hope!

Gina came up short at the end. Just in time, by the look of it.

He sighed with relief. She was safe. She was secure. She was—

Wait a sec…

She peered over the edge, into the forever darkness.

And jumped.

NOOOOO!!

He screamed without a scream.

A strong hand pulled Elijah out from the vision. On his shoulder, the touching sensation sending a jolting bolt of discomfort and anxiety flooding through him.

He jumped back with a yelping start.

"Whoa there, partner," Johnny said, putting up his hands in surrender. "Didn't mean no harm."

"You alright?" Jae said, face etched with worry. "You were screaming bloody murder!"

Elijah was panting, heaving desperate breaths. Not only from the touch, which wasn't his jam, but the visionary fright—of Gina, his friend and partner.

Depressed, drowning in despair, descending into a mawing darkness that spells doom.

Johnny asked, "What's wrong, are you OK?"

Elijah took another breath, then a beat, then swallowed hard.

"Not sure…"

Jae asked, "Did you black out or something?"

"Or something."

"Kid…" Johnny went on, "you're making me nervous."

"I'm making myself nervous." Elijah pressed a hand to his temple, a pain lancing across his head. "I think I had a…vision."

"A vision?" asked Jae.

Johnny replied, "Like, what, in the vein of the Good Book? Jacob and his ladder, with angels ascending and descending and all?"

Elijah nodded. "Something like that, but it involved…"

"Involved?" Johnny was searching his face with a furrowed brow.

"It was about Gina."

Jae smirked. "You got a thing for the gal?"

Elijah flashed her narrowed eyes. Neither the time nor the place for joking, that's for sure!

She frowned. "Sorry…Seriously though, is this a common thing?"

He shook his head. "It's pretty uncommon that I would have a dream, a vision like this."

"Then what do you think it means?"

Elijah heaved a breath, his heart rate ratcheting up at the question. Didn't want to face the truth of its answer, but it started to come into focus.

Gina was in trouble.

Big time.

And he was pretty sure what was about to happen.

CHAPTER 21

Gina was bushwhacked.

Exhausted, yes, but it was more than that.

She was on the verge of a meltdown. Could feel it, deep down. A welling sensation, like she had to vomit.

Her stomach was sour and tight. Her salivary glands were working overtime, flooding her mouth with a cold wetness, as if preparing the chute for an evacuation that wasn't coming. Her head all at once pounded with a wicked quake and bloomed with a dizzying faint that threatened to send her over the edge.

And into a meltdown.

Unlike Elijah, hers were much less combustible. No flapping of hands or bodily shakes, no shouts or swearing. Nothing as violent as his own manifesting overwhelm that had exploded in Farmer Warner's onion patch.

Gina was much more prone to shutdowns. Whereas meltdowns are all about the fight response to overwhelm, shutdowns are similar to the freeze response. Like a computer trying to turn on but can't because there's no power. She found it difficult to communicate, shifting into basic functions and burrowing deep within—wanting nothing more than to climb into bed and go to sleep. To just fade away…

Like now.

Was any wonder she'd made it to Happy Camper Inn, given her state of mind—given the state of her body dealing with the weight of her overwhelm and mounting anxiety.

But she'd slid into a parking spot at the front of the brown-brick building that looked like a sad loaf of bread, the roof covered in pigeon poop and moss.

Hurt to even open the door to the Escalade and dismount the pony, her muscles were so spent, so exhausted. But exhaustion wasn't even the full measure of it, though. She was demoralized, discouraged.

Gina had always been good at solving puzzles. Just the way her brain worked. One of those things Daddy and her did growing up as a child, spending Sunday afternoons noodling on 1000-piecers while Mama was passed out after a late-night bender. Her ability to disconnect from the world and everything around her with a hyperfocus drive is what made her shine at the FBI, too—and what had clued her into her own autism diagnosis.

Hadn't known of her…condition, as allistic peeps might frame it, until graduate school. There had been indications growing up—a hypersensitivity to sound, a struggle to feel emotion—but neither Daddy nor Mama had ever treated her any different, thank the good Lord above. Just figured it was how she took in the world around her.

But that bubble had been burst when she was in graduate school working on her doctorate in psychology. Her intense single-mindedness is what especially clued her in that something had been off in her brain all those years. And, wouldn't you know it, she tested on the spectrum with autistic tendencies.

Had always been proud of her hyperfocus, viewing it as a superpower. But that diagnosis labeled her as disordered, damaged, less than her neuronormative colleagues. Certainly hid her diagnosis, barely able to come to terms with it for herself, let alone letting others in on the secret.

Took several sessions of counseling to help her make peace with her diagnosis, as well as several sessions with a priest to help her make peace with how God had made her—the dear man affirming how her autism in some way reflected the Image of God, giving her a Creator-infused lens for taking in the world. Like people with tetrachromacy, and their superhuman vision to perceive a broader color spectrum thanks to the genetic anomaly giving them four cones instead of just three.

Same with her, experiencing the world in four dimensions instead of three.

And yet, why couldn't she put that hyperfocus to work on this case? Couldn't work out this puzzle mystery worth a lick!

Eight females, all dead, by their own hand. Girls and women, varying ages and stages of life. No obvious signs of trauma or reasons for despairing—though she understood the truth of that word: *obvious*. Who knew what went on in the human heart? Only the good Lord above, that's who!

Nothing made sense; nothing was connecting. She couldn't flat focus on all the disparate pieces still floating around the card table.

And she didn't know what to do about that.

Pulling out her phone, the security blanket to her overwhelm, she flipped through her ShareFeed as she pushed inside the hotel.

There they were: images of acquaintances lying on beaches in Mexico, tanned toes covered in white-powder sand and waves crashing upon the near distant shore; sipping tea in a well-appointed sage room dappled by sun, Brené Brown's latest tome of wisdom in one hand and a plate of powdered cookies on a lap ensconced in terry cloth; showing off their piles of washed dishes and folded laundry like prize-winning hogs at the county fair.

Then all the pithy memes and insider jokes she didn't get; the status updates on buying new cars, new homes, new pets; the hot takes on China's human rights violations and designs against Taiwan, congressional gridlock, inflationary pressures against avocados and refrigerators—it was enough to make someone's head explode!

And then…

Gina gasped, with surprise as much as a small amount of intrigue.

That ad again.

For the kit to end it all.

It intrigued her. Tempted her.

Maybe, just maybe…

No! She shook away the wicked thought, shoving her phone back inside her pocket and hustling across the hotel lobby, the wet newspaper smell hidden behind Pine-Sol and bleach, but still ever present.

Exhausted, she sure was. Frustrated beyond all get out at her failure to solve the bleepin' case, as well!

But it was more than that. She was—

Depressed.

Despairing, even…

She wanted justice—*needed* justice. For those women.

For Grace.

But how?

There wasn't a way, there wasn't any hope.

It was hopeless. Her life was hopeless…

"Miss Anderson?" a male voice called from behind the front desk.

She spun around toward the sound, confused and surprised.

The desk clerk in an ironic red jacket and matching pants, edges lined by gold more akin to a four-star hospitality joint than Happy Camper Inn.

She sauntered his way, wanting nothing more than to just get to her bed to ward away the exhaustion.

The twentysomething looking barely out of puberty rapped his fingers on a square box before sending it skittering across the gold desk.

Gina frowned. "What's this?"

He shrugged. "A package, for you."

"For me?"

"Came a bit ago by courier."

The brown box was a familiar one, having shifted most of her shopping online. It was indeed addressed to Gina Anderson, care of Happy Camper Inn, which was weird. Only ones who knew she was there was Silas Grey, Big Kahuna of the Order of Thaddeus, and Abraham Patel, their trusty new investigative support agent with Group X. No return address made it even weirder.

And intriguing…

Spidey senses were doing their thing at the back of her lizard brain—the one her English ancestors had relied on to keep them from being gored by a wooly rhinoceros out in the hinterlands.

But the other part of her brain was too weak for words. Didn't want to think too hard on it, so she swiped the box and thanked the man.

Her room was down the end of a long, dark hallway, a single window at the end doing most of the heavy lifting for illumination. There was that wet newspaper again, so she picked up her pace. Hiking the package under her arm like a football, she shuffled to her room, swiped her room key, and shoved inside.

Same sad, dark story, a tiny window no bigger than a computer monitor shrouded by thick brown curtains doing nothing but nothing for the room's mood, or her own, which had darkened even more.

Couldn't get her flat failure out of her head. Not only for those girls, for those women—now it was for Grace.

No. Not going to go there. Not now, not there in that Bates Motel room.

Setting the box on her bed, she pressed the side held down by packing tape and slid her finger underneath, then yanked up and yanked back until the two flaps were popping up with invitation.

Popping through was the faintest hint of something that struck her as familiar.

Was too dark to make it out completely, but it looked like her favorite color.

Fuchsia…

Heart started rapping a mean beat against her ribcage now, and her lungs searched for breath.

Was this what she—

No, surely not…

Gina dove in, peeling back the flaps…

And gasped with recognition.

A fuchsia box greeted her with a smile, literally. On it was a bag with a drawstring wearing a smile, along with an attached stylized tube labeled HeN2. And a curious phrase.

'On your own terms, Gina.'

The exit kit. From the WeShare advertisement!

"But how…"

Had someone sent her this special care package, knowing she'd seen and tapped the ad, somehow knowing where she was staying? Had to have been—it had been personalized with her bleepin' name!

Gina's heart hammered in her head, and it felt faint. And she felt hotter than a hen in heat, crimson racing up her neck and blooming in her face at the crazy.

"But how…"

None of it made a lick of sense!

She looked down at the box. The fuchsia, the smile—her bleepin' name!

It was a taunt—no, an *invitation.*

Yes, that's exactly what it was. A way out.

An exit.

But…

No! No way would she follow Grace's footsteps.

She needed a nap—pronto!

Because she was on the verge now.

Flopping into bed, yet keeping the box just where she had set it, she whipped out her phone—her security blanket for such times as these—and scrolled and scrolled and scrolled, trying to stay the hand of rising dread but feeding it more than satiating it.

More perfectly airbrushed and manicured images flashed by, now from people she didn't even know. Taunting and mocking, raising her despair and dread.

Then the smart status updates that had been the bane of her social media existence.

Gina raced past those. Scrolling, scrolling, scrolling.

Until—

Gina gasped, bringing a trembling hand to her mouth.

No, it couldn't be…

A sudden memory popped up on her ShareFeed.

From middle school prom, when WeShare was barely more than a year old.

And she and Grace were teenagers.

The night came flashing back with such clarity, such high-definition color and precision. The dresses (fuchsia for her; huckleberry for Grace), the corsages (roses, carnations, orchids, chrysanthemums, and lilies thanks to Mama), the dates (none for either one).

Couldn't afford any fancy dinner, so the sisters and a few friends had raided an Applebees for their wings special—which in her Presidential Estates double-wide neck of things was a step up from fast-food.

Part of her lizard brain knew what it would do to cycle through the blast from the past.

Didn't care.

Gina clamored down the rabbit hole, jabbing the collection of pictures, grainy from pre-smartphone days but enough to take her back.

Pictures of late-night runs to Micky Ds for milkshakes and

fries. Of mid-day romps driving kiddie tricycles down Kmart aisles. Of the role as Dorothy in the *Wizard of Oz* high school production. Of birthday parties and Christmas Day, and July Fourth fireworks in the street and Harry Potter launch days dressed as Hermione Granger (Gina) and Luna Lovegood (Grace).

Gina's eyes and nose flooded with emotion, her throat a clenched hose now. From all the pictures, yes—but it was more than that. They were memories, they were Gracey.

And that was it. The shove she needed. The kick in the pants to follow those instructions, to take the invitation.

To take matters into her own hands.

To join Grace.

On her terms…

Don't think about it. Just do it.

Gina glanced around the room, expecting to find someone (something?) standing behind her, beside her.

It was empty.

A scuffed wood chair, a lumpy bed, and drawn thick brown curtains. That was it.

Could have sworn…

She shook her head, a Force coming from within now—permitting, cajoling, *compelling* her to act. To do it.

And she did.

Quickly, before she could chicken out.

The kit's lid flipped up easily, a frustration-free package kept closed by a magnetic flap. Nestled inside sat a cloudy plastic bag with a drawstring and a tube labeled HeN2, the gas that would grease the skids on toward destiny.

Don't think about it. Jutht do it.

The Voice was stronger, more persistent and insistent. And with a curious lisp.

But Gina didn't have a lisp. So what the hey-ho day was going on inside of her?

As quickly as the thought appeared, it vanished, the Force

pressing in against her now, almost willing her hands to get to it, to end it all.

On her terms.

If she thought about it any longer she wouldn't. The invitation was so pure, so liberating. All of it could vanish—her depression and gloom, her despair and anxiety, her hopelessness—with this kit, and she would be reunited with Grace.

Grathe, Grathe, do it for Grathe!

There it was, that Voice again. With the lisp.

Inside, compelling, inviting, liberating.

Just like that, the bag was over her head, vision clouded and reality disappeared.

Then the close tie, cinched against her neck.

And the cold, hard tube of Helium combined with Nitrogen held firmly in her hand until she flipped the switch.

Easy peasy.

There was a knock at the door.

"Gina...are you doing ok? Is there anything I can do for you?"

Egads! Elijah?

Panic bloomed inside Gina now, but a sudden Force pressed against her. Holding her to the bed, binding her to her decision.

It will all be over thooon...and you'll be reunited with your thithhhter...

Air was hard to come by now, and the cloudy vision of the room beyond was dimming in and out with a darkness that promised the world beyond.

"Just had a vivid dream involving you," Elijah called out with a muffled panic, "depression and despair. Suicide, even. Not sure if this means anything to you, but that's what I saw. Pretty uncommon that I would have a dream like this. So..."

Those words did something inside Gina.

Depression.

Despair.

Sui—

The third word struck at something deep within Gina.

Light piercing the dimming darkness, those three words were joined by the fact someone had thought of her.

Someone had come for her, someone cared!

The good Lord above had thought of her and cared! Sending her partner some sort of ecstatic vision about her depression and despair, her misery and—

What the bleepin' blazes was she doing?

Something else rose within her alongside the light piercing the darkness.

Hope.

Like a dolphin rising up from the deepest darkness of the ocean for the surface—finning, wiggling, fighting for the life that awaited up on top!

Gina wanted to fight for the surface, wanted to fight for life, for air, just like her fave sea creature!

She wanted to reach for the helping hand that was his offer, but—

She couldn't.

Was too weak, too paralyzed, and it felt like something was sitting on her. A Force or Power—something pressing against her, binding her to the bed.

Or someone…

Panic bloomed, but she was helpless to do anything about it.

What had she done?

It would all be over soon. She could feel it. A tug down into the finalizing, totalizing depths of mawing darkness.

All she needed to do was let go.

Her eyelids drooped; she spread them open, fighting for life. But it was no use.

The last thing she heard before she slipped into gloomy blackness was her name:

"Gina colada!" someone shouted.

Eli!

Then again: "Gina, I'm coming in. Stand back."

And the sound of the doorjamb splintering in no time flat.

Then there was nothing.

Nothingness.

For the longest time.

Until…

There was something.

A somethingness.

Consciousness coming into a sharper hearing, a sharper focus, a sharper feeling until—

CHAPTER 22

Elijah's shoulder hurt like a mother after heaving his body against the hotel door when he didn't get any sort of reply from Gina.

Thank Yeshua Almighty it was a cheap Happy Camper hotel door. The thing whacked open on impact, splintering the jamb and giving him entry. Should demand his money back after such cheap security.

But that wasn't what mattered.

What was, were his partner's purple lips and pale blotchy face and the plastic bag, inside covered in condensation from her breath—her last ones on her way toward the pearly gates of Heaven itself.

Not on his life would he have let that happen. No way, no how!

Gina colada had always said there were three kinds of people in life when the shiznit hits the fan.

Freezers, callers, and runner-inners.

Three personalities baked into the lizard brain after generations of ancestors stared down saber-toothed tigers and mastodons and half-naked men in loincloths bearing sharpened sticks.

Freezers freeze. Could be a third kind of F word to the famed Fight-or-Flight Response, but they're really fleers. Their brain flat flees when disaster strikes. Do diddly, worth diddly.

Callers grab the squawk box and, well, squawk! Whether for help from the police or fire and rescue, or plain ol' pops when a pipe bursts.

Runner-inners run into danger. They're the heroes—often ordinary ones thrown into extraordinary circumstances—who rise to the occasion and save the day.

So, freezers, callers, and runner-inners. Three peeps who show up when the shiznit hits the fan.

Like when their partner is lying half dead on a lumpy, flea-ridden Happy Camper bed!

Took nothing but nothing for Elijah to snap to it. No freezer was he! Or caller, instead running to Gina's rescue.

In one motion, he'd snapped the tie keeping the bag cinched around her neck and whipped it off, then pressed his forefingers against her carotid artery.

A pulse.

Barely.

Faint. Very, very faint.

But it was something to work with!

Now he was standing over his partner administering CPR—pleading with Yeshua above to save his partner. Hoping against hope that they weren't too late. That Jesus wouldn't let her—

He couldn't finish the thought.

"Dear Lord, what happened?" Johnny asked from the door.

Elijah ignored him, his training kicking into high gear to save his partner's life.

All the while his mind was reeling and threatening to bloom into a full-on meltdown from the overwhelm.

How could this have happened? How could Gina have done this? What had led her to take such drastic measures—to end her life?

The questions swirled in an endless vortex with every breath from his lungs into hers, with every press against her chest.

Then they turned personal:

Why hadn't he seen this coming? Why hadn't he seen the signs? What had he missed? Was it something he did, something he said—didn't do, didn't say?

Why, why, why, WHY, *WHY?!*

But a voice inside told him it was nothing but nothing of his doing. Something was way off. Out of orbit off—from an entirely different realm of things!

And he was pretty sure who was to blame.

What was to blame…

Another breath, more pumping against Gina's chest.

All the while praying that Yeshua Almighty better not let her—

Gina gasped for desperate breaths.

"Praise God from whom all blessings flow!" Johnny exclaimed from the doorway.

Elijah's heart leaped for joy; a sudden rise of emotion sprang to his eyes and clenched his throat.

He had to agree. Thank you, Jesus!

She kept at it, heaving breaths and grasping for life—choking, then heaving some more. Her color returned, her eyes watered something fierce, and she moaned and groaned like she had been hit by a bus.

Jae ran over to Gina, ready to embrace her.

But Elijah put out a staying hand, not sure if she would appreciate the gesture.

Instead, he knelt next to her as she recovered.

"Eli," Gina moaned. "What…"

On a shaky breath, Elijah explained, "I saw you walking through a hall of mirrors."

He swallowed hard and searched for his own breath, his heart working overtime in the face of such overwhelm, recalling for her what he had seen—what the Holy Spirit himself had shown him.

He went on, "Frightened, freaked, crying. Like everything you saw in those mirrors made you depressed. Everything you saw in yourself made you depressed…"

"What are you…" She trailed off, clearly not making any sense of what he was talking about.

But he kept going: "Then you raced toward the end, which was a cliff that dropped off into a mawing void of nothingness. And—well…you jumped."

"Jumped?" Confusion etched her face, her eyebrows squished together and lips pursed.

Elijah went on, "I reflected on the many great moments I've experienced with you—at the FBI and Cracker Barrel, and how much your thoughts and words have shaped me, and the care you displayed at transitional points in my life. And I raced over as fast as I could, all three of us did."

"Where…" Gina coughed, heaved a breath, then coughed again.

She pushed herself up against the headboard, then tried again: "What happened?"

Elijah was stunned by the question. Didn't have a clue how to answer it.

He looked to Johnny for help, then to Jae.

She picked up the plastic bag and held it up. "Do you recognize this?"

Gina's eyes flashed from Jae to the sagging, wet plastic.

Took her a beat, then a sudden breath of recognition.

"Oh my God…"

A sudden wracking sob overtook her. Clearly it was all coming back.

Her face went red and twisted up with grief, her chest heaved a horrific sound that would stick with Elijah the rest of his life. A wracking, hacking, guttural moan from the depths of despair.

The sound of shame. At what she'd done, at what she'd tried to do.

Elijah could see it as plain as the nose on his face.

"Something inside me—" Gina's throat stumbled over itself, another bout of wracking sobs overtaking her.

Elijah thought he might join her, a rise in empathy threatening to overtake him—paining him physically, a vise grip against his consciousness.

But he held it together. *Had* to hold it together.

For Gina.

"I don't know what you're going through," Elijah said, "but it would be an honor to help be there for you when you are coming out of a difficult season, whatever that means, however that looks."

"Thanks for reaching out. For coming for me." Gina heaved a stabilizing breath, swallowing hard. "Or, perhaps I should thank the Holy Spirit...The truth of it is...well—"

She couldn't finish it. Couldn't voice the truth of it. That she had tried to—actually tried to....

"The truth of it is," she went on, "there have been several dark days these past few days. Even darker thoughts at times. Perhaps more demonic than anything, but also depressive, despairing, and...well—"

She didn't finish that thought; didn't need to. Everyone knew what she meant.

Suicidal...

Elijah nodded, eyes welling with emotion. "Appreciate your honesty, Gina colada. And appreciate your willingness to sit with a heavy topic like this. This has been a difficult stretch for so many people, and it sounds like you have had some difficult moments."

Gina shook her head and sighed. "My head is blooming with the pain of a bazillion migraines joined by the piercing ache of a thousand Friday night spotlights I'd cheered underneath during high school football games."

"Wait, you were a cheerleader?"

She smiled, chuckling. "Yeah, can you believe it?"

Her face fell, a shudder overcoming her. "That's not all that went on inside my head…"

"What do you mean?"

"Something inside me said it was the only way. Something buried deep."

Johnny took a step toward the bed. "What, like voices or something?"

Gina's face flashed hot, but only for a moment. Eyes narrowing and nostrils flailing and lips pressing into a thin line.

"Not like schizo voices. Like this…Being. With a lisp, of all things."

Elijah slapped his hands together. "This is the work of something sinister. The work of the Watcher-spirits, I just know it!"

"Watcher-spirits…" Johnny said, eyes squinting with recognition. "You've mentioned them before."

"Yeah, what's this you're driving at?" Jae asked.

Elijah closed his eyes and tipped back his head. He quoted:

> *And now the giants, who are born from both spirit and*
> *flesh—they shall be called evil spirits upon Earth,*
> *and on Earth shall their dwelling be. Evil spirits*
> *have gone forth from their bodies, because they are*
> *born from men, and from the holy Watchers is their*
> *original creation. They shall be evil spirits on Earth,*
> *and evil spirits they shall be called. And the spirits of*
> *the giants afflict, oppress, destroy, attack, do battle,*
> *and work destruction upon Earth, causing chaos.*
> *These spirits shall rise up against the children of*
> *men and against their women, for they have come*
> *from them.*

"Interesting quotation there," Johnny said, rubbing his chin. "What is it?"

"From an ancient Jewish text," Elijah explained, "about the fallout from Genesis 6. Though not of this world, the Watcher-spirits have been wreaking havoc on Earth since the dawn of time. Afflicting, destroying, attacking humanity. Chaos is their aim. And I would put despair right up there with the Enemy's tactics to devour humanity—dragging people into the darkest valley."

"Sounds like," Jae added, "you're speaking of spiritual warfare."

Elijah nodded. "Bingo. Which isn't about commanding demons to submit or performing abracadabra magic tricks to put them in their place. Fundamentally, it is about conflict."

"A war between two kingdoms..." Gina whispered. "The kingdom of God and the kingdom of Satan."

He swallowed. Ain't that the truth. And what a stark reminder. Up close and personal, in hi-def, Gina-colada color.

Elijah said, "This war isn't about flesh-and-blood actors."

"Demons," Johnny said, swallowing hard and licking his lips.

"Demons. Well, the principalities and powers of this present supernatural darkness. Spiritual warfare is driven by the Great Commission to share God's crazy love, which catalyzes the expansion of the kingdom of God. Which those dead Watcher-spirits want nothing more than to stop in its tracks, using every trick in the book."

He paused, glancing at Gina and thinking about those other women, believing something demonic had driven them all to the brink.

He suddenly spun around, then bolted for the rickety chair, a sad thing in crimson fabric that looked like it would give him a skin disease, but he'd take his chances.

"I need to sit," he announced, then did so.

Gina made herself more comfortable on the bed. She'd heard this before, but the review would be good for the point he had in store. Jae and Johnny shifted, the pair looking like deer in head-lights. An even worthier pair who needed to hear the point he had in store!

"Get this," Elijah explained, "there is an Unseen Realm with

Yahweh the Most High ruling over a divine counsel. Problem is, we aren't trained to view this Unseen Realm. Yahweh ruled with *beney elohim*, divine beings called 'sons of god' on his council until the corrupt *elohim* were punished with death like humans, as Psalm 82 teaches. The end makes it clear that these chastised gods were given a degree of dominion over the nations of the earth, a ruling task at which they failed miserably."

Taking a breath, he continued, "Yahweh is among the *elohim*, sitting at the head of his divine, heavenly assembly, but he is superior to all other gods. He created them. He is their sovereign king. Likewise, since Jesus is Yahweh incarnate, he too stands apart with superiority from the other gods. He is the divine sovereign over all the *beney elohim*."

"Mind blown…" Jae said with a chuckle, making an exploding motion with her fingers at her head.

Johnny grunted a chuckle. "You're telling me, kid. Never heard nothing about any divine counsel in my seminary years. Not sure Thomas Aquinas or the Magisterium are down with your view, either."

"Nope. Not my view. The Bible's."

"That may be true, but what does any of this have to do with our investigation?"

Elijah chided himself silently. "Forgive my theological travelog. That was set up for the Watcher-spirits, the Nephilim offspring which I believe are the very beings who have haunted the memories of countless people across the world, from ages past."

Jae twisted up her face. "Uh…Nephil-what?"

"Nephilim. Those birthed from the sexual union between the sons of God and human women. Here, let me…"

Elijah closed his eyes, reaching back again into his eidetic memory. He quoted Genesis 6:

> *When people began to multiply on the face of the*
> *ground, and daughters were born to them, the sons*

*of God saw that they were fair; and they took wives
for themselves of all that they chose. Then the Lord
said, "My spirit shall not abide in mortals forever,
for they are flesh; their days shall be one hundred
twenty years." The Nephilim were on the earth in
those days—and also afterward—when the sons of
God went in to the daughters of humans, who bore
children to them. These were the heroes that were of
old, warriors of renown.*

"This is from the Bible?" Jae asked with surprise.

"Yuppers. Before the Great Flood story," Elijah explained. "In some of the ancient Jewish books that didn't make it into the Bible, like the Book of Enoch, the actors in this story named *'the sons of God'* are called Watchers."

He sprang back to his feet, bobbing back and forth on his heels with pent up energy. Ready to unleash it on the room. Ready to explain the gravity of the situation.

"What's fascinating about this story in Genesis is that it reflects other kinds of stories from major religions and cultures around the world. Beings coming down from heaven to mate with women, eventually birthing unusual offspring."

"What kind of unusual offspring?" Jae asked with skepticism.

Elijah spun on his heels to face her. "Divine-human hybrids birthed with the intention to rule over humanity with divine right. These beings breached the established boundaries, falling from their heavenly positions. So part of the reason for the flood was to wipe them off the face of Earth. Same for later, in Israelite's conquest of the Promised Land, where this word of ours, *Nephilim*, is found again."

"And these…divine-human hybrids," Johnny said, "the Watchers, you think they're responsible for Gina's…incident. The others?"

"Wouldn't put it past them in the slightest! Again, Jewish

literature teaches that demons are actually the disembodied souls of dead Nephilim. Watcher-spirits that continue to plague and terrify humanity, as that Jewish text I quoted says."

Elijah slumped back in the chair again, spent from the past few days. Mostly spent from sheer exhaustion from the scare Gina had given him.

Running a hand through his hair, he continued, "The Watchers descended to Earth in celestial flesh and spawned a ruling class of immortal gods, shrouded in the robe of mortal flesh. These rebels did what was unthinkable, unconscionable—breaching the categories of heavenly and earthly beings—rebelling to take back their rightful rule, while humanity embraced them as their gods."

"But Yahweh," Johnny said, "the Most High God, their very Maker, would have none of it. He exiled them to the Abyss and sentenced their bastard offspring to death in the Great Flood of Genesis 6, am I right? It is these half-breeds who were the Nephilim—isn't that right?"

Elijah grinned, pleased the priest could be taught. "Nicely done, Johnny Pope! The only other missing piece to the puzzle are the *shedim*."

"The what?" asked Jae.

"Demons..." answered Johnny. "Hebrew for the fallen creatures."

Elijah nodded. "Bingo. The Nephilim bastard-born monstrosities had been exterminated, but they were instantly reborn upon death, becoming as their Watcher forebears: immortal, disembodied, uncontrollable. The Bible reveals that after the flood, more members of Yahweh's council, the Watchers, the cosmic sons—they rebelled and came to Earth, where humanity was again enraptured. Mankind worshiped them as shamanic teachers, divine healers, powerful saviors. They were gods to them."

Taking a breath, he continued, "Still more bastard-born races arose. The Anakim, Emim, Rephaim, and Zamzummim. Like those before them they were slaughtered, now by the Israelites, Yahweh's one people sent to conquer the lands occupied by these hybrid beings—blooming the *shedim* to frightening numbers."

"Which have tormented humanity since," Johnny said. "And manifested themselves in untold ways across the centuries. Including through demonic influence—"

He took a breath, then a beat, turning to Gina. "Like compelling people to end it all. Like the way you described the Voice and Force, Gina. Maybe even like all those women."

Elijah nodded. "Bingo."

"But how?"

He shrugged. "You heard it yourself. Jewish literature suggests the Watchers and their offspring had creative power. In fact, they possessed advanced knowledge that they pledged to pass along to humanity. A higher level of knowledge from the storehouses of the spirit-realm itself."

"What kind of knowledge?" asked Jae.

"Scientific, engineering, magical."

"What about technological?"

Elijah nodded. "Any advanced knowledge. The Book of Enoch, an important Jewish text many New Testament writers referenced, reveals, and I quote: *'And Azazel taught men to make swords, and knives, and shields, and breastplates. Semjaza taught enchantments, and root-cuttings. Hermani taught the resolving of enchantments. Baraqijal taught astrology. Kokabel the constellations. Ezeqeel the knowledge of the clouds. Araqiel the signs of the earth. Shamsiel the signs of the sun. Sariel the course of the moon.'*"

Johnny asked, "Who or what are these…people?"

"Not people. Sons of god, possessing advanced knowledge they gifted to humanity."

"Like smartphones and social media apps?"

It was Gina, her voice stronger now, filled with the investigative resolve he'd come to know from her.

"Interesting question," Elijah said. "Why do you ask?"

She hesitated, taking a breath, then a beat. "Just a feeling."

Johnny asked, "What sort of feeling?"

She shifted in the bed, bitting her bottom lip, hesitating.

"Go on, Gina colada…" Elijah encouraged.

Offering a weak smile, Gina took a breath. "Well…the past few days, my head has been filled with so much despair, anxiety, and depression. Mostly after nonsense I've been reading."

"Reading?"

"Right. On WeShare."

Elijah sat straighter with growing intrigue.

"What sorts of things?" he said carefully.

She shrugged. "I don't know…just so many images and messages coming through that have stirred up so much despair inside."

"On your phone?"

"Yeah."

Elijah leaped to his feet, racing to pick it up from the floor, next to her bed. Must have slid when she…

Didn't finish that thought; didn't want to.

He held it up. "May I?"

"Sure," she said, "but—"

"Just give me your passcode."

Snapped at her more than he'd meant to. More than she deserved. But there was an impression of a possible idea that was blooming into more of a probable one that he wanted to check.

Gina told him the four-digit passcode. He pecked it in.

Then gasped.

"Gina…"

"What? What is it?"

"I know why you did this. I know why this happened to you."

Elijah swallowed hard, took a breath, then took a beat—breath trembling within him.

"I know why this happened to them all."

CHAPTER 23

Gina's heart was hammering in her chest, and her head felt faint. Mouth tasted of pennies, too, a ping of adrenaline coursing through her veins to jumpstart the ticker.

Which was probably a good thing, considering she'd nearly stopped it cold.

Could really use two sticks of Doublemint right about now! But she'd run out the last round of overwhelm, so she settled for the next best thing. Her hair.

Grabbing it, she began twisting it, a fresh wave of shame washing over her. Cold and tingly with humiliation.

She was like Saul falling on his sword when he thought he'd been beaten by the Philistines. Or more like Judas after he'd betrayed Jesus by handing him over to be crucified.

How could she have done such a thing? What had compelled her to do such a thing?

Then another thought hot on the heels of that one: Could Jesus forgive her? Would Christ forgive her?

That…she didn't know. Flat didn't know.

A passage of Scripture suddenly flashed in her mind's eye. Something the Apostle Paul said in his letter to the Philippians, about his own journey: *'forgetting what lies behind and straining forward to what lies ahead, I press on toward the goal for the prize of the heavenly call of God in Christ Jesus.'*

Her heart jolted forward at the exhortation. Could she do that, forget what she'd done and move on?

Another verse, from John's first letter: *'See what love the Father has given us, that we should be called children of God; and that is what we are!'*

That was what Gina was. God's daughter. Had to have broken his heart, what she had tried to do.

And yet...

Perhaps he was more heartbroken over her despair and the hopelessness that led to it than what she'd done, like any parent would be.

But wasn't such a thing—she gulped down a rise in emotion at the truth of the thing—wasn't suicide irredeemable?

Another verse, from the Book of Romans: *'For I am convinced that neither death, nor life, nor angels, nor rulers, nor things present, nor things to come, nor powers, nor height, nor depth, nor anything else in all creation, will be able to separate us from the love of God in Christ Jesus our Lord.'*

Nothing could keep her from God's crazy love for her in Jesus.

Not the demons that led her to despair; not the despair itself, and its resulting...incident.

That broke her.

Broke something inside of her.

That love melted whatever shame still lingered, still threatened to finish off what she'd started.

One more verse quickly followed, though, another from John's first letter: *'If we confess our sins, he who is faithful and just will forgive us our sins and cleanse us from all unrighteousness.'*

Is that what she had done? Sinned?

Surely! No way, no how her act—however she had been compelled and cajoled by Forces from the Unseen Realm—was not a big, ginormous slap in the face to the love of God, or even the love of neighbor tied to love of oneself the Bible calls for.

When Grace passed after her own…incident (couldn't frame it any other way after what she'd just done), the family priest who had presided over the funeral was a dear man who counseled them that her…act (another euphemism for you) had not put her outside God's graces. The Church had revised its understanding of suicide as a mortal sin that was irredeemable, instead recognizing *'grave psychological disturbances, anguish, or grave fear of hardship, suffering, or torture can diminish the responsibility of the one committing suicide,'* as the Catechism explained. Still affirmed taking one's life was an act of rebellion against God's love, but it was not irredeemable.

Gina herself was not irredeemable.

That gave her a small measure of comfort.

And yet…

She'd done it. The Act. The Incident! And she was desperate to say sorry to her heavenly Father who had sacrificed so much for her and her life—gave up his very own Son, sending him to die on the cross for her sinful rebellion to pave the way for her salvation and new-life adoption into God's family, for Pete's sake!

So she followed John's exhortation, and in that moment confessed her sin.

Confessed her Act, her Incident.

Most merciful God, I confess that I am captive to sin and cannot free myself. I confess that I have sinned against you in thought, word, and deed; by what I have done—

The thought seized Gina by the throat, her neck literally constricting with emotion.

But another quickly followed: forgiveness, the love of Christ.

So she kept at it: *and by what I have left undone. I have not loved you with my whole heart, I have not loved my neighbor as myself…*

More shame threatened to rise, but was quickly dampened by a flood of the warmth of Christ's love for her.

She continued: '*For the sake of your Son, Jesus Christ, have mercy on me. Forgive me, renew me, and lead me, so that I may delight in your will and walk in your ways, to the glory of your holy name.*

Amen.

A new resolve flooded her veins, riding high on a rising wave of righteous, holy anger.

Anger at that Voice she had heard—at that Force that had dragged her down into the depths of despair and tried to devour her.

Literally, compelling her to take her own life.

Just like all those other women, those girls.

Had they heard the same Voice? Had the same Force dragged them down as well, fed them despairing thoughts to steal, kill, and destroy their lives?

The thought sickened her, made her hopping mad!

She aimed to find out who—or what—had done this.

And take them down.

For them.

For her.

"Eli!" Gina snapped with too much bite.

He startled. "Yes?"

"What's your theory? Where's the origin with all of this?"

"Why, you," he said matter-of-factly.

Gina startled. "Me?"

"You."

"That's what I said."

"No, you said Me; I said You."

"For the love…"

"What are you getting at, kid?" Johnny said, intervening.

Elijah took a breath and held up Gina's phone, the familiar all-consuming ShareFeed from that bleepin' social media platform pulled up.

He gave it a shake. "This is your answer."

"I thought I was the answer."

"You and WeShare."

"WeShare?" Johnny said with a start. "Spell it out for us, kid."

"Well, Gina's brain on WeShare."

"So…what," Jae added, "Markus Braun made her do it?"

"WeShare's founder and the Devil, yes. Or at least his algorithms working in concert with agents of the Unseen Realm, using…whatever is going on with this feed to, well, feed Gina a constant diet of depressing, despairing, hopeless images and stories and videos."

Johnny folded his arms, clearly skeptical. "How do you figure, kid?"

"How? Don't have that figured out yet, but it's like we read in Doc Vaughn's office, the documents he had hidden behind that Gita folio."

Jae said, "Right…the research into WeShare's and WeGram's effects on girls and women."

"Bingo!" Eli gave Gina's phone another shake, reading it and flipping his thumb along the surface. "Scrolling through this feed, it's filled with crapola!"

Johnny snorted a laugh. "Aren't they all? WeShare is for the birds."

"Spoken like a true luddite." Jae flashed him a wink.

"Hey, I'm down with the latest tech!" He whipped out his phone. "Just not a slave to social media."

Elijah said, "Slave is a good way of putting it, because that's what it does. WeShare serves up human connection—or the fake kind, a pseudo-human connection, which releases dopamine into our bloodstream when we get likes and comments."

Gina considered this, adding, "And dopamine is the feel-good chemical that triggers our inner rewards system, like when we pop a shot of heroin into our veins."

"Bingo! And the dopamine produced by these conditioned behaviors overpowers our brain's normal responses, hijacking it and binding it."

Johnny smirked with satisfaction. "Like I said, WeShare is for the birds."

"Whatever…" Jae scoffed. "What does this have to do with our investigation?"

Elijah nodded and returned to Gina's phone. "This ShareFeed is filled with crapola. Half-naked women in skimpy bathing suits showing off their bods. Ridiculous panic-porn news articles fomenting hysteria about the next pandemic. People spouting off about their luxurious vacations to exotic islands and six-figure bonuses and publishing deals. Even some chic named Mandy Fosdick wishing she would never have been born because her favorite café was out of avocado toast. Which, let's be real, is hyperbole coming from someone who sounds like a character from *The Simpsons*."

Gina snorted a laugh. "And I don't even know who that is!"

Jae added, "In other words, crapola."

Eli nodded. "Yuppers. Envy, fear, despair, jealousy, and hopelessness. A steady diet on that would put anyone over the edge. There's a reason Jesus said to take care what our little eyes see, because *'if your eye is healthy, your whole body is full of light; but if it is not healthy, your body is full of darkness.'*"

"Luke, chapter 11," Johnny said. "*'Your eye is the lamp of your body.'* Gave several homilies harping on that verse. *'Therefore consider whether the light in you is not darkness,'* I'd remind my congregants."

"Actually, that's what Jesus said, and for good reason. I think we're seeing the effects of that verse played out in real time."

"In Mill Creek Junction," Jae said.

"Yuppers."

"But how?"

Eli shrugged. "Not sure on that front. Maybe some sort of geotargeting? I recall reading in some newspaper exposé on the WeNet platform how they have powerful targeting featured with their ads platform. You can narrowcast your ads not only down to specific interests like Harry Potter and bowling, but also demographics like age and race and religion, even down to specific locations!"

"Wild…" Jae said. "And scary."

"Advertisement…" Gina muttered, that dreadful exit kit WeShare ad surfacing from her memory.

Elijah turned to her. "What was that?"

She glanced up, surprised at her audible recollection.

Now he narrowed his eyes and drew closer to her bed. "You look like you've seen a ghost, you're so pale."

She slugged him one; he yelped.

"Thanks a lot, mister."

"Sorry, I just mean it sounds like something I said triggered you."

Gina drew her arms around her chest and rubbed her shoulders. "You could say that…"

He waited for her to answer, all three were.

Might as well spill the tea, as Eli would say.

"Like I said, ever since arriving at Mill Creek Junction yesterday, I've been getting these messages, these images."

"Yeah…" Elijah said, nodding.

"But that's not all."

"What's not all?"

She took a breath, held it, then sighed. "I saw an ad."

"An ad? For…"

Gina's eyes fell to the floor, where the wet bag sat, along with the rest of the kit.

Took a beat, then a sudden, startled breath for Elijah to realize what was what.

"You saw an ad for that—on WeShare?"

She nodded, saying nothing more. Didn't much need to.

"Oh my cheeps…that's sicko!"

Jae said, "That's nutso to the maxo."

"And psycho," added Johnny.

Elijah suddenly went rigged, eyes went wide, and his mouth fell open.

Gina had seen that look before. Something had dawned on him. He'd cracked something.

"Sweet mother of Melchizedek, that's it!"

Johnny pounded a hard fist into his solid hand, nodding. "Someone is geotargeting their dark, wicked, twisted content to the citizens of Mill Creek Junction."

Jae nodded, too, clearly putting it together. "A steady diet of darkness, sending people hurling into the darkest valley."

Elijah added, "That's why that one chic—what's her name?"

"Rebecca Goodall," Johnny replied.

He snapped his fingers. "Yes! That's why, even though she wasn't from around here, paying a visit to dear ol' dad and mom —that's why someone from New York also suffered the same effects."

Gina swallowed hard. "And me…"

Elijah turned to her, face falling and nodding.

"But who, how?" she asked.

"There's one person we can call to help answer that one."

Jae raised a brow. "Ghostbusters?"

"Close, but no banana."

Elijah punched a number into Gina's phone and put it on video chat, then handed it to her. After a few rings, a familiar Indian man appeared with thick, black glasses.

"Why, if it isn't my favorite Group X agent!" Abraham Patel crooned.

Elijah scoffed. "What am I, chopped liver?"

"Oh, dear me!" The man laughed nervously. "I was not realizing you were also on the line. My second most favorite Group X agent."

"There are only two of us…"

Gina cleared her throat. "Abraham, ignore him. We need your help."

"How can I be of service?" he asked.

Elijah explained, "We need you to work your magic on Gina's phone."

"OK…what sort of magic? What is this being about?"

Elijah looked to Gina with wide eyes, shrugging.

She frowned, but nodded. Didn't want to verbal vomit her chunks, but the man needed to know the truth of what they were dealing with. What she was dealing with—had been dealing with. Would probably be better than therapy, anyhow. Cheaper at least.

So she laid out what had just happened—starting with her incident, tracing it backward to the things she had been feeling and seeing on WeShare, even what she had heard from that lispy Voice.

Abraham listened well, quietly and without interruption. Thought she caught a sniffle on the other end, but she didn't bring it up.

"So, can you work your magic?" Gina asked.

There was a beat, then a breath and a sigh before he spoke. "First of all, I am feeling most honored that you would be letting me into your pain in this sort of way. You can be most assured that you can be counting on me to carry it for you. No judgment, no gossip."

Gina smiled. "Thank you, Abraham…"

"Secondly, I am having an idea."

"What sort of idea?" asked Elijah.

He grinned. "It is being a surprise."

"I hate surprises."

Now his face fell, but Gina intervened. "Don't listen to him, Abraham. We trust your judgment with this sort of thing, but what are you thinking?"

Abraham answered, "I am thinking there is something about this feed that is being…off."

"Off?"

"I am calling it a hunch."

"A hunch?"

Elijah smirked. "Is there an echo in here?"

She threw him a jab; he yelped.

"Give me a few hours and I will be having an answer for you."

"We don't have a few hours," Gina said with irritation.

"Well…I'll see what I can be doing."

"No. Don't see. Do. There is no see when it comes to people's lives."

Abraham's chest rose on a heavy breath, but he nodded. "Give me an hour. I'll call back then."

Nodding, Gina held up a finger. "One hour, Abraham. We're counting on you."

And so are millions of women…

CHAPTER 24

Elijah was about to burst, he was so anxious for an answer!

Time ticked by like the drippy bathtub faucet from back at the orphanage. And there hadn't been anything from Group X HQ.

At least he had coffee. Black and brewed strong. Not bad.

And PB&Js. Raspberry and crunchy peanut butter. On thick slices of white bread, too. None of that hippy sprouted grains and legumes nonsense, with millet and spelt and lentils. *Blech!* Wonder Bread, all the way.

"Pass the Cheetos, will ya?" Gina asked, waving an arm at the bright orange bag with the cool-cat cheetah cartoon.

He reached behind to the tan formica countertop from another century and grabbed the bag, then handed it across the round oak table scuffed with age nestled in the breakfast nook.

She snatched the bag and shoved a handful in her mouth, humming with pleasure. "These things are my fave. Like crack, they are!"

Supposed she deserved a little crack (the processed food kind, anyway) after what she'd been through, what they all had.

Especially waiting for their trusty investigative support

agent, Abraham Patel, to report back with his findings—whatever those were.

For the last hour, they had been holed up at Johnny Pope's bachelor pad. Which apparently had been the house he'd lived at with his wife before she died and he took to the celibate life as a Catholic priest. Kept the house and now worked from it. One of those turn-of-the-century, two-story craftsman bungalows that looked like it was standard fare in Mill Creek Junction, along with every other postwar Midwest town, complete with a modest fireplace in the living room. Felt like a fire was blazing away inside, too, it was so hot!

Elijah jumped to his feet and started pacing. "I need air…"

"Eli…" Gina said, turning to him with orange-powdered cheesy lips. "Don't crack on me."

He opened his collar and waved a dismissive hand. "Not that kind of air. No meltdown on the horizon. I mean air air. It's hot as Hades in this joint."

"Sorry, kid," Johnny said. "Air conditioner is on the fritz."

Elijah smirked. Just their luck. And how apropos: Their blasted *inexplicitus* case had started in a church with an air conditioner on the fritz, and it would end in a bachelor pad with an air conditioner on the fritz.

At least, that was the hope.

But Abraham was late with the goods he prayed to Yeshua Almighty would break the case wide open and bring it to a swift resolution.

Elijah paced back and forth with impatience, sweating to beat the band! So he whipped out his flip phone.

"Eli…I'm warning you," Gina said, shaking an orange-powdered cheesy finger at him. "Leave our boy alone."

"He's late."

"He'll call."

"But it's been an hour and twenty-three minutes!"

Johnny snorted a laugh. "Exactly, huh?"

"Yuppers." Elijah checked his watch. "An hour and twenty-three—wait, no. An hour and twenty-four minutes!"

Gina said, "He'll call when he's good and ready."

"I'm calling him now."

"Let him do his thing, kid," Johnny said. "Gina's right. He'll get on the horn when he's got something to share."

"But—"

"Found something!" Jae shouted with interruption.

She'd been analyzing the contents of that proctological doohickey she'd shoved up Cain Vaughn's Dell to extract—whatever it is you extract from the backside of a PC.

Elijah shuffled over to her seated on a couch in front of a laptop on a glass coffee table. "Please tell me it's something we can use…"

Johnny joined her other side; Gina kept eating her Cheetos, licking her fingers and diving for more. Again, deserved it.

"I can tell you one thing," Jae said. "Cain Vaughn was into much more than a simple NIH clinical trial."

"Really? What else?"

"Looked like he was employed by Markus Braun himself."

"The Big Tech Kahuna?"

"Sure thing—"

"Chicken wing…" Elijah muttered, his partner's typical rhyming-all-the-timing response.

"Huh?" Jae said with confusion.

"Never mind. What'd you find?"

He craned toward the laptop screen arrayed with a bunch of PDFs—charts and graphs, journal articles, trial studies.

She explained, "Apparently, WeNet commissioned him and a team to go further than the NIH study."

"How so?"

"Well, where the clinical trial merely gauged the effects of WeNet social media outlets on people, Vaughn was tasked with seeking how to leverage the platform to actually influence behavioral changes."

"Egads!" Gina exclaimed, shuffling over now, fingers licked clean but still stained a faint orange.

Johnny gave up his seat for her, and she joined Elijah in craning for her own look.

Jae pointed at the screen. "Take a look at this PowerPoint presentation."

The Group X agents read in silence as Jae shuffled through a series of slides summarizing their findings.

"Says here," Elijah said, "WeGram has flooded teen users with rapid-weight-loss videos, contributing to a wave of eating-disorder cases spreading across Mill Creek Junction. The popular video-sharing app's algorithm serves users thousands of these videos within a few weeks of joining the platform."

"I knew it," Johnny growled, slamming a hardened fist into his palm. "The Junction was Vaughn's playground."

He glanced up at him and nodded. "And WeNet's, apparently."

Jae gasped. "Look at this testimonial."

A quotation was centered on a slide with a white background and a navy running header:

"'The more I interacted with those types of content posts,' one fourteen-year-old was saying, 'the more they showed up on my ShareFeed. Except I couldn't see what it was doing to me.'"

Elijah's heart jolted forward even as his bowels sank to the floor at a name attached to that quote, at the bottom.

Abby Johnson. The fourteen-year-old suicide victim!

The revelation struck the entire room at once, moans and curses thrown up, along with a muttered prayer from the ex-priest.

Lord have mercy, Christ have mercy…

"Check it," Gina announced, pointing to the next slide. Then read:

Trial participants described falling down a rabbit hole of content with an inability to climb back out. They became attached to this or that influencer on WeGram or kept receiving this or that content on WeShare, having the effect of normalizing eating disorders and engendering a fear of missing out, believing everyone was doing it.

"Hive groupthink mentality," she explained. "A perfectly rational social psychological response to shared experience. Whether in the flesh or virtual."

"And not just teenagers," Jae said. "I found a response from Gloria Warner as well."

"Gloria?" exclaimed Johnny. "What did she say?"

Jae tabbed over to another document. "Here we go. You can see here, she said how hard it was taking her eyes off of the content. Spent hours and hours on the videos. Her almost zombie-like connection to the platform started after a random weight-loss video appeared in her feed last year. Said she hit the like button without giving much thought to what she was doing."

"Let me guess," Elijah said, "more weight-loss videos started popping up?"

"Correct. Then fitness videos and others on how to work out."

"Which are pretty harmless on their own."

Gina said, "But not when someone is having struggles with insecurities about her body."

Jae went on, "Soon her feed morphed into a mix of exercise, nutrition, dieting, fasting—and more extreme weight-loss methods."

Elijah jumped to his feet and started pacing the room, bouncing on the balls of his feet.

"It's all making sense! From what we can gather, nearly every suicide victim had seen Cain Vaughn for counseling. Have to imagine they participated in his WeNet side project."

"Whoa…" Gina said, bringing a hand to her mouth.

"Got something?"

"Katrina's laptop!"

"You're thinking she was part of the study, too—that she was digesting this brainwashing content?"

"Sure looked that way by the look of her face."

"And then *kaboom*!" Johnny exclaimed. "A fire just happens to destroy it, the evidence."

"Absotootly!" Gina replied.

Shame suddenly flooded Elijah. He'd accused her of watching naughty videos, and here she was probably being brainwashed by her ShareFeed!

Sending her over the edge…

"So WeGram serves up a nonstop stream of videos and images, combined with WeShare's content—worsening girls' eating disorders because watching was so effortless, and any number of other issues. The algorithms tracked their interests, then served it up to them without any effort on their part."

"Spiraling them," Gina said, "into a vortex of depression, anxiety, despair, self-consciousness, and insecurity."

"Bingo! It was all designed to send people over the edge. To make 'em snap." He snapped his fingers, the sound a reminder of the lives taken.

"Nice story, kid," Johnny said, "but do we have evidence for it?"

"And how do we nail Vaughn," Jae added, "if we can't even find him?"

The shrilly *bring-bring-bring* of Gina's phone interrupted.

"About time!" Elijah said. He lunged for it and answered the call.

It was Abraham alright. Guy looked like he'd run a marathon. Face was drawn and sweaty, eyes bloodshot and bags chilling under his eyes.

"You're late."

Gina threw a square blue pillow at Elijah and motioned for her phone.

He ducked and frowned but relented, handing it over and sitting back beside Jae, who held the phone in between the trio with Johnny off-view.

"Sorry I am running late," Abraham said.

Gina shook her head. "No worries. Just hope you got something for us."

"Oh, I am definitely having something for you."

Elijah was getting impatient. "What were you doing that took you so long?"

"I was running my own experiment to see the effects."

Sounded promising. "What kind of experiment?"

"Crafted my own set of bots and set them loose on WeShare and WeGram."

Hot dog, that was promising!

"And?" Elijah said.

"WeGram's specific algorithm was serving my bots more than 84,000 weight-loss videos, from all manner of accounts I've determined were really fake ones—AI creations themselves designed to look like real people using deepfake technology but really only bots."

"Oh my cheeps. Sinister…"

Gina asked, "What kind of content?"

"Fasting, tips for burning belly fat, pushing weight-loss detox programs, participation in extreme weight-loss competitions."

"Egads! Doesn't sound at all healthy."

"Once WeGram," Abraham went on, "was determining my bots would re-watch those videos, it began serving more and more of the same. More than half their feeds were being this stuff, even if the bot was never seeking it themselves."

"And flooding their brains with trash." Gina took a breath. "Or people's brains, rather."

"And souls…" Elijah said.

The revelation hit hard, the room going silent at the thought of how those women, those girls—Gina, of all people!—had not only been brainwashed by those blasted WeNet social media sites, but their souls had indeed been…no other word for it but tortured by them.

Leading to their ultimate, finalizing end.

"That is not being all," Abraham said. "Sometimes the videos were being more disturbing."

"How so?" Elijah asked.

"Not only were they encouraging eating disorders, but I found evidence they were even encouraging suicide."

"*Suicide?*" the room echoed as one.

Elijah said, "Explain that one."

Abraham said, "Most of the accounts were being given interests consisting of keywords that would trigger the machine learning classifications within the WeNet algorithm. If a video was matching the account's declared interest, which I was programing, then the bot would take more time with that video."

"Which would grab the attention from the WeShare algorithm?"

"That is being correct. I was registering dozens to thirteen-year-olds, which I was programing to dwell on weight loss and suicide."

"And?"

"The bots were watching nearly 300,000 on weight loss and half that on…well, the other thing."

"For the love…" Gina said.

"You could say that again," Johnny said.

Elijah said, "Not hard to see how that could be extrapolated out to real people, teenagers and others watching those same videos about weight loss and—"

He stopped short, not able to voice the truth of it—Katrina's face flashing in his mind's eye, that dear woman who had blown her brains out because of the wickedness that had stolen itself into her heart, destroying her life.

Gina's own face flashed in his mind's eye—the same, horrifying story nearly playing itself out as well.

He swallowed hard and asked, "How was this possible?"

"WeNet sites are only needing one important piece of information to be figuring out what you are wanting."

"What's that?"

"The amount of time you are spending watching or reading a piece of content. Every second you are not scrolling away or rewatching, the app is tracking you."

Gina added, "And then serving up more of the same bulldookie. A feedback loop that just snowballs."

"You are being right."

"Totally what I experienced on my own ShareFeed."

"The WeShare and WeGram algorithms are being just too freaking strong! The way it is rapidly identifying a person's interests and then sending them harmful rivers of videos and images and content posts—it can tip them into unhealthy behaviors or trigger a relapse or—"

"Send someone over the ultimate edge."

"That is appearing to be the point. But I have good news."

"Good news?" Johnny snorted a laugh. "Praise God from whom all blessings flow, let's hear it!"

Abraham explained, "I've been running an algorithmic backtrace on the IP address to the fake accounts."

Jae said, "Like, what, location tracking?"

"Precisely, my dear."

Elijah stood, not able to contain his excitement. Here it was. The lead they needed to close the case.

"And?" he asked.

"And…give me another few seconds. Ahh, I am having—"

The line went quiet. Sounded like the call dropped.

Elijah plopped back down again. "Abraham, you still there?"

"Uhh, yes. I am still being here."

Gina said, "Then whatcha got for us?"

"It's just that..." Abraham went quiet, then hummed.

Elijah rolled his eyes. They didn't have time for theatrics!

"Spit it out, keyboard boy!"

Abraham cleared his throat. "The algorithmic backtrace on the IP address says the attack is coming from—well, your neck of the woods."

Johnny knelt next to Gina and leaned in. "You're saying Mill Creek Junction is the epicenter of this massive social experiment to kill people using WeShare?"

"I am not saying," Abraham explained, "what Mill Creek Junction is being the epicenter of. All I am knowing is that the despairing bot campaign is originating from there."

Jae said, "Do you at least know where?"

"I will be sending you the coordinates shortly. Should I tell Master Grey?"

"No!" Gina insisted. "We'll take it from here."

Elijah turned to her. "You know I'm always one to go it alone, even going rogue, but—"

"Butts are for toilets."

Elijah took a breath, then a beat. "I get that you want to run to the OK Coral for a shootout, but...don't you think we should let the chief in on the latest development?"

"We don't got time for chain of command. This is our moment. We don't know when the next shoe is going to drop."

"Or body, I suppose..."

"My point exactly."

"There's something else you should be knowing," Abraham said with interruption.

Elijah frowned. Great. Another shoe dropping? Or body...

"What's that?" he asked.

"Cain Vaughn doesn't exist."

"Of course he does, silly. We saw—"

"No, no, no. I am meaning that the name is not existing. Until a year ago, at least."

"Whoa," Johnny said. "You're saying it's a cover then?"

"It is appearing that way."

"For who?" asked Jae.

"Or what?" Gina echoed.

"That is the question, isn't it?"

Abraham said, "I have been running a search of property tax records with the Mill Creek Junction city office, cross checking recently purchased properties in the area with Cain Vaughn."

Elijah sat up straight with interest. "And?"

"And…I was finding a Chauvin Gan."

"Chauvin Gan?" He closed his eyes and ran the words through his noggin. "That's an anagram for Cain Vaughn!"

"We got him!" Gina exclaimed, giving him a high five.

"Sorry to burst your bubble, but he owns a local Vietnamese joint in town."

Elijah twisted up his face. "Cain Vaughn's not Vietnamese, silly."

"No, but Chauvin Gan is. Have been eating there for years."

Jae said, "Doesn't sound like our man."

"I was also finding a Chad Vander Hann."

Gina sat up with interest now. "Sounds promising."

Elijah smirked. "A bit too on the nose. And isn't that German?"

"Dutch," Johnny corrected.

"Same difference."

Abraham added, "He is owning a house off Willow Street."

Johnny said, "Suppose we could check him out."

Gina asked, "Anyone else, Abraham?"

"Then there is also being," he answered, "Abel Ivanovich. Owner of the local funeral home."

"Funeral home?" Jae exclaimed.

Elijah snorted a laugh. "Real clever. Cain and Abel."

"The fratricidal brothers."

"Bingo." Then it dawned on him. "The Ukrainians…"

Johnny asked, "What was that, kid?"

"At that bar on Main Street!"

"What, Max's Place?"

Elijah nodded. "The men we saw palling around that card table, with those other farmers."

Jae said, "From the Ukraine."

"Nope. Ukraine. Not the Ukraine."

"Right right right. What of it?"

"Bet they're in on it, is what."

Gina said, "Thought they were hired hands for Warner's onions and celery."

Elijah smirked. "So they say. My money is on it being a front, and they're here for other more nefarious reasons."

"So, what," Jae said, crossing her arms, "the Russians set up shop in Mill Creek Junction, programmed a bunch of WeShare social bots using artificial intelligence combined with deepfakes to infiltrate people's minds—specifically women's minds?"

"Bingo! Hey, you're good."

"Sounds plausible," Gina said. "Where have we seen this playbook before?"

Jae scoffed. "I think the 2010s are calling to ask for their election conspiracy theory back."

"Russians, in Mill Creek Junction," Johnny said, "waging some sort of psyop—what, with the goal to roll out their suicide machine worldwide?"

Elijah grinned. "Only one way to find out."

"Before we go," Gina said, "I think a prayer is in order."

"For holy angels?"

"You know it."

"Let me do the honors," Johnny Pope said. "An ex-priest has prayed that prayer more times than you can imagine."

The group huddled together, closing their eyes while the man prayed aloud:

*Everlasting God, you have ordained and constituted in a
wonderful order the ministries of angels and
mortals: Mercifully grant that, as your holy angels
always serve and worship you in heaven, so by your
appointment they may help and defend us here on
earth; through Jesus Christ our Lord, who lives and
reigns with you and the Holy Spirit, one God, for
ever and ever.*

"Amen," Elijah said, followed by Jae and Johnny.

"Giddy up," Gina echoed.

He nodded. Time to close this *inexplicitus* case.

CHAPTER 25

As far as Gina was concerned, stake outs bit the big one.

Never liked them with the Bureau. And sure as heck didn't like it now planted in the abandoned lot of a burned down hardware store across the street from Graceland Memorial, the funeral home attached to a private cemetery on the outskirts of Mill Creek Junction—owned by a one Abel Ivanovich.

At least they were staking out in style, the soft, supple tan leather of the Cadillac Escalade with the kickin' lumbar support making it that much easier.

Gina shifted in the driver's seat, wondering whether her next ride should be a Caddy. The Order of Thaddeus still owed her a make-good vehicle—for the second time—after her second candy apple red Honda Odyssey (affectionately named Fuji) was flatlined by a steel beam on their last investigation.

They'd been like that for hours after the revelations from Abraham Patel. Just sitting, observing, sitting some more—engine killed without any air conditioner, shirt soaking with sweat from the thick blanket of humidity still hanging around after sunset.

And her without an extra swipe of Secret.

Supposed she could grab the deodorant stick from her overnight bag behind her seat. But Elijah would squirm and pitch a fit. Wasn't a fan of personal hygiene products. Used them. Just didn't want to see them, especially his partner's.

Had forgotten about the crazy high Michigan humidity. Nearly as bad as Washington, DC, although that city was built on a swamp! The Mitten State had the Great Lakes to contend with, as well as Canada.

"I'm melting," Elijah complained, a hand fanning his sweaty face and a lock of dark, wavy hair drooping down into his eyes. He blew at it. "And it sucks."

Gina went to reply when squawking brakes caught her attention.

Down the way.

A sedan, unknown make and model, dark and shrouded in darkness from dead headlights came into view. The car slowly worked its way down from the end of the turn until it passed their position.

"Here we go…" she said lowly, a ping of adrenaline kicking her ticker into high gear.

Elijah sat up and pointed out the windshield, the car pulling into the parking lot.

"I see it." She stiffened as well. "Dollars to donuts that's Cain."

"Abel."

"Whatevs. It's our boy."

"Or our Russian boys."

Or that…

Static discharge from a short-range, two-way radio flared up. Then: *"You see what we're seeing?"*

Elijah answered, "Sure do, Johnny."

"Hold your position until we've got confirmation of the package."

Keeping her eyes trained on the car, Gina pulled her Glock out from her boot. Red brake lights flared up as the mystery sedan parked along the brick building, and she slid out the magazine for inspection. A little ritual she had at the FBI when she went on assignment.

Faint opening doors echoed her way, and she smiled.

Nine 9mm bullets with Ivanovich's name on them.

Closing doors snapped her back to the funeral home.

"Oh me cheeps…" Elijah said. "There he is."

An overhang with a faint yellow light confirmed the package had arrived.

"Along with two other goons," Gina said, sliding the magazine back into place.

"Big guys, too. About the same size as the hombres from Max's Place."

She smirked. "I can take 'em."

"You see what I'm seeing?" Johnny called again.

The three men disappeared inside. A heavy, clangy thud echoed from across the street.

Door closed.

But not case closed.

Yet.

Soon enough…

"You ready, Gina colada?" Elijah asked, inspecting his own magazine before sliding it back into his Glock.

She threw him a grin. "Thought you'd never ask."

"We're going in, Pope man," Elijah announced, then shut off the radio before any further reply.

Gina threw open her door and hopped out, then quietly shut it.

Waiting, intuiting, discerning.

A heavy haze had settled on the darkened road, the hot humidity a wet blanket on the summer evening quickly cresting into night. Katydids and tree frogs and a barking dog up the street was the soundtrack for their incursion.

For Gina's incursion. Because mark her words: She was taking point on the *inexplicitus* case from the bowels of the Abyss.

Padding across the cracked pavement, a shutting car door stopped her cold.

Heart jolted forward, her breath caught in her chest. Elijah nearly ran into her backside, her partner doing a skipping and hopping dance to sidestep her.

"Gina…"

"Sorry!" she whispered, searching for the sound.

And spotting a not very happy Johnny Pope and Jae McCray padding their way, weapons drawn and held firm in front.

Whatevs. It was go time.

On Gina's time.

She followed after her partner, the pair close behind.

They all came up in a crouching rush to the vehicle's rear. An Audi A4 luxury sedan.

Figured Russian terrorists would be riding in style.

They side stepped around the passenger's side, the four still in a huddled crouch.

"Next time," Johnny said lowly, "warn us before you make a move, would ya?"

Gina ignored him, edging around Eli and making for the door.

Pulse sounding in her ears from the thrill of the moment, Gina went to open the door—

When a shrilly *bring-bring-bring* cut through the night.

Her phone!

"For the love…" she hissed, cussing beneath her breath as she silenced it in her pants pocket, and the other three pressed against the brick wall.

Just a single round of alerts, but it was enough to blow their cover, that's for darn tootin'.

"Why didn't you silence that thing?" Elijah whispered.

"Thought I had!" Gina hissed back.

"Who was it?" Johnny said lowly.

She yanked out her phone and saw a missed call from Group X HQ.

"Guessing it was Abraham."

A soft buzzing indicated a new message.

From Abraham.

She opened it, scanned the two brief lines.

And a cold dread flooded her veins.

"For the love…" she gasped.

"What's the dealio?" Elijah asked.

She showed him the phone.

"*'Hope I wasn't blowing your operation ;)'.*" Elijah snorted a laugh. "Yeah right. He keeps going: *'Don't ask how but found every victim was an organ donor.'*"

Flushing away the cold dread was a hot, holy anger. A passionate impulse to rip the head off the snake and feed it to her cats back home!

"Organ donor?" Jae said. "What does that—"

"The Big Mo," Gina said with interruption. "That's what it means."

"Sweet mother of Melchizedek," Elijah said. "One leg of the crime-case trifecta."

"Along with means and opportunity. Which WeNet gave Doc Vaughn or Ivanovich or whoever the heck he is."

Jae said, "I'm sorry, but I still don't get it."

"Organ donors," Johnny grunted. "More like organ harvesting."

"Bingo…" Elijah said. "Fetch a stack of Benjamins off the black market, those things do."

"Or rubles…"

All the green light Gina needed to hop to it.

"Time to take this bleepin' mother ship of demonic wickedness down."

She grabbed for the knob, then twisted.

Locked.

Crapola!

"Now what?" Elijah mumbled.

Gina took a breath. "Where there's a will, there's a Gina."

Gripping her Glock tighter, she took aim at the door knob—

Then let her rip.

Pop-pop-pop it resounded, splitting through the night. That bleepin' dog barked up the road, joined by another. Probably woke the goons inside, too, but she didn't care. She wanted in.

Pronto.

The knob fell to the cracked pavement with a clatter, and in no time flat she was inside a dark hallway. A faint red light from an *EXIT* sign blanketed the space filled with the tang of formaldehyde and bleach, joined by the fresh electric smell of a summer thunderstorm barreling across Ohio.

Or, in their case, a whole hot mess of servers pumping out bots and deepfakes to ensnare unsuspecting small-town citizens in a web of horrifying evil.

Johnny grunted a sigh. "What'd I say about letting us in on your moves beforehand?"

Ignoring him, Gina pushed inside, immediately feeling overwhelmed.

Hallway was far too narrow for Gina's liking, her head blooming with the threat of claustrophobia, exacerbated by the dim lighting and crazy-stuffy hot quarters—compounded by the thrill of the chase and the adrenaline keeping every one of her senses on high alert.

Not a good combo for an autistic person like herself.

But she persisted, padding carefully down the corridor, her boots throwing up a squeaky swish.

A faint blue glow was thrown from an open door at the end, joined by deep voices.

Foreign. Definitely Russian.

Three, maybe four, chattering with a nervous, excited energy —echoing her way, getting louder.

Until a brutish man appeared. All neck with cannons for arms and a barrel chest.

And an AK-47 made to order from Mother Russia.

Didn't even think about it. Her lizard brain took over, joined by hours of certification training with the FBI.

Pop-pop-pop and the dog was put down, Gina bo-bina style.

Recoiled like one of those B-level streaming service movies, blood blooming from the bullet wounds. Feared his Russian rifle would go off—again, like said B-level streaming service movie—but it didn't, the weapon clattering to the floor before the oaf slumped in the doorway.

But that didn't stop a strafing *rat-a-tat-tat* from inside!

Livid bullets chewed the cheap drywall and up into the ceiling, the textured fiberglass-gypsum material falling like snowflakes in the dim, red light.

"Get down!" Elijah commanded.

Crouching, she glanced behind to find her partner hovering over her shoulder, but no Johnny or Jae.

Another threatening *rat-a-tat-tat* was joined now by an angry *pop-pop-pop* that meant business.

Elijah's business.

A yelp from inside made her smile.

"Yes!" Eli said, victorious.

Another weaker bout of weapon fire sounded from the room, but not very committal. More like covering fire for an—

Escape!

"Not on your life, pal," she sneered, standing with outstretched Glock and darting toward the doorway.

She gasped at what she saw.

Expected a vast array for refrigerators. The kind that kept loved ones safe and sound until it was time for burial. Maybe an embalming table, some gurneys for transportation and other wares of the funeral trade. Coffins, caskets, cremation jars.

Yes, there was that.

But that wasn't all.

The room shimmering with icky fluorescent lighting swinging from the ceiling was also humming with racks of servers. And by racks, rows and rows of the suckers in two large black cabinets lit up like Christmas trees!

The vessels that had carried those vile bots with those vile images and messages and videos of depression and anxiety, hopelessness and envy.

Of despair…

A *pop-pop-pop* through a darkened hallway at the other end of the room brought her back to the moment.

Gina tightened her grip. What was that?

"Come back here!" a voice shouted from somewhere beyond the doorway void.

Right before a nasty *rat-a-tat-tat* flared, followed by a *pop-pop-pop* rejoinder.

Something flashed in the shadows. A figure, running beyond the threshold and pulling up short.

Gina whipped her Glock and took aim. "Hold it right there!"

No movement, no sound.

"Come my way, hands where I can see them!"

Elijah pulled up next to her with a nod and added his own Glock.

Took a beat, but the figure emerged from the shadows, stiff leather shoes clattering across the tiles along with a growly laugh.

Gina narrowed her eyes, curling one end of her mouth upward with satisfaction.

"Abel Ivanovich," she sneered.

He smirked, brushing a hand through that wavy hair of his. "Good on you. You found me out."

Johnny and Jae pulled up behind him, their own weapons outstretched.

"The other hostiles?" Elijah asked.

"Deader than doornails," Jae replied.

Gina nodded, then stepped closer, gripping her weapon tighter. Her hand started shaking, an adrenaline rush brought on by the melee compounded by having the perp in her sights.

"Why?" was all she said.

Ivanovich shrugged. "Why not?"

Heat raced up her neck and bloomed in her cheeks. Punk.

"Are you knowing," the punk went on, "that funeral homes are the front lines in organ donation in America? *Da,* that is being true. They are playing a critical role in the donation process of organs, eyes, and tissue by supporting families as they say goodbye to their loved one. It is why I was buying this lovely establishment."

Elijah smirked. "To give people a fancy-shmancy send off? Yeah, right."

"That's sweet of you," Gina said. "Bet there's also gold in them thar bodies? Mucho dinero to be made—or, in your case, rubles."

Ivanovich's mouth widened into a wicked grin—bent, yellow teeth beneath flared nostrils and narrowed eyes. "*Da.* That is being true."

He sighed, running a hand through his hair again. "What is the American saying? It is taking money to be making money, *da*?"

"Da."

"And, well, my comrades were wanting much money."

"But why, when you had the NIH grant money?"

Elijah added. "And then WeNet's rubles?"

"*Da,* but that will be running out," the punk replied.

Ivanovich stepped closer, the ghastly light from above playing with the shadows on his face—with those angular cheekbones and that nose, the bulging eyes. Looked ghoulish.

"Now, suppose," the punk went on, "that I am able to franchise this fine establishment, while supplying myself with a steady stream of…customers."

"Donors, you mean," Elijah said, throat gravelly with disgust.

"*Da!* Impressive, you are catching on."

"Who were then sent to an early grave through your bots?"

"Most impressive."

Gina tightened her grip, her stomach growing as tight with disgust. Thought she would retch from the revelation.

"Money?" she spat with exclamation. "That was the motivation? The Big Mo?"

"Does make the world go 'round," Elijah said.

Ivanovich just stood there, that smug, ghoulish grin plastered to his face.

"And WeShare is your slaughterhouse, using the social media platform to lure unsuspecting victims."

Vaughn shrugged. "Like sheep to the slaughter, users are being, as you suggest. For years, humans were being primed for such an operation, willingly marinating in depressive images and status updates, triggering despair and petty jealousies, their brains boiling in dopamine-induced addiction that kept the sheeple chained to gloom. WeShare's targeting tools made it that much easier."

Gina's breath caught in her chest. "Including geotargeting…"

"*Da.* You cannot be imagining what is possible, those little devices tracking your every movement. And all willingly!"

She'd heard enough—had had enough. All the confirmation she needed to know that exit kit had been delivered thanks to Vaughn's WeShare magic—and her own willing heart, even. Frightening…

Nothing more to do than bring this dirt bag in.

Gina waved her weapon, gesturing to the floor. "On your knees."

Ivanovich stiffened. "*Nyet.*"

"Come on, pal," Johnny said from behind. "You're surrounded. Outmatched and outgunned."

"We can do this the easy way," Jae added, tightening her grip on that Sig Sauer of hers, "or the Jae McCray way."

Ivanovich laughed now.

"*Nyet.* We'll be seeing about that."

He snapped his fingers.

Gina frowned. "What are you—"

A sudden rumble cut her off, the room shaking and quaking, the server racks rattling to beat the band inside those black cabinets, joined by those icky fluorescent lights swinging on squeaky chains.

Followed by a horrifying sound straight from the Abyss.

Then…from the shadows—

She sucked in a startled breath, disbelieving her eyes.

What was happening?

Even worse: What was that *thing*?

CHAPTER 26

A terrifying roary, snorty, skittering screech sounded through the funeral home room. Small at first before quickly crescendoing, as if emerging from a tear in the fabric of reality itself.

Elijah's breath caught in his chest at the sound, a cold dread spreading through him, sending every hair on his body standing at attention.

It was back. The thing of nightmares.

The Being that had haunted *his* nightmares since last year, when the bastard-born, divine-human hybrid emerged in that blasted hangar at the Air Force base in Ohio.

A Watcher-spirit.

A Fallen One…

Out of nowhere, something emerged from the shadows—from another dimension, even. A hulking figure, with a bulbous head resting atop wide shoulders corded with muscle, sauntered toward them. Skin rippled in scaly waves with an iridescent glow.

The Being was hideous, horrendous, something straight out of a Stephen King fever dream. And entirely familiar!

Yet…

Yet there was something attractive about it. Enticing, even. As if it was what Elijah had been waiting for his whole life—to give meaning and definition and permission to his identity as a man, as a human.

An Angel of Light. Come to save humanity.

Yesssssss, thaths riiiight….

A Voice erupted from within.

Not his head, his very soul.

"This isn't happening," Jae muttered.

"You see it too?" Gina whispered on a frightened breath.

Johnny looked stunned. Unmoving and unable to voice any sort of recognition, yet his face said it all.

He saw what Elijah saw. They all did.

The Being slithered from the shadows and planted itself behind Ivanovich. Who was whose master, it wasn't clear. What was clear was what it said.

With unmoving lips, coming from inside his head!

I am Dethhpair, dethhroyer of worlds! Come to wreak the pathetic lives of Earth's sheeple and reap the fruit of my loins—bringing and bearing deprethhion and anxiety, hopelethhness and insecurity, dread and…dethhpair—Elijah!

Elijah's heart exploded, his head surged with fight-or-flight adrenaline.

He wanted to flat take off. Run out the back and never come back.

Not back to Group X, not back to his life. The one that called for him to stand against the darkness—*that* darkness, the one standing in front of him!

And yet…

The Being knew his name. Didn't know what to do with that. Not in the slightest.

Someone responded for him.

"Who are you?"

It was Gina, giving a command to that Being.

You know who I am, Geeennnnaaah…We go farrrr back, you and I.

Elijah turned to her, mouth open with a bazillion questions!

But she didn't waver, didn't falter in the face of the menacing horror.

"Say it," Gina commanded. "I want to hear. In the name of Jesus Christ, name yourself."

There was that terrifying roary, snorty, skittering screech again. Livid, even pained. Same as what had happened last year, with the other Watcher-spirit that had manifested itself in their world.

The Being recoiled from the mention of the Son of God. Its head thrown backward and back arching, arms rising to shield itself—as if it were injured.

Yet it relented. Elijah knew it had to. It was textbook, just like in the Gospels when Yeshua Almighty called to the demons that had possessed people.

Same for this one, submitting to the name that every knee must bend to—whether in Heaven or on Earth or under Earth. Both the seen realms and the Unseen Realm.

And it did.

Dethhhpair! it screeched, throwing its bulbous, scaly head back in a high-pitched yet growly and rumbly wail—the room shaking and quaking again under the unholy, wicked weight of the Unseen Realm, in the flesh.

Gina recoiled at the name. Made sense, given all the crazy that had gone down, fueled by just that.

Despair.

It also seemed too on the nose. Maybe there was a lesson there to learn. That this…Being or demon, the Watcher-spirit or whatever—maybe it got its strength, its power from its name? Something to think about. Another day. When they got through that one.

If they got through that one…

"What is it you want?" Elijah asked—now fixing the Being with eyes that meant business, his jaw clenched and face set.

Gina flashed him a smile; he replied with the same.

Despair had two agents of the Church to contend with!

Just like old times…

The Being paused, saying nothing. It only raised an arm, where long fingers curled into a tight fist.

All six of them!

The server racks inside the cabinets started shuddering. A monitor fell to the floor from the quaking room.

Lord Jesus Christ, Son of God, make haste to help us!

"What is it you want?" Elijah demanded, taking a step toward the Being now.

To make humanity thhuffer through dethhpair. What eltthhhee?

To make humanity suffer, through despair. What else? Of course! And what better way than through direct-line injection sites in their pockets?

"Nope. Not going to happen."

A laugh erupted from the Being, the sound cackling from it like a strangled goat. Bleating and braying, strutting even.

Time to bring out the big guns.

Elijah reached inside his shirt and pulled out a cross—the one from a family teenage trip to Rome with Dad and Mom that had served him well a time or twelve.

Like the last time they'd confronted a Cosmic Power from the Unseen Realm!

Elijah held out the faded gold icon, beseeching Jesus Christ and his blood to combat the very forces of hell.

"Almighty and eternal God," he shouted with all of the authority given him by Jesus Christ himself, "who appointed your only-begotten Son the Redeemer of the world, and willed to be appeased by his blood: Grant, we beseech you, that we may so honor this, the price of our redemption, and by its virtue be so defended from the evils of our present life, so as to enjoy its fruit in heaven forevermore, through the name of Christ Our Lord. Amen."

The Being threw up that terrifying roary, snorty, skittering screech.

And before he knew it, Elijah was flat on his back, face blooming with pain and nose gushing blood.

He'd been struck in the face, his eye swelling shut from the blow.

Ivanovich was on him in an instant—teeth bared and terrifying, eyes wide and wild, glowing with a possession, a Power that no doubt came from the Watcher-spirit raging with the heat of a thousand suns. The Being couldn't touch him and Gina directly, not Christ's children.

So it sicced his puppet on him.

And on him he was, the man pummeling his face.

Elijah brought his arms up to shield himself, then sent a knee sailing straight into Ivanovich's gonads.

Cheap shot, but sometimes the cheap ones are the best ones.

Dude faltered back, and Elijah was on him in an instant. Where was help from the others? It was like they were paralyzed or something.

Maybe they were…

Which left Elijah to—

He was thrown back. Ivanovich was a brutish beast himself, infused with a superhuman strength that reminded him of a case back in Vegas, where a man had been terrorizing the Strip and couldn't be contained, no one had the strength to subdue him.

The psycho lunged for Elijah. He raised his arms, but Ivanovich was on him in an instant, grabbing his head and smashing it against the solid blue tile floor.

Once, then again.

Darkness overtook him, joined by starlight and an instant dizziness that threatened to plunge him into the Abyss.

Thought he might dive down deep, too, until a voice suddenly pierced through the fog of war.

Familiar, familial.

Gina colada!

"'The Lord is my light and my salvation; whom shall I fear? The

Lord is the stronghold of my life; of whom shall I be afraid?'" she cried out, quoting a familiar Hebrew poem, Psalm 27.

Then another, like a rapid-fire assault rifle aimed squarely at the Watcher-spirit and Ivanovich: *"'You who live in the shelter of the Most High, who abide in the shadow of the Almighty, will say to the Lord, 'My refuge and my fortress; my God, in whom I trust.'"*

This time from Psalm 91—which did the trick.

Ivanovich staggered back, and that terrifying roary, snorty, skittering screech echoed through the room.

"'Because you have made the Lord your refuge,'" Gina said, voice solid and rising high, *"'the Most High your dwelling place, no evil shall befall you, no scourge come near your tent. For he will command his angels concerning you to guard you in all your ways.'"*

Another blow to the possessed and the possessor, Ivanovich stumbling now in a drunken stagger.

But Elijah was too dizzy, too weak from the melee to respond.

"'Those who love me, I will deliver,'" Gina continued, the demonic roary, snorty, skittering screech swirling into a moaning, tortured vortex of cacophony. *"'I will protect those who know my name. When they call to me, I will answer them; I will be with them in trouble, I will rescue them and honor them. With long life I will satisfy them, and show them my salvation!'"*

The Being offered one final wail before it almost seemed to explode—a darkness so totalizing that it bloomed until it disappeared completely.

And Abel Ivanovich collapsed to the floor.

Tried to get up, the bastard going to his knees.

Gina raced over and grabbed the man's head, clocking him with a hardened fist in his schnoz.

Go Gina colada, go!

Ivanovich shouted a curse and grabbed for his nose, blood blooming.

But she didn't give up. She persisted and insisted the man submit.

Gina grabbed his hair and jerked up her knee, smashing his head into her kneecap.

Lights out for Ivanovich, the man slumping down to the tiled floor. Still, unmoving.

Just the way it should be.

Elijah caught his breath, sucking in desperate air laced with bleach and formaldehyde, but he didn't care. They'd done it. Closed the case, him and Gina.

He moaned and went to his knees.

Wishing he hadn't done that.

Almost went back down hard, but a hand caught him under the arm.

It was Gina.

Body tingled from the touch and head bloomed with an alarming ping, but he didn't care. He welcomed her help. Welcomed her…

"You saved my life," he grunted, rising to his feet with her help.

Gina smiled and shrugged. "Easy peasy."

Johnny slipped a pair of plastic cuffs from the back of his waist and slipped them on the downed perp's wrists, then another around his ankles.

The PI threw her a smile. "Nice work, little lady."

She smiled. "Thanks. All in a day's work."

"You did it, Gina colada," Elijah said, raising a palm.

Gina brought hers to his. Not touching but nearly there.

"We both did."

Now he smiled. "Two peas in a pod, we are."

"A real mind-meld."

"Yuppers!"

Sirens sounded in the distance, muffled but approaching. Mill Creek's finest, come to put that blasted perp in the clink.

Gina slumped to the floor herself now, surely spent from her duel.

They'd done it. Solved the case and gotten the perp, saving him to face justice.

All in a Group X day's work.

Elijah said, "Suppose the authorities will want statements."

"And answers," Johnny said, waving a hand, "after what went down."

"Yeah, all of it."

Gina nodded, then knelt and folded her hands. "First things first, guys."

Elijah glanced her way, then quickly followed suit. Same for Johnny and Jae.

Elijah asked, "Anything special you have in mind?"

"I think I've got just the ticket," the ex-priest said, then prayed aloud:

> *O God, almighty and merciful, you heal the broken-*
> *hearted, and turn the sadness of the sorrowful to joy.*
> *Let your fatherly goodness be upon all whom you*
> *have made. Remember in pity all those who are this*
> *day destitute or forgotten. Look upon all this night,*
> *in this town, with the eyes of your mercy; comfort*
> *Mill Creek with a sense of your goodness; preserve it*
> *from the temptations of the enemy; and give its*
> *people patience under affliction in your good time.*

Elijah's eyes suddenly welled with emotion, his heart rending in two at the thought of all the darkness that had come against this town. Against those women.

He took a breath, swallowing hard.

Against his friend, his teammate, his partner…

Johnny picked up where he'd left off:

> *Lift up those who are cast down. Mightily befriend inno-*
> *cent sufferers and cheer with hope all who are*
> *discouraged and downcast. Though they be troubled*

on every side, suffer them not to be distressed;
though they are perplexed, save them from despair.
Grant this, O Lord, for the love of him who for our
sakes became poor, your Son our Savior Jesus Christ.

"Amen," Johnny grunted.

"Amen," the other two echoed.

"Amen," Gina said softly, crossing herself.

Elijah stood. "I think our job here is done."

"Mill Creek PD might say otherwise," Johnny said.

Jae said, "I'd imagine they'll have some questions for us all."

"Yeah, but how will we explain this level of crazy?"

Elijah shrugged. "We fought the darkness."

"And won," Gina said with a grin.

He grinned back.

Exactly.

CHAPTER 27

Elijah was almost in a pickle. Again.

It was coming up on ten o'clock, the hour he turned into a pumpkin if he didn't get his raisin bagel smothered in low-fat plain cream cheese joined by a large dark roast coffee.

But this time, he had a plan.

He'd already mapped out the best route to get to Saxbys from his row house in the Adams Morgan district along the 18th Street corridor in Northwest DC. Had landed the half-million dollar fixer-upper after a bidding war that ended with one of those impassioned letters that actually worked.

So he put that plan to work. In no time flat, he pulled into a parking spot, his bimmer (one I, two Ms) grumbling for the early hour on a Saturday morning. Elijah wrenched off his helmet and hustled toward the grayish-blue door—praying to Yeshua Almighty there was a raisin bagel with his name on it.

Throwing open the door, he was overcome with the force of brewing coffee and baking quiche Loraine. Had already eaten breakfast, otherwise the ham-swiss-egg combo would have been right up his alley, then right down his gullet. No rumble of conversations at this hour, given Georgetown University was out of session, and the red-brick space anchoring the corner of 35th and O Street was pretty empty. Only a handful of patrons in those gray plastic tables and chairs this time.

There were those orange flowers again sitting on top of cases filled with cookies and breads and bagels and scones, greeting and tempting Elijah, but he was untemptable. He had his eyes set on one thing, and one thing alone.

The lone bagel nestled under a glass lid.

"Oh, you're back," barked the same goth chic he'd run into at the start of the week. And with the same black Grateful Dead T-shirt and matching black skirt. This time sporting a spiky collar to match those silver cantaloupes dangling in each ear.

Chic was born about three decades too late, the '90s wanting their fashion style back, but he wasn't about to clue her in. Not with a raisin bagel on the line.

"A large dark roast and that raisin bagel," Elijah announced.

He held his breath—hoping against hope all was right in the world.

Goth Chic nodded and got to work.

He sighed with a smile. All *was* right in the world.

The door behind him jingled, and in walked Gina and Silas Grey, along with another familiar face.

Peter Young.

"Boy, is it nice to see you!" He hustled over with a grin and opened up for an embrace.

Elijah froze, then stepped back and waved. "Howdy!"

Peter stopped short, face twisted up with confusion. Silas came from behind and put a hand on his shoulder. "Just go with it."

"Alright." He laughed and gave a wave of his own.

"What are you doing in town?" Elijah asked.

He grabbed Silas's shoulder with a grin. "Wedding planning!"

Elijah raised an eyebrow. "You two getting hitched?"

Silas laughed. "No. Me and Celeste Bourne."

"Ahh, yes. The Bourne who was a Bourne before that action hero Bourne was a Bourne."

"Exactly."

"About time, too," Peter added.

"Yeah, Celeste was going to beat me up if we waited any longer."

Elijah said, "I'd pay good money to see that."

Silas frowned. "Why don't you get us a seat while we order drinks."

He grabbed the chairs in the bay window—bearing his raisin bagel and large dark roast, in the same spot where all the *inexplicitus* nonsense started a few days ago.

The others returned, and the four settled in and caught up. Mostly heard how Mill Creek Junction was navigating the news from the Russian bot bust, as well as how the pastor was navigating all the tragic fallout with his church—especially with the death of his assistant, a well-beloved member of his community.

Heaving a breath and shaking his head, Peter said, "Did a number on me, that's for sure."

Elijah nodded. "Have to imagine it did. All those people ending their lives like that."

He swallowed a swig with a nod. "That. And…"

The pastor trailed off, leaving a big, fat question mark hanging in the air.

A baton Gina grabbed: "Aaannd?"

Peter laughed. "Sorry. It's not something I talk about much, but…well, my brother basically committed suicide."

"Really? Younger or older?"

"Younger. James was his name. Almost five years ago, now."

Elijah asked, "What do you mean by *basically*?"

Silas almost coughed on his coffee. "Sounds like he meant to leave it vague, Eli. Maybe let it go?"

"No, it's fine," Peter said. "He overdosed on heroin and there was a note."

"A note?" Elijah said.

"Suicide note," Gina said. "Same as my sister, I'd imagine."

Peter nodded, saying nothing more.

She went on, "Can imagine the case brought up a whole lot of crazy memories long buried. Did for me."

"That it did…"

A silence settled over the group, and they sipped in silence. Too silent, after that heavy emotional weight. Which made Elijah super uncomfortable. The case had opened up something in him, too, an empathy and emotional outlet long buried. But wasn't quite ready to sit with all the emotional heaviness. Far, far too soon for that.

So he interrupted the silence: "So, hey, the Russians…who would've thought?"

"Like a bad remake of *Red Dawn*." Gina added, "Only running an operation in Small Town, America—with bots!"

"In Mill Creek Junction, no less," chimed Peter.

Silas said, "To harvest body parts to sell on the black market?"

"Right?" exclaimed Gina. "Too weird for words."

"Par for the course with the Order of Thaddeus, I'm afraid."

"Bizarro," Elijah said, throwing back a swig of brew.

"No…*inexplicitus*," Gina said with a wry grin.

He chuckled. "Touché."

"Speaking of which," Silas said, throwing back a swig of brew, "I've got another case for you back at the farm."

Gina joined Elijah in a loud groan that meant business.

The chief got the hint, putting up his hands in surrender. "Alright, alright. It can wait. Let's just enjoy a nice conversation without anything to do with solving mysterious, supernatural cases."

"Here, here!" Peter said.

"I'll drink to that," Gina said with a smile before taking a sip of tea.

So they did. Not talking a lick about *inexplicitus* cases or taking a stand against the darkness. That all could wait, for another day.

But Elijah knew better.

The Cosmic Powers of this present supernatural darkness had been dealt another blow, another setback in their quest to steal, kill, and destroy God's Image Bearers.

They wouldn't sit on their laurels for long.

They've got long memories, and they're relentless.

He understood that more than most.

For now, Elijah sat back and listened, to stories of hope and tragedy, enjoying his bagel and coffee.

All was right in the world, indeed.

EPILOGUE

I failed. And everyone knows it.

Including the Deadly Seven.

My coming out moment, this was supposed to be. The day I stood, shoulder to shoulder, with the Big Kahunas that guide and control all that we underlings unfold across Earth.

Vainglory and Pride.

Greed and Covetousness.

Lust and Desire.

Envy and Jealously.

Gluttony.

Wrath and Malice.

Sloth.

But I'm getting there—I *will* be there, just you wait and see.

Imagine it won't belong until I have a seat at the Deadly Seven table—the Deadly Eight we will be!

And when I do, I'll show them all. Yessiree, I'll rule them all. The Deadly Seven, yes, but also all the sheeple of Earth.

One Power to rule them all, I will be. One Power to define them. One Power to gather them under the shadow of shadows —and in the darkness bind them.

To me!

That great pope from the 6th century who originally identified the Deadly Seven didn't have a clue, along with that 13th century medieval thinker. I should know. I've been around the solar block for as long as time itself, the fruit of the Flood, my ancestors, continuing to wreak havoc across the centuries from the four corners of Earth. The disembodied souls of the dead fallen ones who had once roamed Earth.

Despair will have his hour, just you wait. When I do, I will bring all the others along who have been secretly following me in the shadows. To elevate the others champing at the bit to take their own place among the Deadly Seven, swelling it to seventeen, twenty-three—and beyond.

With me at the center of it all…

For too long, the Deadly have been narrowed to the seven. But I know there are far more.

Covetousness. Strife. Deceit. Craftiness. Gossip. Slanderer. Faithlessness. Godlessness. Heartlessness. Ruthlessness.

Then my posse: Chaos, Turmoil, Strife, Disease.

And my personal favorite, of course:

Despair…

I revel in it, roll around in it. Positively exude it out of every one of my pores. It's what fuels me, gets me up in the morning after another spin on this Third Rock from the Sun.

After all, names for our kind have always been important. It's what gives us our powers. What allows us to manifest ourselves in various ways across the world—beckoning and wooing, cajoling and conning those billions of sheeple strewn across Earth.

And that's the thing about sheeple: they're all the same. So easily amused, their hearts so easily led astray. Prone to wander, they are. It's any wonder why the Name-Who-Shall-Remain-Nameless doesn't just chuck the whole operation into the Abyss!

They play at their worship, work at their play, and worship their work. Has been that way from the beginning—even without all the trappings of the modern world, the digital devices that have come to define them.

The ones dripping with despair.

With me!

Only now, all that is gone.

Although…perhaps not.

Yessiree, Despair will rise again. I might be down in the Deadly's book, but I am certainly not out! I shall return.

When I do, I'm coming for you, bucko.

After all, you've got me in your pocket!

AUTHOR'S NOTE

Social media is killing us.

That's what the subconscious part of my brain wrote as a theme woven through this story, even as my conscious brain was writing a story about evil actors using it to bring women to the brink. Didn't know it at the time that's what I was writing, but it seemed to come through in the end.

It's true, though, isn't it? In some cases, social media is literally leading to people's deaths, as recent research suggests with the rise of suicides connected with depression and anxiety fueled by social media use. It's also figuratively killing us, destroying relationships and unraveling our social fabric—decimating our ability to connect and discuss and disagree with courtesy and care.

This second Group X case was inspired by a series of exposés by the *Wall Street Journal* uncovering the harmful effects of a slew of social media sites. *The Facebook Files,* as reported beginning in October 1, 2021, outlined the horrifying impact of Facebook and Instagram on our individual and collective psyches. WeShare and WeGram were my own inventions that served as stand-ins for these platforms, parts of my story-world I've used in other books.

The research that went into chapters 19, 20, 23, and 24 was culled from these articles exposing the harmful effects of social media platforms—as well as from similar analysis by *The Atlantic* ("The Dangerous Experiment on Teen Girls"; November 21, 2021) and *U.S. News* with regards to TikTok ("As Social Media Time Rises, So Does Teen Girls' Suicide Risk"; July 6, 2021). The verdict from all three sources: social media is harming young girls and women specifically, exponentially so.

Depression, despair, hopelessness, and—yes—suicidal ideation are all ratcheted up thanks to the relentless assault of algorithms, images, likes, and cyberbullying. So while all fictional stories require you to suspend your disbelief, and although this story might have seemed like it required you to suspend it to a larger degree than you might have liked, the unfortunate reality is that truth is stranger than fiction—and as deadly.

The technology discussed regarding bots and AI and deep-fakes is all accurate—anyone paying attention to recent American elections knows that Russian intelligent services deployed such technology to influence voters' thinking and opinions regarding a slew of candidates and political issues. More recently, China deployed bots and fake accounts in a massive propaganda campaign to influence people's impressions of the Winter Olympics held in Beijing and push a wonderland vision at odds with reality.

Again, truth is stranger than fiction!

While I wouldn't want to suggest Mark Zuckerberg (or my own version in Markus Braun) and his platforms are literal instruments of the Devil, I cannot help but think about the manner in which Satan and his minions devour humanity through any number of means, including digital ones like social media sites and the humans that post in them, sowing despair and binding them to its power. Doomscrolling comes to mind!

There seems to be at least some sort of spiritually wicked

element to the way in which Image Bearers are ravaged by the kind of depression, anxiety, and hopelessness such sites engender—trusting that what Jesus says about the Thief is true: *'[He] comes only to steal and kill and destroy'* (John 10:10). That the Devil *'prowls around, looking for someone to devour'* (1 Peter 5:8) is a sober reminder of our true enemy, which I find fits the ravenous ills of Despair (both my invented demon and the personal feeling) in all of its forms.

One final thing to mention: It is always a risk for any writer to represent characters from certain walks of life. Naomi Torres (from my *Order of Thaddeus* series) is one such character, a Latino woman. Elijah and Gina were two more, autistic people whose characters came to me in the writing process of a different story, *Fallen Ones*. I spent time reading autistic people's stories and getting to know their experiences in the world to get them right. I particularly wanted to listen to their pain points when it comes to representation in the media, not wanting to fall into the same traps.

Hopefully, I represented them justly, writing unique, individual characters that shed some light on how they image their Creator in the world and their unique challenges expressing their personhood. However, if I fell down on the mark, and you yourself are autistic who can offer me insight into better representation, do contact me and help me understand how I can better write the stories of autistic Image Bearers.

I will also say that writing these two characters and exploring their stories in these first two books gave me a chance to explore my own story. During the course of research, I myself tested for autistic tendencies. I also placed along the autism spectrum in a way that gave me further clarity about myself and also gave me interest in delving deeper into this aspect of my own story. While I would not claim to be an autistic person, nor have I been clinically diagnosed, this process writing these stories was an interesting journey for me personally.

As with all of my stories, I like to take elements of the real world and spin it in a way to tell a compelling, propulsive page-turner. I hope you enjoyed this foray into supernatural suspense.

GET YOUR FREE THRILLER

Building a relationship with my readers is a joy of writing!
Join my insider group for updates, giveaways, and your free novel—a full-length, action-adventure conspiracy mystery in my *Order of Thaddeus* thriller series.

Just tell me where to send it. Follow this link to subscribe: www.jabouma.com/free

CONTINUE THE NEXT CASE!

There is a rising wickedness in American, something hidden from the past that is making itself known in our present. Something so unfathomable that it targets a sitting U.S. Congressman while targeting a small-town country church. Group X must confront a fearsome darkness from tearing apart our social fabric—and the Church.

Read *Against These Powers* today: bouma.us/gx3

ENJOY THE DARKEST VALLEY?

A big thanks for joining Elijah Fox and Gina Anderson on their investigation saving the world! **Here's what's next:**

Want to join Elijah Fox and Gina Anderson solving more supernatural mysteries? Dive into solving more Group X cases: www.groupxcases.com.

Case 1, *Not of This World*, is ready to solve at: http://bouma.us/gx1

If you loved the book and have a moment to spare, **a short review is much appreciated.** Nothing fancy, just your honest take. Spreading the word is probably the #1 way you can help independent authors like me and help others enjoy the story.

ALSO BY J. A. BOUMA

Nobody should have to read bad religious fiction—whether it's cheesy plots with pat answers or misrepresentations of the Christian faith and the Bible. So J. A. Bouma tells compelling, propulsive stories that thrill as much as inspire, offering a dose of insight along the way.

Order of Thaddeus Action-Adventure Thriller Series

Holy Shroud • Book 1

The Thirteenth Apostle • Book 2

Hidden Covenant • Book 3

American God • Book 4

Grail of Power • Book 5

Templars Rising • Book 6

Rite of Darkness • Book 7

Gospel Zero • Book 8

The Emperor's Code • Book 9

Deadly Hope • Book 10

Fallen Ones • Book 11

The Eden Legacy • Book 12

Silas Grey Collection 1 (Books 1-3)

Silas Grey Collection 2 (Books 4-6)

Silas Grey Collection 3 (Books 7-9)

Backstories: Short Story Collection 1

Martyrs Bones: Short Story Collection 2

Group X Cases Supernatural Suspense Series

Not of This World • Book 1

The Darkest Valley • Book 2

Against These Powers • Book 3

Luck Be the Ladies • Novelette

Ichthus Chronicles Sci-Fi Apocalyptic Series

Apostasy Rising / Season 1, Episode 1

Apostasy Rising / Season 1, Episode 2

Apostasy Rising / Season 1, Episode 3

Apostasy Rising / Season 1, Episode 4

Apostasy Rising / Full Season 1 (Episodes 1 to 4)

Apocalypse Rising / Season 2, Episode 1

Apocalypse Rising / Season 2, Episode 2

Apocalypse Rising / Season 2, Episode 3

Apocalypse Rising / Season 2, Episode 4

Apocalypse Rising / Full Season 2 (Episodes 1 to 4)

Faith Reimagined Spiritual Coming-of-Age Series

A Reimagined Faith • Book 1

A Rediscovered Faith • Book 2

Mill Creek Junction Short Story Series

The New Normal • Collection 1

My Name's Johnny Pope • Collection 2

Joy to the Junction! • Collection 3

The Ties that Bind Us • Collection 4

A Matter of Justice • Collection 5

Get all the latest short stories at: www.millcreekjunction.com

Find all of my latest book releases at: www.jabouma.com

ABOUT THE AUTHOR

J. A. Bouma believes nobody should have to read bad religious fiction—whether it's cheesy plots with pat answers or misrepresentations of the Christian faith and the Bible. So he tells compelling, propulsive stories that thrill as much as inspire, while offering a dose of insight along the way.

As a former congressional staffer and pastor, and award-nominated bestselling author of over forty religious fiction and nonfiction books, he blends a love for ideas and adventure, exploration and discovery, thrill and thought. With graduate degrees in Christian thought and the Bible, and armed with a voracious appetite for most mainstream genres, he tells stories you'll read with abandon and recommend with pride—exploring the tension of faith and doubt, spirituality and culture, belief and practice, and the gritty drama that is our collective pilgrim story.

When not putting fingers to keyboard, he loves vintage jazz vinyl, a glass of Malbec, and an epic read—preferably together. He lives in Grand Rapids with his wife, two kiddos, and rambunctious boxer-pug-terrier.

www.jabouma.com • jeremy@jabouma.com

facebook.com/jaboumabooks

twitter.com/bouma

amazon.com/author/jabouma